Darlin'.

Jake's endearment gave Shah sustenance and strength when she felt as if her knees were going to cave in beneath her. She lost herself momentarily in the warm gray of Jake's gaze—that same feeling of powerful protection again embracing her.

"I'm glad you're okay," she quavered.

He gave her a grim smile. "You're the one I was worried about."

Turning away, she blinked back tears. Tears! Her emotions frayed and raw, Shah didn't try to rationalize them away this time: they were tears of relief that Jake wasn't dead. A gamut of emotions smothered Shah, making her dizzy. How could Jake Randolph mean that much to her in such a short amount of time?

He was her enemy.

Dear Reader,

Last year, I requested that you send me your opinions on the books that we publish—and on romances in general. Thank you so much for the many thoughtful comments. For the next couple of months, I'd like to share with you quotes from those letters. This seems very appropriate now, while we are in the midst of the THAT SPECIAL WOMAN! promotion. Each one of our readers is a special woman, as heroic as the heroines in our books.

This August has some wonderful books coming your way. *More Than He Bargained For* by Carole Halston, a warm, poignant story, is the THAT SPECIAL WOMAN! selection. Debbie Macomber also brings us the first book in her FROM THIS DAY FORWARD series—*Groom Wanted*. MORGAN'S MERCENARIES, Lindsay McKenna's action-packed trio concludes this month with *Commando*. And don't miss books from other favorite authors: Marie Ferrarella, Susan Mallery and Christine Rimmer.

I hope you enjoy this book, and all of the stories to come! Have a wonderful August!

Sincerely,

Tara Gavin
Senior Editor
Silhouette Books

Quote of the Month: "Romance books provide the escape that is needed from the sometimes crazy and hard-to-live-in world. It takes me away for that three or four hours a day to a place no one else can come into. That is why I read romances. Because sometimes there is not a happy ending, and going to a place where there is can uplift the spirit that really needs it."

—J. Majeski
New Jersey

LINDSAY McKENNA

COMMANDO

Silhouette®

SPECIAL EDITION®

Published by Silhouette Books New York

America's Publisher of Contemporary Romance

To my brothers and their families:
Gary, Debby, Brian and Kimberly Gent,
and Brent, Jeanne, Erin and Lauren Gent.
A sister couldn't get luckier, believe me.

SILHOUETTE BOOKS
300 East 42nd St., New York, N.Y. 10017

COMMANDO

Copyright © 1993 by Lindsay McKenna

ISBN: 0-373-09830-8

First Silhouette Books printing August 1993

All the characters in this book have no existence outside the imagination of the author and have no relation whatsoever to anyone bearing the same name or names. They are not even distantly inspired by any individual known or unknown to the author, and all incidents are pure invention.

®: Trademark used under license and registered in the United States Patent and Trademark Office and in other countries.

Printed in the U.S.A.

LINDSAY McKENNA

After the publication of *Return of a Hero* (SE #541), I received hundreds of letters asking what happened to the story's hero, Morgan Trayhern. Well, in my latest trilogy, *Morgan's Mercenaries,* the question is answered.

I loved returning to the characters of Morgan and his wife, Laura, and am thrilled to give you three very exciting, adventurous and intensely romantic stories about the men in Morgan Trayhern's employ.

Mercenaries have always fascinated me—they are loners in our world, with mysterious pasts and brooding secrets deep within their hearts. I hope you enjoy reading about Wolf, Killian and Jake as much as I did writing about them!

Prologue

"Mr. Trayhern, I want my daughter out of the Amazon jungle. Now. No questions asked."

Morgan Trayhern eyed the man who stood tensely in front of his large desk. Ken Travers, a millionaire real estate developer, wore a Saville Row suit; his black hair was peppered with a few white strands. Right now, he looked angry. Morgan rested his finger against his chin and allowed his instincts to take over. Travers might be rich and influential, but Morgan didn't like his attitude.

"Mr. Travers—"

"Call me Ken."

Morgan allowed a brief, perfunctory smile to cross his mouth as he eased forward in his leather chair. He clasped his hands in front of him and rested them on top of his cherrywood desk.

"All right. Ken. Perseus doesn't do anything without asking a lot of questions first. You come bursting into my office without an appointment, and—"

"Yes, yes, and I apologize." Travers raked his hand through his short hair, his blue eyes narrowing. "It's just that my daughter, Shah, has no business being down in the Amazon! She's headstrong and opinionated." Travers paced for a moment, halted and pinned Morgan with a glare. "On top of that, she's half Sioux, and wears it like a damned badge of honor. She calls herself a warrior for Mother Earth. What rubbish! She's a hellion who goes off half-cocked on ridiculous, fanatical quests."

"Please, Ken, sit down and let's discuss this matter intelligently." Morgan wondered which of his Perseus employees might be available for the assignment. Marie Parker, his intrepid assistant, kept him supplied with a complete, updated list of who was open. Quickly perusing the list, Morgan noted the "not available" status of Wolf Harding, who had recently quit. At least he was happy with his ranger's job in Montana—and he would be marrying Sarah Thatcher shortly. Marie had penned a date in the margin near Wolf's name to remind Morgan that he and Laura would be attending that wedding.

Hiding a smile, Morgan's gaze moved down the list. Killian had requested only American assignments, and low-risk ones at that. Judging from Ken Travers's agitated state, this potential assignment was probably not low-risk. Besides, Killian was still on his requested three-month leave, working to get his life back together, and Morgan respected that request. With Morgan's own sister-in-law, Susannah Anderson at his side, and his recent move to Glen, Kentucky, to be with her, Killian's focus was on the personal right now, anyway.

Morgan was nearly to the end of the list when he noticed that one of his men, Jake Randolph, was due to come in off an assignment today. That meant he'd be checking in with Marie tomorrow morning as a matter of course. Every employee, after coming off an assignment, wrote up a detailed report at the main office to be submitted to Morgan. Then the employee was given two weeks—or more, if he or she requested it—time off to rest and regroup.

Frowning, Morgan sat back in his chair, rubbing his jaw. Jake had been on a brutal assignment in Peru. He'd been responsible for getting all the parties together regarding the contract on Susannah Anderson by José Santiago's drug cartel. If it hadn't been for Jake's brazen approach to Santiago's estate, demanding that those now in command talk with the Peruvian government, as well as with U.S. officials, the contract would never have been lifted from Susannah's head. Yes, Jake had clearly been a key to saving Susannah's life.

Jake would be tired, Morgan knew. He'd risked his life time and again, carrying messages to the drug cartel on behalf of the U.S. government when the cartel officials refused to talk directly. Quickly glancing to the end of the list, Morgan realized that Jake was the only operative potentially free to take this assignment for Travers.

But would he? Morgan looked up at Travers. "I've got one of my operatives coming off an assignment tomorrow morning. Why don't we discuss some of the details of what you want done, and we'll have a meeting with him tomorrow?"

Travers nodded brusquely. "Fine with me. I just want this thing settled. I want my daughter the hell out of Brazil."

Chapter One

"Welcome home, Jake," Marie said with a smile.

Wiping his eyes, Jake Randolph smiled tiredly as he got off the elevator that led directly to the main office of Perseus. "Hi, Marie." He moved slowly across the thick rose-colored carpeting toward her desk. "Got something you've been wanting."

With a smile, she took his report. "Handwritten, no doubt?"

"Yeah. You know me—I can't type to save my soul." He stretched and yawned. "I'm taking that two weeks off. I'm beat."

"Not so fast," Marie murmured apologetically. "Morgan left word for you to come directly to him when you came back."

"Oh?"

"Yes. I'm afraid he's got another assignment, and you're the only person available to take it."

Jake frowned. "Listen, I'm wiped out from that Peruvian fiasco."

"I know you are. Just go in and talk to Morgan, will you? There's a gentleman in there with him. They've both been waiting for you to show up."

Groaning, Jake rubbed his face, which needed a shave. "Okay, but I'm turning it down."

Marie smiled understandingly and pressed the button on the intercom that sat on her desk.

"Jake is here, Mr. Trayhern. Shall I send him in?"

Jake opened the door to Morgan's spacious office and entered. Morgan looked up and nodded to him.

"Come in, Jake. Meet Ken Travers. Ken, this is Jake Randolph. Jake's our Brazilian specialist. He knows Portuguese, the language of the country, and he's been there on assignment a number of times in the past few years."

Travers leaped from the couch like an overwound spring and held his hand out.

"Mr. Randolph."

Jake sized up the lean, restless-looking businessman, taking an immediate dislike to him. It was an intuitive thing, Jake thought as he extended his hand to shake Travers's manicured one. Intuition had saved his life on a number of occasions, and he wasn't about to dismiss a gut feeling.

"Mr. Travers."

Jake turned to Morgan, whose face showed no expression. Not unusual, Jake thought—Morgan knew how to keep his feelings hidden until the proper time. Jake noted Travers's expensive suit, his perfect haircut, the gold watch on his wrist—and his arrogance. Hiding a wry smile at the thought, Jake realized that he must look like a country bumpkin by comparison. He wore jeans, rough-out boots and an off-white fisherman-knit sweater. November in Washington, D.C., was cold, and there was a threat of snow today.

"Have a seat." Morgan gestured to a wing chair positioned to one side of his desk.

Jake nodded, his attention still on Travers. There was a feeling of electricity in the air, and it was coming from him. Jake had learned a long time ago to say little and observe a lot. Travers was pacing like a caged animal, his hands behind his back and his brow furrowed. His full mouth was set in a line of decided aversion. But aversion to whom? Morgan? Him? Probably both of them, he surmised.

Marie, dressed in her tasteful and conservative navy suit with white piping, came in moments later bearing a silver tray that contained coffee and a plate of cookies for the three men. She set it on the coffee table in front of the couch.

"Please call my wife," Morgan told her, "and tell her I have to cancel my luncheon date with her."

"Yes, sir. Shall I order in the usual lunch from the restaurant?" Marie asked.

Morgan glanced over at Jake. "Would you like something to eat?"

"No, thanks. My stomach's still on Peruvian time."

Morgan grinned. "How about you, Ken? Hungry?"

"No!"

"Just bring me the usual," he told his assistant.

"Yes, sir." Marie gave Travers a deadly look, turned and left.

Jake was fascinated by Travers's snappish mood. He was like a pit bull waiting to eat someone alive. Fighting jet lag, Jake got up and ambled over to the coffee table, where Morgan was already helping himself to a cup of coffee. He needed help keeping himself awake. Originally he'd planned to drop his report off at Morgan's office and then make his way home to his condo in Alexandria, Virginia, not far from the office that he used only when necessary. Jake's real home was located in Oregon.

Travers paced while the two men got their respective cups of coffee and sat down again. Jake saw amusement in Morgan's eyes, and he realized the look was for him alone. With a slight nod, Jake spread out his long legs in front of him. Holding the dainty gold-edged white china cup in one of his large, scarred hands, a cookie in the other, he leaned back and relaxed.

"Ken, why don't you start from the beginning?" Morgan suggested, sipping the black, fragrant Brazilian coffee.

Agitated, Travers came to a halt, his hands planted imperiously upon his hips. "I just don't like having Mr. Randolph here. This is strictly private."

"Mr. Travers," Morgan told him, his voice a deep rumble, "if you want Perseus to help you, we need to know the facts. Furthermore, I'm not sure we *can* help you. You're in luck that Jake is here, because, *if* we decide to take your case, Jake will be the man sent on the mission. So why don't you sit down and start from the beginning?"

Jake watched as Travers vacillated. The man acted as if he were going to explode.

"Very well." Travers strode to the couch and sat down, his spine as rigid as the rest of him.

"My daughter, Shah Sungilo Travers, is down in Brazil. She's thirty years old, and a damned fanatic!"

Morgan tipped his head. "Fanatic? In what sense of the word?"

Grinding his closed fist into the palm of his hand, Travers snapped, "She's a damned ecology fanatic. She's down there in the midst of all the hell breaking loose about the Amazon Basin trees being cut down. Global warming, and all that scientific garbage. Shah could be killed!"

"How long has she been down there?" Morgan asked.

"Three months."

Jake raised his eyebrows. "And you're just getting around to asking for help?"

Travers scowled, and his gaze dropped to his expensive-looking black leather shoes. "I didn't know. I— Oh, hell, I'm divorced from Shah's mother. I happened to be in Rapid City, South Dakota, on business, and I decided to drive out to the Rosebud Sioux reservation to visit Shah, who lives with her mother. But she wasn't there. That's when I found out she'd galloped off on another damned windmill-tilting adventure. Only this time it's to Brazil, and it could get her killed."

Travers stood up, his voice tight. "I want her out of there. She's in danger. It's that Sioux blood of hers. She loves a fight. She sees herself as a protector. A steward, she says."

Jake sat up, his interest piqued. A woman with Sioux blood and an unusual name like Shah interested him. But the picture Travers was painting didn't sound quite accurate. He gave Morgan a searching look.

"You can ask him anything you want," Morgan said, reading the question in Jake's eyes before he could voice his request.

"Mr. Travers, if your daughter is thirty years old, she's old enough to realize if she's in danger or not," Jake pointed out.

Travers gave him a withering look of pure disgust. "You don't know my headstrong daughter, Mr. Randolph. This isn't the first time Shah has been in the thick of things. Her mother named her Shah Sungilo, which means Red Fox in the Sioux language. She's got a temper to match any fox's red coat, and she's as clever as the damned animal she's named after." And then, with a snort, Travers added, "You'd think she would pick some worthwhile cause, and not put her life on the line for some lousy trees in Brazil!"

"What's her educational background?" Jake asked, realizing he wasn't going to get many facts from Travers under the circumstances. The man was clearly fit to be tied. But who was he angry at? Shah? Jake could understand a father being concerned about his daughter possibly being in danger, but where was this anger coming from? His gut told him there was a hidden agenda here, but could he get it out of Travers?

"Although she was born on the Sioux reservation, my daughter has had the finest education my money could buy. She has a master's degree in biology from Stanford University in California. I tried to persuade her to go after her Ph.D., but she said there was no time left, that Mother Earth was dying. Hell!" Travers raked his fingers through his hair again. "She's got her mother's firebrand temper and stubbornness. She's bullheaded and won't listen to anyone!"

He turned away and stared out the windows at the distant city. "Shortly after I divorced Shah's mother, I went to court to have my ex-wife pronounced an unfit mother. I didn't want my daughter raised on a Depression-level

Indian reservation. Unfortunately, my ex-wife won. Shah spent the first eighteen years of her life on a damned reservation. What kind of place is that? They're backward there. Shah's mother is a medicine woman, and she forced Shah to live the old ways of her people. She was raised a heathen—never baptized. I should have—"

"Your daughter is a biologist down in Brazil," Jake said impatiently. "Is she on an assignment?"

"Yes. For a television station in Los Angeles that has paid her to investigate the destruction of the tropical rain forest in Brazil. Shah is an environmental activist. She thrives on confrontation." He shook his head. "She just won't back down."

Jake cast a look at Morgan, who was listening intently. "In a businessman, those attributes are often applauded," he noted mildly.

Travers glared at him. "Believe me, I tried to force my daughter to follow in my footsteps, but she didn't want anything to do with real estate. I tried to tell her it was about land, which she's so close to, but she said no Indian would ever sell the land, because it isn't ours to sell. She asked me one time, 'How can you sell Mother Earth? We're her children. All we can do is steward, not greedily buy and sell it.' Can you imagine? My own daughter calling me greedy because I buy and sell land?"

"Sounds like a cultural difference of opinion," Morgan murmured.

Jake liked Shah's attitude. He didn't particularly care for greedy people, whatever their business. "What makes you think your daughter's in trouble?" he asked.

Travers snorted and came over to them. He put his hands on his hips. "Shah goes out of her way to get into trouble. This isn't the first time, you know. She married that no-good half-breed Sioux when I told her not to—

that it was a mistake. Well, it turned out to be one hell of a mistake. Shah's divorced from him now, but she had to be put in the hospital by that alcoholic husband of hers before she came to her senses.'' He nailed Jake with a dark look. ''My daughter lives for confrontation. Being physically attacked doesn't bother her. It's almost as if she expects it. Well, I've put too much money into her education to let her waste it, or herself, on some damned trees in the Amazon!''

''Calm down, Ken,'' Morgan ordered. ''Do you know what her exact assignment in Brazil is?''

''No. As I said, I just found out from my ex-wife that Shah left a month ago for Brazil.''

''And what do you want us to do?'' Morgan asked quietly.

''Bring her home! Get her out of there!''

''If she has a valid passport, approved by the Brazilian government, and she wants to stay, there's nothing we can do,'' Jake pointed out.

''Kidnap her, then!''

Morgan grimaced. ''Mr. Travers, we're not in the kidnapping business. We're in the business of providing protection and help to those who ask for it. But in this case, your daughter isn't asking us for help, you are.''

''I can't believe this! I'll pay you any amount of money to bring her out of Brazil! Shah should be home!''

Ordinarily, so soon after returning from a mission, Jake would be falling asleep in his chair, but this time he wasn't. He liked what he heard about Shah—a woman who evidently believed deeply and passionately in something beyond herself. It was too bad more Americans didn't have that kind of commitment.

''Maybe,'' Jake said, glancing over at Morgan, ''I could go down there and be a bodyguard of sorts.'' He turned to Travers. "I won't bring back your daughter against her will. Kidnapping is against the law in every nation in the world. What I can do is be there to protect her *if* she gets into trouble."

Morgan nodded. "Okay, that's what we can do, Mr. Travers. Jake is ideal for the mission, and I don't see a problem in him being a bodyguard for your daughter. What I want you to understand is, Jake won't haul her out of Brazil unless she wants to go."

Looking defeated, Travers spun on his heel. "I guess it's better than nothing," he muttered. He halted and turned his head in Jake's direction. "But I want you to do your damnedest to convince her to leave Brazil as quickly as possible. Can you do that?"

With a shrug, Jake finished off the last of the coffee and cookie. "No promises, Mr. Travers. Your daughter is an adult, mature and educated enough to know what she's doing. All I can do is wage a diplomatic campaign to try to get her to see your side of the issue."

"Then," Travers said unhappily, "I guess that's what I'll have to settle for." He took a photo out of his wallet and handed it to Morgan. "That's my daughter. You'll need to know what she looks like."

Morgan got up and came around the desk. "My assistant will have a number of papers for you to fill out and sign. She'll take you to another office to complete them. When you're done, we'll talk some more."

"Fine."

Jake watched Travers leave. Marie entered with Morgan's box lunch and set it on his desk. When she'd left, Jake stood up and placed his coffee cup on the silver tray.

"That guy has problems," Jake began seriously. He returned to his chair by Morgan's desk. Curiosity was eating him alive as he leaned forward to look at the small color photo of Shah Sungilo Travers.

Morgan smiled. "I don't care for his abrasive attitude, that's for sure. Go on, take a look at her."

Jake picked up the photo and studied it intently. Shah looked Native American, from her braided black hair to her light brown eyes, high cheekbones, full mouth and oval-shaped face. The photo was a close-up, but Jake could see that she was wearing a deerskin dress that was beaded and fringed. In her hair was a small eagle feather, along with several other decorations that hung to one side of her head. Her braids were wrapped in some kind of fur.

"She looks like she stepped out of the past," Jake said, more to himself than to Morgan.

"Doesn't she?"

"If she's half-white, she doesn't look it."

Morgan nodded and continued slowly eating his sandwich. "You looked interested, Jake," he noted after he swallowed.

"Maybe."

With a chuckle, Morgan wiped his mouth with a linen napkin. "That's one of your many traits that I like, Jake—you're noncommittal."

Jake had to admit that he was feeling anything but noncommittal as he continued to study the photograph of Shah. She wasn't smiling; she had a very thoughtful look on her face. Pride radiated from her in the way she stood, shoulders squared, with a glint of defiance in her wide, intelligent eyes. But there was something else, something that Jake sensed and felt but couldn't put his finger on. What was it? Was that a haunted look he saw in her eyes?

"I wonder how old she was when this photo was taken."

"Why?"

"Dunno." Jake laid the photo back on Morgan's desk. "Travers is hiding something from us," he said.

"I think so, too."

"But what?"

"I don't know." Morgan offered Jake some potato chips. Jake took a handful and munched methodically, frowning as he considered the question.

"Travers seems more angry than anything else," Morgan offered.

"Not exactly what I'd call the concerned-parent type," Jake agreed dryly.

"He's posturing, that's for sure," Morgan said. "It's obvious he's a real controller and manipulator."

Jake chuckled. "Yeah, and it sounds like his daughter rebelled very early on and leads her life the way she sees fit."

"Travers is also prejudiced against Indians."

"Noticed that, did you?" Jake rolled his eyes.

"I know you're a walking encyclopedia of knowledge. . . ." Morgan said.

"I prefer to think of myself as a philosopher," Jake corrected, "despite being an ex-marine."

"And a mercenary," Morgan added. "So how much do you know about Indians?"

"Native Americans is the preferred term," Jake noted. "A little. Enough to realize that Shah is like some of the younger generation of Native Americans who are trying to reclaim their heritage. Her fierce pride isn't unusual."

"Ever been on a reservation?"

"Once, a long time ago. I had a marine friend who was Navajo, and I went home with him for Christmas one year. His folks lived near Gallup, New Mexico, and they had a hogan made out of wood and mud. I stayed with them for nearly two weeks, and learned a hell of a lot."

"You had a good experience?"

"Yeah."

"Sounds like Travers didn't."

"Travers," Jake intoned, "would hate anything or anyone who disagreed with him or got in his way."

With a grin, Morgan finished off his sandwich. "Once Travers fills out the papers, I'm going to have a security check run on him."

"Good idea. He looks a little too slick to me—one of those greedy eighties business types."

"Sounds like his daughter is just the opposite of him—clear ethics, strong morals, and decided values."

"I agree."

"So, if all of our info comes back in order on Travers, do you want to be a bodyguard for a while?"

Jake shrugged. He tried to appear nonchalant, but his protective feelings had been aroused. He looked down at the photo. "Yeah, I'll go to Brazil and see what's going down."

"She's a very pretty young woman."

"The earthy type," Jake agreed.

Jake sat there for a long time, simply feeling his way through the photo of Shah. There was an ageless quality to her, as if all the generations of the Sioux people were mirrored in her classic Indian features. She didn't have a common kind of model's prettiness, but Jake never went for that cookie-cutter type, anyway. He liked women who had their own special and unique features. Character, as far as he was concerned, should be reflected on a person's face, and Shah's face intrigued him.

Unconsciously he rubbed his chest where his heart lay.

"Memories?" Morgan asked quietly, breaking the comfortable silence of the office.

"Huh? Oh, yeah." Jake loved Morgan like a brother. They had both served as marines, and that bound them in an invisible way. Once a marine, always a marine— that was the saying. Even though they hadn't served together, they'd come from the same proud service. Marines stuck together, and supported each other and their families. Maybe that was why Jake liked working for Morgan so much—he understood Jake's tragic loss, and, like any marine brother, supported him as much as possible.

He gave Morgan a quick glance. "Bess was always spunky, too," he whispered, his voice strained. "Shah kinda reminds me of my wife in some ways."

"You always want me to give you assignments that deal with drugs," Morgan said. "This one won't involve drug trafficking."

"It's okay." Jake tried to shake off the old grief that still clung to his heart. "Maybe I need a change of pace. Something different."

"I feel this assignment may be more than it appears to be on the surface," Morgan warned him.

"What else do I have to do with my life?" Jake said, pretending sudden joviality. "Go home to an empty log house? Sit and watch a football game and drink a beer? No plants in the house. No animals..." *No family. No wife.* Not anymore. The grief grew within him, and he got up, rubbing his chest again. He saw Morgan's face, which was no longer expressionless. Morgan knew about personal loss as few men ever would. Jake stood there, unable to put into words the feelings unraveling within him.

"Well," Morgan said softly, "maybe it would do you good to have this kind of assignment, then." He attempted a smile. "Where you'll be going, there'll be plenty of plants and animals."

Jake nodded and moved to the windows. The November sky was cloudy, and it looked like either rain or the first snowfall of the year for the capital. "Brazil is having their springtime," he said, as much to himself as to Morgan. "It'll be the dry season down there, and the jungle will be survivable."

"Just make sure *you* survive this mission," Morgan growled.

Jake rubbed his jaw. "I always survive. You know that."

Morgan nodded, but said nothing.

Jake turned toward him. "You've got a funny look on your face, boss."

"Do I?"

"Yeah."

With a slight smile, Morgan said, "Well, maybe I'm hoping that Shah and her situation can lighten the load you've been carrying by yourself for so long, that's all."

Jake halted at the desk. "Well, time heals all, right?"

Morgan sat back. "Time has been a healing force for me, Jake. I hope it will be for you, too."

With a grimace, Jake ran his finger along the highly polished surface of Morgan's desk. "You know what William Carlos Williams said about time? He said, 'Time is a storm in which we are all lost.' I agree with him. I've never felt so lost since Bess's and the kids' deaths."

"I know."

Jake forced a smile he didn't feel. "Well, who knows? Maybe this storm surrounding Shah will be good for me. It can't get any worse."

Chapter Two

Manaus was the Dodge City of Brazil, Jake decided as he left the seedy-looking gun shop. Less than an hour ago, he'd stepped off the plane into the sweltering noontime heat that hung over the city. Now, standing on a cracked and poorly kept sidewalk outside the shop, Jake looked around. Disheveled houses, mostly shacks, lined both sides of the busy street. Odors in the air ranged from automobile pollution to ripe garbage to the muddy scent of the two mighty rivers that met near the city.

Sweat was rolling off Jake, but that wasn't anything new to him. Manaus sat at the edge of the Amazon Basin, home to one of the largest rain-forest jungles in the world. Rubber trees had been the cause of Manaus's rise to fame—and its downfall. Once chemical companies had learned to make synthetic rubber better than what the trees of the Amazon Basin provided, the city's boom had ground to a halt, leaving Manaus destitute.

Jake flagged down a blue-and-white taxi and climbed in.

"Take me to the docks. I need to hire a boat to take me down the Amazon," he said in Portuguese to the old man who drove the cab.

Nodding, the driver grinned and turned around.

Jake sagged back against the lumpy rear seat as the cab sped off. The asphalt highway leading to the docks was bumpy at best. Not much had changed in Manaus, Jake decided. Skinny brown children with black hair and brown eyes played along the edge of the road. Dilapidated houses lined the avenue. Although Manaus was struggling to come out of the mire of depression that had hit it so long ago, it had remained intrinsically a river town, filled with a colorful assortment of characters, greedy money-seekers willing to turn a quick dime and the now-impoverished "wealthy" who had depended upon their income from the rubber trees to keep them that way.

The docks came into view after about half an hour. Up ahead, Jake could see the wide, muddy ribbons of the Solimoes and the Rio Negro coming together to create the enormous Amazon. A number of boats—some small, some fairly large—dipped and bobbed, their prows either resting on the muddy river bank or tied off with frayed pieces of rope to some rotting wooden post on one of the many run-down wharves. As the taxi screeched to a halt, Jake paid the driver in cruzeiros, Brazil's currency, and climbed out. His only piece of luggage was a canvas duffel bag that was filled, though only partially, with clothes and other essential survival items.

Standing off to one side where the asphalt crumbled to an end and the muddy slope began, Jake reached into the duffel bag and pulled out a large knife encased in a black leather sheath. He put the scabbard through his belt loop and made sure it rode comfortably behind his left elbow. Tying a red-and-white handkerchief around his throat to use to wipe the sweat from his face, Jake rummaged in the duffel bag again and came up with a few badly crumpled American dollars that he'd stuffed away in a side pocket.

Recession had hit Brazil big-time, and over the past few years inflation had risen from three hundred to six hundred percent. One American dollar was worth hundreds of cruzeiros, and Jake knew he'd have no trouble finding a willing skipper to take him where he wanted to go if he showed he had American money.

Jake also had a huge wad of cruzeiros stashed in a hidden leg pouch. Americans weren't common in Brazil, and those who did come were seen by the local populace as being very rich. Jake wasn't about to become one of the robbery or murder statistics on a local police roster. Manaus was a wide-open city, and it paid for any foreigner to be watchful and take nothing for granted. All of Brazil's large cities held areas of homes surrounded by huge wrought-iron fences, sometimes ten feet tall, to protect them from thievery, which was rampant in Brazil.

Pulling the leather holster that contained a nine-millimeter Beretta out of his bag, Jake strapped it around his waist. He wanted the holster low, so that he could easily reach the pistol. Because of the constant high humidity, Jake wore khaki pants and a short-sleeved white shirt, already marked with sweat.

Looking around from his position just above the muddy bank of the river, Jake smiled faintly. The cottony white clouds, heavy with moisture, barely moved above the jungle that surrounded Manaus. The noon-time sun was rising high in the pale blue sky, shafting through the fragments of clouds. As Jake zipped up the duffel and slung it across his shoulder, he knew that for the next couple of days he'd be adjusting to the brutal combination of ninety-degree temperatures and ninety-percent humidity.

He heard cawing and looked up. A flight of red-and-yellow macaws flew across the river, barely fifty feet above the surface. They looked like a squadron of fighter jets, their long tails and colorful feathers in sharp contrast with the sluggish brown headwaters. Watching his step, Jake gingerly made his way down to what appeared to be the most seaworthy craft available, a small tug. The captain was dressed in ragged cutoffs. His legs were skinny and brown. His feet were large in comparison to his slight build, and he wore no shirt, pronounced ribs showing on his sunken chest. He was balding, and his brown eyes turned flinty as Jake approached.

"I need a ride," he called to the captain, "to a Tuca-nos village about three hours down the Amazon. Think that tub will make it that far?"

The captain grinned, showing sharp and decayed teeth. "This boat of mine isn't called the *Dolphin* for nothin'. She floats even when we have the floods!"

Jake stood onshore, haggling with the captain over the price of such a trip. In Brazil, everyone bargained. Not to engage in such efforts was considered rude. Finally, when Jake flashed a five-dollar American bill in the captain's face, negotiations stopped. The captain grabbed the money and held out his hand to Jake, a big, welcoming grin splitting his small face.

"Come aboard."

With an answering grin, Jake hefted himself onto the small tug. It had once been red and white, but lack of care—or more probably lack of money—had prevented upkeep on the paint. With a practiced eye, Jake slowly walked the forty-foot tug, checking for leaks.

"You know the name of this village?" the captain called as he slid up onto a tall chair that was bolted to the deck in front of the wooden wheel.

"Yeah, they call it the village of the pink dolphins."

Nodding sagely, the skipper waved to the children on-shore, who, for a few coins, would untie the tug and push it away from the wharf. "I know the village. There's a Catholic hospital and mission there."

Jake dropped his duffel bag on the deck and moved up front as the tug chugged in reverse. The hollow sound of the engine, and the blue smoke pouring from it, perme-ated the humid air. Narrow strips of wooden planking served as benches along the tug's port and starboard sides. Jake sat down near the captain and looked out across the bow.

"What else do you know about the village?" Jake asked.

The captain laughed and maneuvered the tug around so that the bow was now pointed toward the huge ex-panse of the headwaters, which were nearly a mile in width. "We hardly ever see an American who speaks fluent Portuguese." The man eyed the gun at Jake's side. "You go for a reason, eh?"

"Yeah." Jake decided the skipper wasn't going to an-swer his question—at least not on the first try.

The crystal-clear tea-colored water of the Solimoes was beautiful in its clarity. Its color was caused by the tannin contained in the tree roots along its banks, which seeped out and tinted the water a raw umber. The Solimoes's temperature was far lower than the Rio Negro's. As a result, the river's depths were clear, icy and pretty in comparison to the milky brown waters of the warmer Rio Negro, which Jake could see beginning to intersect it up ahead. Soon, the water surface around the tug mingled patches of tea-colored water with lighter, muddied water, reminding Jake of a black-and-white marble cake Bess used to bake.

"They say there's trouble at that village," the captain said as he maneuvered his tug against the powerful currents of the two rivers mixing beneath them.

So the skipper *was* going to answer him, if obliquely. Jake was pleased. "What kind of trouble?"

The captain shrugged his thin shoulders, his hands busy on the wheel as he kept the tug on a straight course for the Amazon River. "Pai Jose—Father Jose—who runs the Catholic mission there at the village, is said to have trouble. That's all I know."

Rubbing his jaw, which needed a shave, Jake nodded. He knew that the Catholic missionaries had had a powerful influence all over South America. The Indians had been converted to Catholicism, but the numerous missions along the rivers of the Amazon Basin were places not only of worship, but also of medical help—often the only places such help was available.

"You know this priest?" Jake asked.

"Pai Jose is balding," the skipper said, gesturing to his own shining head, "like me. He's greatly loved by the Indians and the traders alike. If not for his doctoring, many would have died over the years." The skipper wrinkled his nose. "He is a fine man. I don't like what I hear is happening at the Tucanos village where he has his mission."

Jake ruminated over the information. Communications in this corner of the world were basically nonexistent outside of Manaus, except by word-of-mouth messages passed from one boat skipper to another. Few radios were used, because the humidity rusted them quickly in the tropical environment. Was Shah involved with Pai Jose? Was she even at the village? Jake didn't know—the information Travers had provided was sparse.

"They doing a lot of tree-cutting in this area?" Jake wanted to know.

"Yes!" The man gestured toward the thick jungle crowding the banks of the Amazon. "It brings us money. My tug is used to help bring the trees out of the channels along the Amazon to the Japanese ships anchored near Manaus."

It was a booming business, Jake conceded—and the money it supplied could mean the difference between survival and death to someone like the skipper.

"Besides," the man continued energetically as he brought the tug about thirty feet away from the Amazon's bank, where the current was less fierce, "the poor are streaming out of the cities to find land. They must clear the trees so that they can grow their own vegetables. No," he said sadly, "the cities are no place for the peasants. They are coming back, and we need the open land. Manaus no longer needs the rubber trees, and the farmers need the land. So, it is a good trade-off, eh?"

Jake didn't answer. He knew that the terrible poverty of Brazil, both inside and outside the cities, was genuine. Here and there along the muddy banks he could see small thatched huts made of grasses and palm leaves. Curious children, dressed in ragged shorts or thin, faded dresses, ran out to stare at them. He looked out across the enormous expanse of the Amazon. It made the Mississippi River look like a trickle.

"Look!" the skipper shouted with glee. "Dolphins!"

Sure enough, Jake saw three gray river dolphins arc into the air then disappear. They were playful, and soon they saw many more.

"This is a good sign," the skipper said, beaming. "Dolphins always bring luck. Hey! If you are truly lucky, you may get to see a pink dolphin near that village! They are very rare."

"What do the Indians say about pink dolphins?" Jake was enjoying the antics of the sleek, graceful gray animals that were now following the tug, playing tag.

"There is an old legend that if a pink dolphin falls in love with a beautiful young village girl, he will, at the time of the full moon, turn into a handsome youth. Once he has legs and lungs, he leaves the river to court this beautiful girl. He will lie with the girl, get her with child, then walk back into the water to become a pink dolphin again. A girl who has such an experience is said to be blessed."

Jake wondered about that legend, but said nothing. The legend could have been created to explain a young girl's sudden and unexpected pregnancy. Heaving a sigh, he allowed himself to relax. There was nothing to do for the next two and a half hours, until they reached the village. Stretching out on the narrow wooden seat, Jake decided to see if he could catch some badly needed sleep.

"Hey!" the skipper called. "We're here!"

Groggily Jake sat up. He was damp with sweat. He untied his neckerchief and mopped his face and neck. The tug was slowing, the engine's forward speed checked as they aimed at a dilapidated wooden dock where several Tucanos children waited.

Wiping sleep from his eyes, Jake stood up and rapidly sized up the small village huts thatched with palm fronds. The tall trees of the Amazon still lined the riverbanks, but just inside them the land had been cleared for homes for the Tucanos. He counted roughly fifty huts, and saw a number of Indian women near fires tending black iron cooking kettles. The women were dressed in colorful cotton dresses, their black hair long and their feet bare. The children raced around, barely clad. The short, barrel-chested, black-haired men held blowguns. Machetes hung on belts around many of their waists.

The odor of wood smoke combined with the muddy stench of the river. As the tug gently bumped the dock, Jake could also smell fish frying. About a dozen Tucanos children gathered, wide-eyed as Jake leaped from the tug to the dock. He set his duffel bag down on the gray, weathered surface of the poorly made dock.

"How can I get a ride back up the river to Manaus?" he asked the skipper.

Grinning toothily, the skipper pointed to the village. "Pai Jose has a radio. He knows the name of my tug. He can call the wharf at Manaus, and someone will find me."

That would have to be good enough, Jake thought. He lifted his hand to the skipper and turned to find the Indian children looking solemnly up at him, curiosity shining in their dark brown eyes. They were beautiful children, their brown skin healthy-looking, their bodies straight and proud. He wondered if Shah, because of her native ancestry, felt at home in the village.

"Pai Jose?" he asked them.

"Sim! Sim!" Yes! Yes! The oldest, a boy of about ten, gestured for Jake to follow him.

Slinging his bag over his shoulder, Jake followed the boy through the village. The ground consisted of a whitish, powdery clay base that rose in puffs around his boots. Most of the village was in the shade of the trees overhead, and the smoke purled and made shapes as it drifted through the leafy barrier. Shafts of sunlight filtered through the trees here and there, and Jake's skin burned. Tropical sunlight was fierce.

A well-worn path through the vegetation wound away from the village and up a small incline onto a rounded hill that overlooked the river, and Jake could see a rectangular adobe brick structure near the top of it. Palm trees, both short and tall, bracketed the path. The calling of birds was nonstop, and sometimes, Jake would catch sight of one flitting colorfully through the brown limbs and green leaves of the thousands of trees.

The path opened into a small, grassy clearing. At the other end was the mission. It wasn't much, in Jake's opinion—just a grouping of three or four structures with a white cross on the roof of the largest building. That had to be the church. The place was well kept, and the path obviously had been swept, probably with a palm-leaf broom. Pink, white and red hibiscus bloomed around the buildings in profusion. Orchids hung down from the trees, turning the air heady with their cloying perfume.

Just as the Indian boy stopped and pointed at the church, Jake heard angry, heated voices. One was a woman's. He turned, keying his hearing to the sound. Giving the boy a few coins in thanks, Jake set his duffel bag on the ground and followed the sound. Turning the corner, he spotted a small wooden wharf down by the river, with several canoes pulled up onshore nearby. Five people stood on the wharf.

Frowning, Jake lengthened his stride down the sloping path. As he drew closer, he recognized Shah Travers in the center of the group. His heart started to pound, and it wasn't because of the suffocating humidity or because of fear. Shah was tall—much taller than he'd expected. Her hair hung in two black, shining braids that stood out against the short-sleeved khaki shirt she wore. Mud had splattered her khaki trousers, and she wore calf-high rubber boots that were also covered with the thick, gooey substance.

What was going down? Jake saw the Catholic priest, an older man with wire-rimmed glasses, dressed in white pants and a shirt, plus his clerical collar, standing tensely. The other three made Jake uneasy. Two of them looked like goons hired by the well-dressed third man. Shah's husky voice was low with fury, and he couldn't catch what she said, but she was squaring off with the man in the light suit and white panama hat.

"I will not stay off that land!" Shah told Hernandez heatedly. "You can't make me!"

Hernandez's thin-lipped smile slipped. He touched the lapel of his cream-colored linen suit, where a small purple-and-white orchid boutonniere had been placed. "You have no choice, Miss Travers! That is my land, and I can do whatever I please with it—and that includes cutting down the trees!"

Shah tried to control her anger over the confrontation. She saw both of Hernandez's bodyguards come forward, trying to intimidate her. Well, it wouldn't work! She was aware that Pai Jose was wringing his hands, wanting to make peace. Her own heart was pounding with fear. She dreaded this kind of conflict. She'd been raised in a family of screaming and shouting, and she hated it.

"Look," she said between gritted teeth, "you can't stop me from going onto that land! I know my rights, and I know Brazil's laws!"

Hernandez glowered down at her. "You are impertinent, Miss Travers. You Americans think you can come down here and cause trouble. Well, you can't! I forbid you to come into the area where we are going to log." He turned and looked at his men. "And if you so much as set foot on my land, I can assure you, my men will take care of you!"

Permanently, Shah thought. Before she could respond, the larger of the two men, a blond, German-looking hulk, moved forward. He gripped her by the collar of her shirt. Gasping, Shah froze momentarily. She heard Pai Jose give a cry of protest.

"Please," Pai Jose begged, "this isn't—"

Suddenly a hand appeared on the hulk's shoulder. "Now, where I come from, you treat a lady like a lady," the new man growled, pinching the man's thick muscles enough to let the lout know he meant business.

Shah's eyes widened considerably. Who *was* this man? Confusion clashed with her shock. He was tall. Taller than any of them, and bigger, too, if that was possible. Momentary fear sent a frisson of warning through her. He looked like an American, yet he'd spoken in fluent Portuguese. Her heart pounding hard in her chest, Shah gulped. His face was rugged and lined. When her gaze flew to his, something happened. Her heart snagged, a rush of wild feelings tunneling through her. His gray eyes were narrowed and nearly colorless, and for a brief second, Shah saw them thaw and felt an incredible sense of safety.

Instantly her heart and head denied those feelings. Men didn't protect, they abused. "Get your hand off me!" she snapped at the blond man, and started to take a step back.

Jake jerked the hulk's shoulder just enough to force him to release Shah. The other bodyguard, a leaner, meaner-looking man, whirled toward him, his hand on the butt of the machete he carried in a long leather sheath at his side.

"Now," Jake drawled in Portuguese, "I don't think any of us should behave like ruffians, do you? This is a lady, and we have a priest here. I know you boys have manners. How about showing them to me?" Jake stepped away, his hand moving to the butt of his Beretta in a not-so-subtle warning that didn't go unnoticed.

Hernandez hissed a curse and spun around. "Who are you?" he demanded.

Jake smiled, but the smile didn't reach his eyes. Both goons were statues, waiting for orders from their thin Brazilian boss. "I'm Ms. Travers' bodyguard," he said levelly.

Shah's mouth fell open. "You're *what?*" The word came out like a croak.

"Darlin', you stay out of this for now. This is male business."

Shah's mouth snapped shut. Fury shot through her. "Why—"

Jake barely turned his head. "Pai Jose, why don't you take Miss Travers back to the mission? I'll finish the conversation with these boys alone."

Hernandez jerked a look toward Shah. "A body-guard?"

"Well, you've got a couple, from the looks of it," Jake pointed out mildly, giving Hernandez a lazy smile. "Why shouldn't she have one?"

"Well—" Hernandez sputtered, then glared at Shah. "It won't do you any good! You hire this, this American pig, and—"

"Hernandez, I didn't hire him!" Shah protested, straightening her shirt and collar. Who was he? Too much was at stake, and she wasn't about to get away from the point of Hernandez's unexpected visit. "And even if I did, I would still go onto that parcel of land where you're going to cut down the rain forest trees. It's my right to film anything I want. You can't stop me."

Jake saw Shah's cheeks flush. Her skin was glistening from the humidity, and she was simply breathtaking. Her body was ramrod-straight, her shoulders were thrown back proudly, and he wanted to applaud her courage. Still, under the circumstances, it obviously was a foolhardy stance to take. This character Hernandez clearly hated everything Shah stood for. In Brazil, he knew women were frequently considered second-class citizens. Too many Brazilian men viewed women merely in terms of how many children they could bear, proof of a man's macho ability.

"Let's call an end to this discussion," Jake suggested amiably. He opened his hands and gestured toward Hernandez and his henchmen. "What do you say, gentlemen?"

Intimidated by the hardware Jake was carrying and by his size, Hernandez snarled, "Come!" at his goons, and they moved back into a dugout canoe with a small motor attached to the rear.

Shah remained tensely beside Pai Jose, breathing hard. She was still shaking inwardly from the man grabbing her by the collar.

"Thank God," Pai Jose whispered. He clasped his hands in a prayerful gesture and nodded to Jake. "I don't know who you are, *senhor,* but you have surely saved Shah."

Shah watched as Hernandez's canoe sputtered noisily away from the dock, heading across the wide river. Then she turned to the American. "Who *are* you?"

Jake held up his hands. "Easy, I'm a friend. Your father sent me down here to—"

A gasp broke from Shah. "My father! Oh, brother, this is too much!" She leaped from the wharf. Once on the bank, she shouted, "Stay away from me! Just leave!" and hurried up the slope.

Nonplussed, Jake watched Shah head for the mission. He turned to the priest.

"Did I say something wrong?"

"My son," Pai Jose said in a sorrowful voice, "you just broke open a festering wound in her heart." He mustered a sad smile and offered his thin hand. "I am Pai Jose. And you?"

Disgruntled, Jake introduced himself. He noticed that the priest's hand was not only thin, but frail, as well. Pai Jose was probably close to seventy years old. His hair was silvered, and his small gold-rimmed glasses slid down on his hawklike nose. There was a kindness to the man, and Jake was glad he wasn't angry with him, too.

"Mr. Randolph, may I ask the nature of your visit?" the priest asked as he walked slowly off the dock with him.

"I'm here to take Shah home. Her father doesn't want her down in the Amazon. He's afraid she'll be hurt."

With a soft chuckle, the priest shook his head. "My son, Shah Travers is committed to saving our precious rain forest. God help her, but she isn't about to go home with you. And certainly not because her father sent you."

His mouth quirking, Jake followed the unhurried priest up the path toward the mission. "What do you mean, Father?"

"It's not really my place to speak of Shah or her personal problems." At the top of the knoll, huffing slightly, Pai Jose pointed to a small white adobe house that sat on the other side of the mission. "Shah is working with me on cataloging many of the medicinal plants used by the Tucanos shamans of the village. She has a hut down there, but it's my guess that she went back to the lab to work on some more plant specimens. Why don't you speak to her? I'm sure Shah can answer all of your questions."

But would she? Jake had his doubts. He nodded to the old priest. "Any chance of paying you to put me up here at the mission?"

"Of course, my son. You may stay with me at the cleric house."

"Money isn't any object."

"A donation would be satisfactory, my son, with our thanks. Red Feather, a dear Tucanos boy who helps me at the hospital and mission, will take your luggage and place sheets on a spare cot for you."

"Thanks, Father. Look, I've got to talk to Miss Travers."

"Of course." The priest smiled, his face wrinkling like crisp, transparent paper. "Dinner is at 8:00 p.m."

Jake nodded. He placed his duffel bag in front of the door the priest had indicated, then walked down another cleanly swept path toward the lab. He couldn't shake the image of Shah's face from his mind's eye—or his heart, to be brutally honest with himself. The photograph of Shah completely failed to do her justice. She had an earthy beauty. And beautiful *was* a word that Jake would use to describe her. Although their meeting had been fleeting, her facial features were forever branded on his memory. Her eyes were a tawny gold color, more intriguing than the light brown indicated in the photo. The Amazonian sunlight gave her eyes the color of the expensive golden topaz that was found and mined in Brazil. Her hair, thick and black, held captive in two braids that nearly reached her waist, was the inky bluish color of a raven's wing. Was it her mouth that intrigued him the most, that made him feel hot and shaky inside? In the photo, her lips had been compressed, but in person her mouth was full and lovely, reminding Jake of the luscious beauty of the orchids that hung in profusion around the mission from the tall, stately pau trees.

He slowed his step as he approached the lab. Shah was a strong-willed woman, there was no doubt about that. She hadn't screamed, fainted or backed down when that goon grabbed her. No, she'd stood her ground, her chin tilted upward, her mouth compressed and her eyes defiant. Jake had been in Brazil three other times, and on one occasion he'd come face-to-face with the most feared of all predators—the jaguar. He'd never forgotten that cat's golden eyes widening, the ebony pupils shrinking to pinpoints. The power he'd felt as he'd momentarily locked gazes with that cat was similarly etched in his memory. Shah's eyes were like the jaguar's: huge, alive with intelligence, and containing a spark of fierceness that he was sure was a gift from her Sioux heritage.

Shaking his head, Jake placed his hand on the lab's doorknob. Suddenly this was more than an assignment.

It was an adventure—an adventure called "life." For the last four years he'd been living in a barren desert of grief. Now, with Shah impacting him like a hurtling meteor filling the night sky with its overwhelming brilliance, Jake felt guarded and uneasy. And, simultaneously, he was afraid—afraid that Shah would hate him and ask him to leave. Would she? He knocked on the wooden door with his knuckles to let her know that he was coming in.

Chapter Three

As Jake stepped into the lab, he heard the click of a pistol being cocked. The telltale click made him snap his head to the left. Shah stood behind a table covered with plant specimens, both hands wrapped around a deadly-looking .45.

"I told you to leave," she gritted out, glaring at him.

Jake's mouth fell open. Her voice was as low as a jaguar's growl. Her golden eyes were narrowed, just like the jaguar's.

"But—"

"I'm surprised my father was stupid enough to send someone else down to try to kidnap me."

His eyes widening, Jake slowly raised both his hands. Shah wasn't kidding around, he decided. She was fully capable of pulling that trigger. "Look," he told her, "we need to talk. Why don't you lower that gun, and we can—"

"Oh, sure," Shah said sarcastically. "Last time, Father sent two jerks who threw a gunny sack over my head and started dragging me toward the river, to a canoe they had hidden in the brush." She pressed her lips together and fought a desire to lower the gun. The man, whoever he was, looked genuinely upset and contrite. She was drawn to his eyes, whether she wanted to be or not. They looked terribly sad, and there were haunted shadows in their recesses. Whoever this hulking giant of a man was, something very painful must have happened to him. Angry at herself, at her tendency to always fall for the potential underdog, Shah hardened her voice. "My father sent you. That's all I need to know! Now get out of here, go back to Manaus, and leave me alone!"

Jake heard the real distress beneath the hardness that she was trying to bluff him with and slowly lowered his hands. "Where I come from, we introduce ourselves. I'm Jake Randolph. I work for Perseus, an organization based in Washington, D.C. It sends people around the world to help those who are in trouble."

With a twist of her lips, Shah moved carefully, the gun still pointed at Jake. "As you can see, Mr. Randolph, I'm not in trouble."

"You were a few minutes ago, lady."

"I could have handled Hernandez!"

"That big goon of his was going to pick you up by your collar and probably throw you into the Amazon. Then what would you have done? Gotten eaten by piranhas?" Jake was teasing her, hoping she'd lower the gun.

Scowling, Shah kept the long wooden table covered with plant specimens waiting to be cataloged between them. The lab had no electricity and had to rely on the natural light that filtered through the three large windows. "I swim in the Amazon and the channels all the time, and the piranhas don't attack me."

Allowing himself a bit of a grin, Jake said, "Because you're the meanest junkyard dog in the neighborhood?" He liked Shah. He sensed she was trying to bluff her way out of the situation. But in her eyes he could see a gamut of very real emotions bubbling close to the surface. He saw fear, real fear, in her eyes, a little anger, and a whole lot of wariness. More than anything, he liked the soft fullness of her lips and those flawless high cheekbones. Her wide, lovely eyes took on a slightly tilted appearance in her oval face. Jaguar eyes.

Jake Randolph's teasing lessened some of Shah's primal fear of him. She ignored his smile and tried to pretend she didn't like the strong shape of his mouth. Despite his craggy features, there was a gentleness to him that threw her off guard. How could anyone who looked that harsh have a gentle bone in his body? Her experience with men had taught her that none of them were to be trusted, anyway—regardless of their looks. "Sit down. Over there, in that wooden chair. And don't try any funny stuff."

Jake nodded, moving unhurriedly so as not to alarm her. He quickly scanned the lab. It was swept clean, and the walls were whitewashed, but green mold still clung stubbornly to the corners near the ceiling, speaking eloquently of the tropics' high humidity. The building held many tables, as well as a microscope and other scientific equipment. He saw a small glass of water with a lovely pink-and-white strand of small orchids in it. It gave off a faint perfume that was light and delicate—like Shah. He sat down.

"Now, with your left hand, very slowly take that gun out of your holster and place it on the floor. Kick it away from you with your foot."

"I'm a southpaw," he offered, giving her a slight smile.

Irritated, Shah moved closer, always keeping the table as a barrier between them. "Then use your right hand."

Jake unsnapped the leather safety, withdrew the Beretta and laid it at his feet. "See? If I was really out to get you, I wouldn't have told you that, would I?"

"On the other hand," Shah snapped waspishly, "you could be lying. You could really be right-handed. Most people are."

He straightened and laughed. It was a deep, rolling laugh that filled the lab. "Your logic is faultless." He held her distrustful gaze. "You know, you ought to think about working for Perseus. They could use someone like you. You think like a marine."

Shah fought to shake off his sudden and unexpected laughter. She saw the light dancing in his gray eyes, as if he truly enjoyed their repartee. Her hands were sweaty, and the gun was heavy. Shah hated guns, but they were a way of life down here in the Amazon. "If that's supposed to be a compliment, then I don't accept it. Now, push that gun away with the toe of your boot."

Jake gave the Beretta a healthy shove, and the pistol slid across the wooden floor. He watched as Shah started to move toward it. If he was going to get her to realize he wasn't her enemy, he had to earn her trust.

"Don't you want me to put my knife on the floor and kick it away, too?"

Shah halted and frowned. "Yes—I guess so. Do it— please."

"Right or left hand?"

There was amusement in his eyes, and Shah knew he was playing her for a fool. "When you get done laughing at me, you can use your right hand."

"I wasn't laughing at you."

"Really?"

Jake placed the knife on the floor. "It's rude to laugh at people. At least that's what my mother taught me."

"Then what did I see in your eyes?"

"Admiration."

Shah watched him kick the knife away. It landed near the pistol. This Randolph stymied her. "Now you stay still while I pick up your weapons," she told him. "One move and I'll blow your head off."

Jake didn't believe Shah's blustering. To disarm her distrust of him, he said, "I admire your courage under the circumstances. Not many women would be living in the Amazon jungle alone." She was shaken, he could tell, and he saw the pistol tremble in her hand. Carefully she moved toward his weapons, all the while keeping her gun trained on him.

With the toe of her boot, Shah kicked the weapons beneath the table. Finally she lowered the gun. There was a good ten feet between the two of them. "Father must have really gotten lucky snagging you. His last two tries failed miserably, so he must have put up a lot of money to hire the best kidnapper he could find—you." She allowed the pistol to hang at her side as she wiped her sweaty brow with the back of her left hand. "Too bad he couldn't have put all that wasted money into a nice donation to save the rain forest here, instead. But then, he wouldn't do that."

"He's sent two other teams down here to kidnap you?" Jake asked. There was indignation in his voice—and anger, too. He and Morgan instinctively hadn't trusted Travers. Now he was beginning to understand why.

Wearily Shah leaned against the wall, tense and on guard. "I don't know why I'm wasting my time talking with you. I've got a million things to do. Just stand up and go back down to the wharf. I'll have Red Feather take you by canoe to the nearest village where the tugs dock when they're working for Hernandez, pushing the logs down the river."

"I don't want to go."

Her spine stiffened, and she glared at him. "You don't have a choice!"

"Sure I do." Jake held up his hands in a peace-making gesture. "I'm not here to kidnap you. Your father hired me to try to *talk* you into coming home."

With a bitter laugh, Shah said, "Sure he did! He's a cold, hard businessman, Randolph. Anyone who gets in the way of his greedy progress is a liability, and he gets rid of them pronto. I'm a liability."

"Why would he want you out of here?" Jake asked reasonably, purposely keeping his voice low and soothing. Every minute spent with Shah convinced him that he should stay around. For the first time, Jake saw the slight shadows beneath her glorious golden eyes. There was tiredness around her mouth, too. Even the clothes she wore seemed a size too big for her. Was she working herself to death down here?

"Because," Shah said wearily, "he probably wants to protect his investment. I'm fighting a one-woman war to stop the destruction of the rain forest. Not that I'm the only one. There are other groups. But this area is especially important. Hernandez is particularly adept at slash-and-burn techniques."

Jake gave her a long look. "That's a hell of an indictment against anyone, especially your father."

Just the roughened tone of his voice soothed Shah's frayed nerves. He had a way of defusing her, and it made her relax. She straightened, making sure the pistol fit snugly in the palm of her hand. She couldn't trust this giant of a man. He could jump her if he got her off guard. His size alone would overwhelm her ability to defend herself and escape.

"Unfortunately, I am his daughter, but that's where any connection between him and me ends," Shah told him tightly. "My mother divorced him when I was twelve years old, and I couldn't have been happier."

"Why?"

Shah gave him a wide-eyed look. "Why would you want to know?"

"Because I care."

He did. It was on the tip of Shah's tongue to deny Randolph's words, but she saw genuine caring in his eyes, and felt that same powerful sense of protection emanating from him that she had on the dock when Hernandez's bodyguard grabbed her. Fighting the feeling, because it was foreign to her, Shah resurrected what little anger was left and snapped, "You care because he's paid you some fantastic sum of money! I know your kind, and I'm not about to trust you, so forget it! Now stand up!"

"I'm telling you the truth, Shah." Jake purposely used her first name to defuse her intent. It worked. He saw a startled expression momentarily flit across her features.

"Truth!" Shah spit out. "The only truth I see is you're a hired gun of my father's!"

"What was it someone said? Truth hurts, but it's the lie that leaves scars? Why can't you believe me? I'm not here to kidnap you. Your father asked me to try to persuade you to come home, but if I couldn't, then I was to become your bodyguard instead.''

Rolling her eyes, Shah moved behind the table. She placed the heavy gun on the wooden surface. Her hand had grown tired from holding it. Wiping the sweat from her upper lip, she glared at him. ''Don't quote philosophy to me. The most dangerous kind of lie is the type that resembles the truth!''

''Who said that?'' Jake asked, truly impressed by her philosophical bent. He was delighted with the discovery; it was just one more amazing facet to Shah Travers.

''Oh, please! I had six years of college. Don't you think I took a course or two in philosophy? Kant? Descartes?''

''Great, we have a lot more in common than even I thought. We'll get along fine.''

''You aren't staying!''

''Now, Shah, I told you the truth. It's obvious to me you need me to stay. Fine. I'll just hang around like a big guard dog and protect you from the likes of Hernandez and his goons.'' Jake grinned, but inwardly he felt sorry for Shah. She appeared unsettled and exhausted. And why shouldn't she feel that way? Hernandez had been ready to have her beaten up if Jake hadn't arrived in the nick of time. She knew it, too, he suspected. Shah was nobody's fool.

''You can't stay because I don't want you to stay.''

''I can be of help to you.''

''I suppose you have a degree in biology?''

''No, but I have a degree in philosophy.''

''That doesn't get these plants identified and cataloged.''

''I'm a fast learner.''

"You're impossible!"

"Thank you."

"It wasn't a compliment, Randolph, so don't sit there preening about it."

He tilted his head. "Are you mad at all men, or just your father?"

The question, spoken so softly, caught Shah off guard. The adrenaline from the confrontation with Hernandez was wearing off, and she felt shaky, mushy-kneed. She pulled over a four-legged wooden stool and sat down. What was it about Jake Randolph that threw her off-balance? Maybe it was his grave features, which looked carved out of granite, or his powerful physical presence. One look into those light gray eyes and Shah had realized she was dealing with a highly perceptive man. She had no experience with his type, so she didn't know how to react to him. Instinctively, she felt him trying to get her to relent and trust him.

Rubbing her brow, Shah muttered, "My track record with men isn't great. I don't trust any of them farther than I can throw them."

"Beginning with your father?" Jake needed to know the truth about Shah's background. It would give him understanding of her distrust toward him.

"I don't owe you my life story."

"That's true." The corners of his mouth lifted slightly. "I was born and raised in the Cascade Mountains of Oregon. Now, I don't know if you've ever been there, but it's one of the most beautiful places on the face of Mother Earth."

Shah's eyes narrowed. He'd used the term *Mother Earth*. What was Randolph up to? No one used that term unless they were Native American or some of the ecologically responsible people who believed in the Gaia theory, which held that the planet was indeed, a living being.

Ah, success! Jake mentally patted himself on the back for using the term *Mother Earth*. Shah had sat up. He had her full, undivided attention. Perhaps the more he revealed of himself the more she'd learn to trust him. Inwardly Jake laughed at the thought. He had been a typical male bastion of silence before marrying Bess. He'd been unable to communicate, unable to share what he was feeling with her. However, Bess wouldn't stand for the one-way communication system, and she'd insisted he open up. He was glad, because their marriage had deepened with joy and sharing as a result. Still, he wasn't used to baring his soul to just anyone, and on one level Shah was a stranger to him. On another level, however, Jake sensed, with a knowing that frightened him, that they were very much alike.

"I grew up on a small farm in a valley where my dad made a living for us by growing pears. We had a huge orchard, and my two sisters and I worked with him when we didn't have school. Dad was a real philosopher. He saw everything in terms of seasonal changes, the earth being alive, and respecting the environment. We never dumped oil on the ground, threw away a battery in the woods or put fertilizer on the soil. Instead, we had a couple of cows for milk, three horses because we kids liked to ride, and plenty of rabbits and chickens for food. He used to compost all the garbage from our household and spread it through the orchard twice a year as fertilizer. Dad had the finest pears in Oregon."

"You said 'Mother Earth,'" Shah growled, uncomfortable.

Jake nodded, placing his hands on his knees. He saw the curiosity burning in her eyes and realized he'd struck a responsive chord in Shah. Jake hadn't felt so excited in years. Shah was a challenge, yet he sensed a fierce, caring passion lurking just beneath her prickly exterior. She had a passion for living life, Jake realized, and that excited him as little had since Bess's and the children's deaths.

"Yes, I did."

"Are you Native American?"

"No, just a combination of Irish, Dutch and English."

"Then why did you use that term?"

"Because my parents always spoke about the planet that way."

Shah sat back, trying to gauge whether Randolph was giving her a line or was really telling her the truth. "Oh..." she murmured.

Pleased that Shah was softening toward him, Jake continued in his rumbling voice. "I think Mom might have had a little Native American in her. Cherokee, maybe, somewhere a long ways back."

"Then that would give you some Native American blood."

Chuckling, Jake held up his hand. "Darlin', I'm about as white as a man can get. No, if I've got a drop of Cherokee in me, it's so washed out that it wouldn't matter."

Shah pointedly ignored the endearment that rolled off his tongue. It had felt like a cat licking her hand. "But it does," she said fervently. "It's a gene type. Even if you have just a drop of Cherokee blood, it would be enough. Genes have memory, and it's possible that your Cherokee gene is a dominant gene, which would give you an understanding that our planet is more than just a planet. She's alive. She communicates, and she breathes, just like us."

There was such burning hope in her eyes that Jake couldn't bring himself to argue with her. Then again, she was a biologist, and she knew all about genes and such, so she could be right. If that meant something important and vital to Shah, then Jake was willing to go along with her logic. "Well, I feel what matters is what we do on a daily basis," he demurred.

"Your walk is your talk. That's a Lakota saying." Thrilled that she was actually communicating with him, Jake heaved an inner sigh of relief. The gold in Shah's eyes danced with sunlight now, as if she'd met a brother of like mind. However, Jake didn't want to be her brother. Far from it.

"Lakota?" he asked, fighting back his less-than-professional thoughts.

"Yes."

"What's that?"

"Whites call us Sioux, but that's an Iroquois word that means 'enemy.' We call ourselves Lakota, Nakota and Dakota. There are three separate tribes, depending upon where you were born and the heritage passed down through your family. My mother is Santee, and that's Lakota."

"I see." Jake smiled. "I like learning these things."

"In Brazil," Shah went on enthusiastically, "the people are a combination of Portuguese, African and native. Brazil is a melting pot, and they certainly don't worry what color you are. And on top of that, the largest concentration of Japanese outside of Japan live in São Paulo. Did you know that?"

"No."

"I like Brazil because of that. You aren't judged on your skin color down here." Shah held out her hand.

"My skin looks tan in comparison to yours. But a Brazilian wouldn't care."

"You have golden skin," Jake told her. Her skin was a dusky color, and he wondered what it would be like to lightly explore its texture—to slide his fingertips along her arm. The thought was so powerful that Jake was stunned into silence. There was such innocence to Shah, to her simplified outlook on life in general.

Heat fled into Shah's face, and she looked away from his kind gray eyes, momentarily embarrassed by her reaction to his statement. "Well," she muttered, more defensively, "you know what I'm saying. Lakota people judge others by their walk being their talk."

"It's a good philosophy," Jake said, meaning it. "So why don't you let me prove myself to you the same way?"

Shah frowned. "What do you mean?" Why did she have the feeling that behind this man's dangerous looks there was a steel-trap mind?

With a lazy shrug of his shoulders, Jake said, "I've already told you the truth about why I'm here. I accept that you don't want to go home. So why don't you let me be your bodyguard? It's obvious you need one, with Hernandez around."

Getting up, Shah began to pace nervously back and forth. "No!"

"I can't go home," Jake told her reasonably, opening his hands. "Your father has paid me for a month's worth of work down here. I'm not the type to gyp someone out of work they've already paid me to do."

"You should have been a lawyer," Shah charged heatedly.

"Thanks. Was that a compliment?"

"You know it wasn't!"

His grin was broad and forgiving. "Calm down, Shah. I'm not your enemy. If I was, why didn't I side with Hernandez earlier? You know, I took a hell of a risk by entering that lopsided fray. If your father really wants you out of here, I could have stood aside and let Hernandez do his dirty deed."

Halting, Shah ruminated over his observation. She eyed him intently, the silence thickening in the lab. "Why should I believe you?" she asked him heatedly.

He held her golden gaze. He could see that she was fraught with indecision. Everything was so tenuous between them, and Jake had never wanted anyone's trust more. He wanted this woman's trust so badly he could taste it. "You're right," he told her quietly. "If your father has had others try to kidnap you, then you've got reason to be paranoid. But I can't prove myself to you except on a minute-by-minute basis, Shah. You'll have to be the judge and jury on whether I'm for real or not."

"I hate men like you!" she gritted out. "They say all the right things. You confuse me!"

"Truth is never confusing."

"Actions are a far better barometer of whether someone's lying," Shah snapped. Worriedly she paced some more. "I don't need you around. I've got enough responsibilities, Randolph. Tomorrow morning I'm going to take my video camera and canoe down the river. I'll make a landing on the parcel where Hernandez has a permit to cut down the rain forest trees. I need that film for the television station that's funding my work."

"Let me go along, then."

She stopped pacing and wrapped her arms against her chest. "No."

"Why not?"

"Because you could throw my video equipment into the river and—"

"I wouldn't do that, Shah," he told her sincerely. "I know you're jumpy about my presence, but I can't go home." He didn't want to, either. Shah fascinated him. She was an amalgam of fire, spirit and passion—all linked with innocence.

"Pai Jose said I could stay at the mission," Jake told her in a soothing tone, "and I'll do that. He said you live in the village. Let's take this relationship of ours one day at a time. I'll be your gofer. I'll do whatever little odd jobs or piddly tasks come up." Looking around, he added, "And judging from the way this lab looks, you need about five biology assistants helping you." Indeed, there were at least a hundred plant specimens in open plastic bags on the four tables. "I'm a pretty quick learner. Just see me as your right-hand man for a month."

Shah sat down, weary as never before. She didn't know what to do or say. Her heart was pleading with her to believe Randolph, while her head was screaming nonstop that he was lying, despite that roughened tone of his voice that sent a tremor of some undefined longing through her. And his eyes! She sighed. The man could melt icebergs with those eyes of his. There was such seemingly sincere gentleness contained in them that Shah had the ridiculous urge to throw herself into his arms and let him hold her.

Of all things! Shah berated herself. Men meant hurt, that was all. Lies and hurt, and not necessarily in that order. Randolph was too smooth, and far too intelligent, and Shah felt she'd more than met her mental match.

"We have a lot in common," Jake said, breaking the brittle silence. "I probably have Indian blood, however little it might be. My parents raised my family to respect Mother Earth." He gave her an imploring look, because her face mirrored her indecision. "What do you say? A day at a time? Let my walk be my talk?"

She glared at him. "A day at a time? Randolph, I'm going to be monitoring your every move one minute at a time."

"No problem."

Pointing to his gun and knife, Shah acidly added, "And these weapons stay with me!"

"Fine."

The man was infuriating! He was unlike any man she'd ever met. He didn't try to argue with her or belittle her decisions. "Just who are you?" Shah asked irritably, sliding off the stool. She holstered her gun, picked up his weapons and stalked around the table. Jerking open the door, she turned and added, "Never mind. I don't want to know. Just leave me alone, Randolph, and we'll get along fine. Stay up here with Pai Jose. The Great Spirit knows, he needs all the help he can get. He'd love to have a hardworking American around for thirty days."

She was gone. As Jake looked around, the lab suddenly seemed darker. Shah reminded him of blinding sunlight; her presence was riveting and undeniable. Rising slowly to his feet, he rubbed his sweaty hands against his pants. A slight smile lurked at the corners of his mouth. Well, their first skirmish had ended in a decided victory for him. As he ambled out of the lab and quietly closed the door behind him, Jake whistled softly. Yes, the world was suddenly looking brighter. Shah was like sunshine on water; scintillating, ever-changing. There was an underlying tenderness to her, too. He hadn't been wrong about her earthiness, either—not judging from all the plants and flowers in the lab, and her work to catalog them and save the valuable information for the world at large.

Shah Travers had many fine qualities, Jake decided as he walked over to the mission. His duffel bag was gone, carried inside by Red Feather, the Tucanos boy who worked with Pai Jose. He stopped in the center of the small yard enclosed by the mission buildings and looked around. The profusion of color, the songs of the birds and the many scents mingling in the humid air made Jake smile broadly. The Amazon could be a cruel killer, he knew. But right now, the area was clothed in a raiment of beauty, because Shah Travers cared—deeply, passionately—for something outside of herself.

Whistling merrily, Jake decided to take a walk around the place. His mercenary side was always close at hand. He didn't trust Hernandez. Although he didn't know the local politics, he wanted to map out the village for his own satisfaction. He felt naked without his knife and pistol, but he was convinced that sooner or later Shah would trust him enough to give the weapons back.

But first things first. Reconnoitering the village like the recon marine he had once been was at the top of his list. Were these Indians friendly? Were they used to white men? Or would they use blowgun arrows tipped with deadly curare to kill him? There was a lot to discover, Jake conceded with a frown. Maybe the Tucanos accepted Shah because she carried native blood in her veins. Maybe Pai Jose was allowed to stay here because of his unceasing humanitarian work with them. He wasn't sure at all.

The dangers of the Amazon were many and real. Jake knew that from his other missions, although he'd never before spent so much time in the rain forest. On guard, he tucked away the warm feelings lingering in his heart regarding Shah. He was astonished by those emotions, because for the past four years he'd felt nothing, numbed by the loss of his family. Shah's unexpected entrance into his life had been responsible for that change. But what was he going to do about it? He wasn't sure. He wasn't sure of anything right now.

Chapter Four

The Tucanos village was a long, haphazard affair that hugged the dry, cracked bank of the Amazon River. At first, Jake was jumpy about the Indians, but soon he had fifteen children following him as if he were the pied piper. The few men present were the old ones, and the women were busy working over their cooking pots. The younger men were probably out hunting during the daylight hours. They were a handsome people, Jake conceded, short but with robust bodies and clean features. Everywhere he walked, the old men and women would look up and stare at him, and some would give him a shy smile. He did the same.

The thatched huts were circular and varied in diameter, depending, Jake supposed, on the number of people living in them. Fires were kept outside of the homes, and Jake spotted woven mats placed on the dirt floor in several of them. The Tucanos people were primitive, without many civilized amenities. There was no electricity, except for what was produced by a gasoline-fed generator that Pai Jose kept behind the small infirmary next to the church. Jake doubted the old priest used it often—perhaps only when light was needed at night for a surgery.

Jake saw that he was coming to the end of the village. One small thatched hut with a dried brown palm-leaf roof sat off by itself. The huts were placed among the tall trees to take advantage of the shade. He slowed, and was about to turn around when he saw Shah emerge from the more isolated hut. Not wanting another confrontation with her, he started to turn, but it was too late.

Shah caught sight of Randolph, walking near her hut. "What are you doing? Snooping around?" she challenged as she walked toward the riverbank, where her dugout canoe was beached. She felt upset to see that Randolph was still around, still so close. Somehow, she hadn't wanted him to know where she was living.

"I was looking around." Jake shoved his hands in his pockets and smiled down at the assembled children in faded cotton shorts who trailed after him. He, too, moved toward the canoe. "It's an old marine habit," he offered.

"Marine?" And then Shah chastised herself for her curiosity. Randolph looked military, she acknowledged. Still, despite his size and his craggy features, she simply didn't feel threatened by him. Unable to understand why, she became angry with herself. She stopped at the canoe. Bento, her Tucanos helper, had found six new orchids along one of the lesser-used channels and brought them back for her to identify. But they had to be properly cared for if she was to try to find out what species they were. She had taught the Indian to place the plants in moist palm-fiber baskets to keep them safe and alive.

Jake stopped at the bow of the canoe and watched as she got down on her knees to gently and carefully gather up a multipetaled yellow flower. Perhaps conversation would ease the scowl on her broad brow.

"I was in the Marine Corps for sixteen years before I joined Perseus," he explained.

Shah glanced up. His towering figure was back-lit by the sun. The shadows deepened the harshness of his features, which would have been frightening if not for his boyish expression. She placed the orchid in a large plastic bag.

"You're a warrior, then." Somehow that fitted him. Shah couldn't picture him in a suit and tie.

He nodded. "Yeah, we saw ourselves as that. Your people were known as warriors, too."

Shah gently lifted the orchid and set it outside the canoe. She took a rusty tin can and walked to the river for water.

"The Lakota recognize that men *and* women can be warriors. It isn't gender-related."

"I didn't know that."

She gave him a dark look, then knelt down, her knees bracketing the orchid. Pouring water around the roots, she muttered, "Nowadays every woman has to be a warrior, to stand up and be counted, because we're the only ones who can save Mother Earth." She lifted her chin, challenge in her low voice. "It's the men who have polluted, poisoned and ruined our Earth in the name of greed, politics and self-oriented policies."

Jake looked up at the slow-moving Amazon. The muddy river's surface was like glass. He considered Shah's impassioned words. Looking back down at her, he realized she was waiting for his reaction. *Good.* He sensed her interest in him; he desperately needed to cultivate that fragile trust.

"I wouldn't disagree with you, Shah. Men have been raping Mother Earth for centuries. Everything's coming due now, though. It's payback time."

"*Rape* is the right word," she muttered, closing the plastic bag around the orchid's stem. She glanced at him, surprised that he agreed with her. Perhaps he was just stringing her along, trying to get her to believe he was really on her side. She was standing, ready to lift the heavy container, when Jake came forward.

"Here, let me carry that for you." He saw her golden eyes flare with surprise. Taking the plant container, he said, "I'm a great gofer. Tell me where you want this plant."

Stunned, Shah jerked her hands away from the container as he slid his large, scarred hands around its circumference. "Well, I . . . in my hut. I was going to try to look up these species before night fell." She dusted off her hands.

Jake walked toward her hut. It would give him the excuse he needed to see her living conditions—and to see how vulnerable her hut might be to attack. Shah hurried and caught up with him. There was a bright red cotton cloth over the front of the door, and she pulled it aside for him.

"Just set it next to the other ones," she told him, pointing to the far wall.

"This orchid smells great," Jake said as he bent low to enter the hut. Obviously it had been built for the short Tucanos people, not for tall Americans.

"I think it's a Mormodes orchid, but I'm not sure," Shah murmured as she followed him into the hut. He was so large! In fairness to him, though, the hut was one of the smallest made by the Tucanos—the type usually meant for an elderly person—and Shah had taken it because of that fact. She didn't want the generous Tucanos people giving up one of their family-size huts just for one person.

Jake's gaze took in the entire hut as he settled the flowering plant next to others against the wall. There was a wonderful scent of orchids mingled with the dry odor of the grass and palm leaves that made up the hut. He noted that a stack of flower identification books, all wrapped in plastic to protect them from the humidity and rain, sat nearby. Furnishings were sparse. Jake straightened to his full height. A grass mat that seemed to serve as Shah's bed lay on the dry dirt floor, topped by a light cotton blanket and a small pillow. Cooking utensils were near the door, for use over the open fire outside the hut. A woven trunk made of palm fiber was the only actual article of furniture.

"Nice place."

"If you like camping out," Shah said, moving back out through the door. She tried to calm her pounding heart. Was it because of Randolph's nearness? *Impossible.*

With a rumbling chuckle, Jake followed her. "I was a recon marine most of the time I was in the corps, and your hut is like a palace compared to what we had out in the bush."

"What do you mean?" Shah wished she could put a clamp on her mouth. Curiosity had been a catalyst throughout her life—too often landing her in hot water. Randolph was an enigma to her, and she tried to rationalize her curiosity about him: after all, if she knew more about him, she might be able to make a final decision on whether he was friend or enemy.

Jake ambled down the bank with her toward the canoe. "Recons are dropped behind enemy lines to gather needed information on troop movements, stuff like that," he explained. "We would sleep in trees, hide on the ground and generally be unseen while we collected the data we needed for the Intelligence boys."

Shah was impressed but didn't say anything, afraid her curiosity would be viewed as interest. But wasn't it? She tried to ignore her questioning heart. "I can get these other orchids," she protested.

"No way. I watched what you did. Why don't you go do something more important?"

Torn, Shah watched him take out the next flowering orchid. She was constantly amazed by the counterpoint of Randolph's size to his obvious gentleness. He picked up the orchid as if it were a vulnerable infant—surprising in such a big, hairy bear of a man. She tried to ignore his blatant male sensuality, the dark hair of his chest peeking out from the khaki shirt open at his throat. His arms were darkly sprinkled with hair, too. Shah swallowed convulsively. Despite his size, he wasn't overweight. No, he reminded her of a man who was not only in his physical prime, but in the best of condition, too.

"Oh, all right." Shah watched as several Tucanos children followed Jake to the canoe. They watched him with solemn brown eyes, and she smiled. She loved the Tucanos, who had welcomed her as one of their own. Once they'd found out that she was an "Indian," too, she'd been adopted by the chief of the village—a great honor.

"Do you like children?" Shah raised her hand to her mouth. Now where had that come from?

Jake frowned, hesitated and drew the next orchid, a purple one, out of the canoe. "Yeah, I like the little rug rats."

"Rug rats?" Alarm entered her voice.

"That's an old Marine Corps term for kids. It's an affectionate term, not a bad one," he assured her as he put the water into the plastic bag that would keep the root system from drying out.

Shah saw his partial smile slip, and when he looked up at her she detected darkness in his gray eyes. There was an incredible sadness that settled around him, and it was overwhelming to her. She was highly intuitive, and had always had an ability to sense a person's real feelings. Her heart went out to him. "Kids mean a lot to you, don't they?" she pressed softly.

With a sigh, Jake gathered up the orchid. As he turned and met Shah's serious gaze, something old and hurting broke loose in his heart. "Well, I..." It was those golden eyes swimming with unshed tears that shook him. Why should she show such compassion for him? She was unaware of his past, of his family's tragic death. He stood there stupidly staring down at her, absorbing her understanding like a plant starved for water. The seconds eddied and halted around them, and Jake felt ensnared within the unspoken emotional web that surrounded him like an embrace.

Shaken by her unexpected understanding, he dipped his head and frowned. "Where do you want this orchid? Next to the others?" he demanded gruffly.

Shah swallowed convulsively. What had just happened? It felt as if they both had been suddenly surrounded by heightened and unexpected emotions. But the mesmerizing feeling had evaporated when Jake became gruff. Blinking, Shah stammered, "In—in my hut, with the rest..."

It hurt to feel, to think. Jake felt himself rebuilding old walls to defend his grieving heart. Adding to the hurt, the Indian children followed him like happy, playful puppies as he retrieved the rest of the orchids for Shah. He was grateful that she seemed aware that children were a sensitive topic for him. His mouth dry, tears burning the back of his eyes, he placed the last orchid on the floor of the hut.

Shah was outside, crouched over a small cooking fire, her tripod and kettle suspended above the coals. Giving him a quick glance, she went back to stirring the contents with a stick. Her heart beat faster as he approached. Suddenly shaky for no reason, Shah refused to look up at him.

"Are you psychic or something?" he demanded.

A small smile touched Shah's mouth, and she forced herself to look up at him. What she saw tore at her heart. There was such raw anguish in Randolph's eyes that she nearly cried out for him, for the pain he carried like a living thing within him. The Indian children had gathered around them. One small girl tucked herself beneath Shah's arm and leaned her small head against her shoulder.

"I'm intuitive," she admitted, and hugged the little girl fiercely, letting her know that she loved her.

Jake considered Shah with a renewed intensity. The little Indian girl looked as if she belonged to Shah. Both of them had shining black hair, brown eyes and golden skin. The child, no more than six years old, put her fingers in her mouth and smiled shyly up at him. It hurt to breathe in that moment, because the girl's expression resembled that of his eldest daughter, Katie, bringing back a flood of wonderful memories—and torment.

Without a word, Jake spun around and stalked away.

Nonplussed, Shah watched him leave. She had seen the questions in his eyes about her intuition. But she had also seen the devastation and bleakness in their depths. Slowly rising to her full height, Shah continued to hold the little girl close. Gently she ran her hand across the girl's long black hair and sighed. What was going on between her and Randolph? It was crazy, she decided finally. Daylight was fading quickly, and in its wake the sky had turned pale lavender and gold. Patting the little girl's shoulder, Shah asked her to stir the fish stew she had made. She needed to get to the identification books to find out if these orchids had been officially discovered before the light failed entirely.

Jake couldn't sleep. He lay on his back, his hands behind his head, in the austere mission room, which resembled a boxcar in size and shape. The palm-thatched door was open to allow what little cross-breeze there was from his open window. The cot wasn't long enough for him, but it didn't make much difference. The boards beneath him were covered by a thin, lumpy mattress that had seen too many years of service. All the night sounds—the calls of the howler monkeys, the insects buzzing outside the open window—provided a soothing chorus to Jake's frayed nerves.

Every time he closed his eyes, the image of Shah's lovely face, her large eyes filled with tears, struck at his wounded heart. After four years he'd thought that most of the loss was behind him, but that one poignant moment when Shah held the little girl in her arms had struck at him with savage intensity. With a sigh, he stared up at the wooden ceiling. If not for the quarter moon low in the night sky, the place would have been plunged into a darkness so inky that he wouldn't be able to see his hand in front of his face.

Although he wore only drawstring pajama bottoms, Jake's body was bathed in a sheen of sweat from the unrelenting humidity. Glancing at his watch, he realized it was four in the morning. He knew he had to get some sleep, but he was too tightly wound from being around Shah. Everything in the Amazon jungle seemed so quiet and serene in comparison to him.

There was no doubt that Shah loved children. He had seen it in her eyes, that special adoration she held for the little Tucanos girl. Shah was in touch not only with the soil beneath her bare feet, but also with the life she held in her arms.

With a soft curse, Jake slowly sat up, his bare feet touching the wooden floor. He buried his face in his hands. Why now? Why? He had to leave his past behind him, but it refused to be buried. Not that he tried to forget, but wouldn't there ever be a reprieve from the loss and the cutting loneliness he felt twenty-four hours a day? Jake raised his head to stare out the open door. He could hear Pai Jose snoring brokenly in the room next to his. Red Feather slept on a grass mat in the room across the hallway. There were three patients recovering from an assortment of ailments in the mission's small hospital wing, and Jake heard some snores drifting down the corridor from them, too. He was envious of the others' ability to sleep while insomnia stalked him.

Getting up, he rubbed his damp-haired chest with his hand. Maybe he needed to take a quick walk around the premises—to get some fresh air. Jake tugged off his pajamas and put on trousers, boots, and a dark green shirt with short sleeves. He missed his knife and pistol, because Pai Jose had warned him that at night, even this more settled area of the Amazon came alive with predators. Jaguars hunted the dangerous wild pigs; cougars, cousins to North America's mountain lions, also combed the tropical rain forest for unsuspecting prey.

Just as Jake came out of the mission doorway, he heard what at first sounded like a string of firecrackers popping. The sound came from the direction of the village, near the riverbank. Jake tensed—he recognized the sound of gunfire when he heard it. Running around the end of the building, he halted, his eyes widening. Fire erupted and exploded in the night sky. Some of the huts were on fire! Between the shadowy trees, Jake could see several men running with torches in hand through the Tucanos village.

Shah! Jake dug his feet into the sandy ground and sprinted down the hill. The village seemed so far away. More gunfire erupted. The cries of the Tucanos, startled out of sleep, spilled into the night air. The gunfire continued.

Suddenly Jake realized that whoever these invaders were they weren't Indian. No, they looked like the men Hernandez had hired. As he tore down the path, the wind whipping past him, Jake's mind spun with options. He was unarmed—unable to defend himself, much less Shah or the unarmed villagers. Veering off to the left, tearing through the jungle itself, Jake decided to hide by skirting around the village. He had to get to Shah's hut! His pistol was there, and so was she.

Shah groggily awoke, the sound of screams filling her ears. Sitting up, her hair cascading around her like a curtain, she smelled suffocating smoke. Firelight danced outside her window. What was going on? She scrambled to her feet, her knee-length cotton nightgown hampering her movement. Just as she reached the window, gunfire slammed through the hut. With a cry, Shah dropped to the floor, covering her head with her hands. What was going on? Who was attacking?

As she began to get up again, a hulking figure appeared in the doorway, jerking the cotton barrier aside. Shah screamed.

"It's me!" Jake rasped. He dropped to his knees. "Where the hell is my gun? We're under attack."

Frantic, the cries of the Tucanos shattering her composure, Shah groped for her trunk. "Here," she told him, fumbling in the darkness. "They're in here...."

"Get them!"

Obeying wordlessly, Shah's hands shook as she located the holster and pistol. "Here—"

"Stay down," Jake whispered savagely, and he forced her to lie on the ground. "Whoever's doing this is playing for keeps."

Sobbing for breath, Shah felt the strength of Jake Randolph's hand in the center of her back as he forced her to lie flat on the floor. "Who is it?" she cried.

"I don't know," Jake breathed as he hitched the holster around his waist. He could take a Beretta apart and put it back together again blindfolded. Despite the lack of light, he quickly drew the pistol from the holster, snapped off the safety and placed a round in the chamber. Getting up, pistol in hand, he went to the entrance.

"Don't you move," he growled to Shah.

She opened her mouth to tell him to be careful, but found that she couldn't speak. Her throat was choked with tears of outrage and terror over the attack. Who was setting fire to the village? Who was firing guns? Why?

Jake pounded down the bank of the Amazon toward five dugout canoes tied to the dock. Each of them had a small motor mounted in the rear, and Jake's suspicion that Hernandez was involved grew. Ten men were fleeing the raging inferno of the village, running hard for the canoes. The shrieks of the Indians hammered at Jake as he halted, got down on one knee and aimed his Beretta.

Suddenly bullets whipped and whined all around him. Hitting the ground, Jake jerked his attention to the left, where the bullets were coming from. He couldn't see who was shooting at him; everything was dark and shadowed by the roaring flames and smoke that clouded the village. More sand whipped up in geysers around him. Someone had targeted him! Jake knew the other men were getting away. He wanted to capture one of them, but right now he had to protect himself. Whoever was firing at him was serious.

Sliding down off the bank, Jake moved into the tepid river up to his waist so that he'd present less of a target and the bank could provide cover. In moments, the firing stopped. Jake turned on his side, his Beretta aimed toward the dock. All but one of the canoes had left. Damn! Out of the corner of his eye, he saw the hulking figure of a man sprinting toward the remaining boat, followed by another, more slightly built man. The big man was the one who had grabbed Shah!

Scrambling out of the water, Jake leaped onto the bank. The big blond man was the one who had had him pinned down! Taking careful aim, he fired the pistol once, twice, three times. The man let out a cry and fell to the dock. Satisfaction soared through Jake as he scrambled to his feet and lunged forward. A tree root caught and captured the toe of his boot. With a grunt, Jake slammed down on the bank. Cursing, he got to his feet, but not in time. The canoe was leaving the dock, with both men in it. Damn!

Jake stood, torn between going after them and helping the Tucanos put out the raging fires that were consuming several of their huts. Shoving the pistol back into its holster, Jake decided to help the Indians. Many were running back and forth to the river with buckets. As he angled through the trees and headed for the first hut, he heard a moan. Looking to his left, he saw a Tucanos man writhing in pain. The light was poor, but Jake knew the man had been wounded in the fray.

He stopped, knelt beside the groaning Indian and tried to reassure him. He drew back his hand. It was covered with blood. Jake frowned. The wounded needed care first. Speaking to him in Portuguese, and trying to persuade the Indian that he was a friend, not his enemy, Jake picked the man up. The Indian was ridiculously light in his arms as he headed toward the hospital up on the knoll. Was Shah safe? Had a bullet found her, too? Jake hurried at a fast walk, weaving around the burning huts, dodging the running Indians who were trying to save their homes. He made his way up to the mission, where he handed the man over to Pai Jose for medical treatment. That done, Jake knew he had to locate Shah.

Jake's heart pounded unevenly in his chest as he approached Shah's hut.

"Shah?" he shouted as he neared it. "Shah? Are you okay? Answer me!"

His heart rate soared along with his anguish when only silence answered him. He broke into a trot, his face grim, his throat constricted, as he tried to prepare himself for the scene he'd see. He envisioned Shah wounded and bleeding on the floor of her hut. Other scenes, scenes from his ugly past, bludgeoned him. He halted at the hut and tore the cotton barrier aside.

Breathing hard, he stood in the doorway, looking frantically for Shah. She wasn't there! Relief cascaded through him, and then, on its heels, sheer terror. What if Shah had been kidnapped by those men? What if she hadn't listened to his orders and had run out of the hut? She could be hurt and bleeding anywhere in the village! The possibilities were too real, and Jake spun around.

Half running, half stumbling back toward the center of the village, he saw that the Tucanos had taken the brunt of the attack. Firelight danced and twisted in grotesque shapes as the huts continued to burn wildly out of control. The Indians were doing their best to put the fires out with the buckets of water, but Jake knew they needed to conserve their efforts for the nearby huts, which could easily catch fire from the sparks floating like red, winking fireflies in the night air.

He grabbed an older man, ordering him in Portuguese to use the water to save the other, vulnerable huts. It took a few minutes, but finally the Indian understood. Jake then raced to form a bucket brigade line, his arms waving, his voice thundering above the roar of the inferno for attention.

The new tactics spread quickly through the populace, and soon buckets of water were being thrown on the roofs and sides of nearby huts. Jake blinked the sweat from his eyes and looked around. He saw several men lying wounded. Gesturing to a couple of Indians, Jake got them to help him take the wounded up to the hospital. Where the hell was Shah? The bitter taste of fear in his mouth wouldn't leave.

Dawn was crawling over the crimson-and-gold horizon as Jake made his last swing of the village looking for

Shah. He hadn't found her. Rubbing his mouth with the back of his hand, Jake suddenly felt weary as never before. The fires had died down—but five of the huts had burned completely to the ground. Smoke hung heavily over the area, mingling with the humid mist that stole silently in and around the trees as dawn continued to push back the night.

The place was eerie, with the mixture of fog and smoke hanging at rooftop level, Jake decided as he tiredly tramped through the village looking for Shah. Perhaps he'd missed her. The darkness had hampered relief efforts, and the hysteria of the Indians hadn't helped, either. Jake couldn't blame them for their reaction, though. At least ten Indians had been wounded at the hands of Hernandez's men.

Shah was nowhere to be found. Jake stood outside her hut, tears stinging his eyes. He tried to attribute them to the stringy smoke that hung in the air like a thick blanket. Glumly he headed back to the mission, where he knew he could be of some help. His steps were heavy, and he felt a bone-tiredness that reached clear to his soul. Jake didn't try to fool himself; he realized it was depression and grief over Shah being missing. Had she been kidnapped? Why hadn't he paid more attention to the men running for those dugout canoes? he chastised himself. But he knew the answer: he'd been pinned down by gunfire. He couldn't possibly have watched the canoes, much less identified who occupied each one.

At the top of the knoll, Indians were racing madly around the mission buildings. The cries of women and sobs of children rent the air. Thick fog blanketed the knoll as Jake slowly made his way through the crowd of relatives waiting to hear about wounded family members.

Bright light from bulbs strung in Christmas-tree fashion around the perimeter of the hospital wing momentarily blinded Jake. He raised a hand to protect his eyes while they adjusted to the change.

"Jake!"

He froze. He pulled his hand away from his eyes. There, not more than ten feet away, working with Pai Jose, was Shah! Realizing his mouth was hanging open, he snapped it shut. Never had Shah looked so lovely, despite her haggard appearance. Her hair hung loose about her body like a raven cloak. Her face was smudged with charcoal, and her white nightgown was splattered with mud and blood. At first Jake thought she'd been wounded, but then he realized she was helping Pai Jose dress the injuries of the Indian lying on the surgery table.

He took a step forward, but then halted, relief surging through him. Euphoria rose in him, and all he could do was stand there helpless beneath her golden gaze. Her huge eyes were shadowed with exhaustion, he noted.

"We need help," Shah pleaded, her voice cracking. "Do you know first aid?" She tried to deny the feelings racing through her, tried to ignore her overwhelming relief at seeing that Jake Randolph was safe. When he'd left her on the floor of the hut, Shah had feared for his life. And when she hadn't seen him throughout the past three hours, she'd feared him dead. The look of astonishment and joy mirrored in his eyes now shook Shah.

"I can help," he told her as he closed the distance between them. "Just tell me what you want done."

Shah reached into a box filled with sterile surgical gloves. "Go scrub over at the sink. Pai Jose can use your help. I'll go help some of the others who are hurt less. Hurry, please!"

Jake nodded to the old priest, whose hair was as white as the surgical gown that covered his clothing. For a moment Jake thought that Pai Jose's silvery hair, glowing in the light, might be a halo around the old man's head. The priest worked quickly over the man who lay on the table before him.

Jake's hands shook beneath the thin stream of water coming weakly out of the faucet. The soap smelled clean and good amid the stench of sweaty bodies, the lurid smell of blood and the odor of antiseptics. Jake felt as if he'd stepped back a century in time. As he scrubbed up, he checked out the antiquated facilities. There was very little here except the most necessary of equipment and medicines, he realized as he gazed at the glass cabinet above the sink. He glanced around the room and saw with growing anger that whoever had attacked the village had hurt at least twenty people. Sickened, he hurried over to where Shah stood waiting for him. Expertly she slipped the surgical gloves onto his hands.

"There are two more men who are seriously hurt," she told him breathlessly. "Pai Jose is so tired. You'll have to watch him, Jake. His hands aren't as steady..."

He smiled tiredly down at her. "I'll take care of this, darlin'. You go do whatever else needs to be done."

Darlin'. The endearment gave Shah sustenance and strength when she felt as if her knees were going to cave in beneath her. She lost herself momentarily in the warm gray of Jake's gaze—that same feeling of powerful protection again embracing her. But this time she didn't fight it or deny it. Absorbing Jake's care, she felt like a plant welcoming sunlight onto its leaves for the first time. Then, forcing herself to snap out of the inexplicable magic that bound them, she stepped away from him.

"I'm glad you're okay," she quavered.

He gave her a grim smile. "You're the one I was worried about."

Shah knew they didn't have time to talk; there were too many wounded to be attended to. Turning away, she blinked back tears. Tears! Her emotions frayed and raw from the attack, Shah didn't try to rationalize them away this time: they were tears of relief that Jake wasn't dead. She headed toward the wall, where several of the less seriously wounded sat or stood, waiting patiently for treatment. A gamut of emotions smothered Shah, making her dizzy. How could Jake Randolph have come to mean so much to her in so short a time? He was the *enemy*.

Chapter Five

"Shah, let me take you to your hut. You're ready to keel over."

The instant Jake's hands curved around her slumped shoulders where she sat at a table in the hospital, Shah capitulated. The heat of the day was rising, and although all the windows were open to allow air to flow sluggishly through the long, rectangular area, the room was stifling. For an instant, she rested against his large, caring hands, but just for an instant. Straightening, she pulled away from the contact with him and got to her feet.

"I guess most of the emergencies are over," she said wearily.

Jake put his hands on his hips and surveyed Shah intently. It was nearly noon, and help had arrived from another mission nearby. Five nuns were now caring for the wounded, but he knew that Shah would stay on to help unless someone made her take care of herself.

"For now," he agreed quietly. Her hair, once loose, was now captured by a rubber band behind her head, the ebony strands drawn into a ponytail that almost reached her waist. He watched as Shah, with some difficulty, pulled the once-white surgical gown off her shoulders. Her golden eyes were dark with anguish.

"Here, I'll take that. One of the Tucanos women is out back with a big black kettle, boiling the hell out of anything used for the surgeries."

Shah forced a tired smile—one that she didn't feel but felt Jake deserved. "Thanks. You sound so chipper—as if nothing had happened." She looked up into his harsh features. Jake's eyes were red-rimmed, as she was sure hers must be, and his mouth was a slash, holding back the unexpressed feelings she knew he carried.

Taking a huge risk, Jake reached over and settled his hand again on her shoulder. "I've been through this kind of thing a few times more than you have," he said. "Come on, I'll walk you down the hill to your hut."

His hand was at once supportive and sheltering. Shah wanted to surrender to the powerful care that emanated from him like a beacon of light slicing through the darkest night. But she couldn't; she didn't dare. Long ago she'd learned that no matter how nurturing a man appeared outwardly, later he would change—withdraw that care and hurt her. Her spongy mind screamed at her to resist, but her instincts persuaded her to accept Jake's attention, just this once. Without a word, she nodded and left the antiseptic smells of the ward behind.

The tropical sunlight lanced through the triple canopy of rain-forest trees, producing bright splotches on the otherwise shaded ground. Everywhere Shah looked, she saw distraught expressions on the Tucanos's faces. Her heart ached for them, for their loss.

"How many died last night?" Jake asked. He forced himself to allow his hand to slide off Shah's shoulder. Every fiber of his being screamed that she needed to be held, but, much as he wanted to draw Shah into the circle of his arms, Jake knew she'd fight him.

"Two. Thank the Great Spirit it wasn't more," she murmured tiredly. The once-swept path was littered with leaves, small branches that had fallen from overhead, and many impressions from bare feet.

"Pai Jose is sleeping," Jake told her. Shah was weaving unsteadily, and he started to reach out, but forced his hand back to his side.

With a slight laugh, Shah said, "He ought to be! He's seventy-two, but he has such strength for his age. I'm sure it's his faith that gives him the grit to keep going when most people would have folded."

"Yeah," Jake agreed, constantly surveying the area. "He was something of a miracle himself last night and this morning. I didn't know he was a doctor."

"Well," Shah said reluctantly, "he isn't a medical doctor, but he's been so isolated out here for the past fifty years that he's had to learn more than just basic first aid." She gazed wonderingly up at Jake. "And you. You never told me you were a paramedic."

He flushed and avoided her admiring gaze. "All part of being a recon marine," he assured her.

"Between you and Pai Jose, the people are going to be fine." Shah walked carefully down the slope, dizzy from fatigue. Swallowing hard, she risked a look up at Jake. "This is all my fault," she choked out softly. "I realize now it was Hernandez and his men who did this. It was a warning for me to leave or else."

Grimly Jake pulled her to a halt. Without thinking, knowing she needed his touch, he swung her around to face him. Her golden eyes were filled with tears of self-incrimination. "Now look," he said gruffly, grazing her cheek with his fingers, "this attack *wasn't* your fault." He tried to ignore the fact that her skin felt like the lush velvet of an orchid petal.

Jake's brief touch sent Shah's senses spinning. She stepped away from him, closed her eyes and inhaled a sudden breath of air. She heard the barely contained emotion in his rumbling tone, the raw feelings that lay just beneath it, and knew that he could shatter her defenses with the intimacy he'd automatically established with her.

Forcing her eyes open and swallowing her tears, Shah tried to resurrect the tough barricade she'd presented to him yesterday. "This *is* my fault!" she insisted. "I should have realized that Hernandez would come back. Sometimes I'm too stubborn, too blind." She held her hand against her trembling lips. "I should have placed these people's welfare ahead of my own ideology! They're the ones who have suffered. What about the two men who are dead? Their families will never see them again, and I'm responsible for that!"

Jake winced inwardly at the logic of her words. He stepped forward, gripped her by the shoulders and gave her a tiny shake. "Listen," he growled, "stop blaming yourself, Shah. You had no way of knowing Hernandez would do this."

Shah tried to pull away, but Jake's fingers tightened their grip. Her voice rose. "I've been here three months, and I knew all about Hernandez! Everyone said he was a killing bastard. Well, he is! The Indians never had a good word to say about him. I should have listened to them, Jake." Sobbing, she tore out of his grip. She stumbled backward, off-balance, then caught herself. Tears streamed down her cheeks as she forced herself to look up into his grim features. "I should have listened," she sobbed again, and spun away.

Jake stood there, angry and helpless, as Shah walked hurriedly down the path toward the carnage in the village below. He wanted to run after her, to grab her and hold her. That was what she needed right now—a quiet harbor in the terrible storm that surrounded her. His wife had taught him about the safety of an embrace early on in their marriage, and he'd never forgotten that wonderful facet of their relationship.

Kicking at sand with the toe of his boot, Jake decided to go on into the village anyway. He wanted to see if the six-year-old girl who had been in Shah's arms yesterday was safe. He hadn't seen her up at the hospital, so he figured she was fine, but he wanted to make sure. He knew that he needed sleep, too, but his nerves were taut and his senses were screamingly alert. Anyway, he wouldn't put it past Hernandez to try another attack tonight. First, he'd check on the little tyke, then he'd grab a quick nap, and then he'd talk to the chief about preventing another surprise attack by Hernandez.

Frowning, Jake shoved his hands into his pockets. What he really wanted to do was go after Shah. But she needed sleep, and perhaps when she was more rested she would realize that this carnage wasn't her fault. Throughout the dawn hours and into the morning, he'd watched her work tirelessly with the survivors at the hospital, always offering a kind word, a soft smile, her healing touch. He believed that her passion for protecting Mother Earth was just as fierce and genuine as her compassion for the people around her, and that was admirable. At first, Jake had been concerned that she might be one of those ecofanatics who couldn't see beyond their own narrow views, but she'd proved that theory wrong. No, Shah Travers was a woman of incredible courage linked to a giving heart. That discovery did nothing but make Jake want to know her—to explore her, to chart the vast, hidden territory of her compassionate heart.

When Shah awoke, sunlight was slanting low through the western window. With a groan, she eased herself into a sitting position on the grass mat that served as her bed. She rubbed her eyes, which were puffy with sleep, and allowed the village sounds to filter into her awakening senses. She didn't hear the usual sounds of children's laughter, dogs barking and the singsong Tucanos language filling the air. Glancing at her watch, Shah was alarmed to discover it was nearly 4:00 p.m.

How could she have slept so long? Hurriedly she got to her knees and opened the trunk where she kept her toiletry items. Retrieving a pair of tan gabardine slacks and a white tank top, she rummaged around some more and found a pair of white cotton socks. Her hair was a tangled mass that desperately needed to be washed and combed. Forcing away her sleepiness, Shah got to her feet and pulled the cotton away from the door.

"You're up."

Shah jerked to a halt. Her eyes widened momentarily. Jake Randolph sat on a decomposing log not more than fifty feet from her hut.

"Jake . . ."

Jake smiled when he heard her use his first name, glad that the previous stiffness that had existed between them was no longer there. Perhaps it was because she had just awakened. Her features were softened, her lids half-open to reveal drowsy golden eyes. Disheveled, her hair mussed, Shah looked absolutely beautiful, in a natural sort of way.

"I figured I'd play bodyguard," he said teasingly.

"I don't need one," Shah groused in return. She frowned and walked toward a small, makeshift shower enclosed by three sheets of plywood. A large piece of black plastic suspended above the shower caught and contained rainwater.

Jake got up and slowly followed her. He watched as she placed a yellow terry-cloth towel on a nearby tree branch and stepped behind the enclosure.

"How are you feeling?"

Shah stripped out of her smelly, damp clothes and tossed them outside the shower. "Like hell."

"You don't look like hell. Now me, that's another thing." He ruefully rubbed his prickly jaw, aware that he needed a shave.

Releasing the small clothespin from the tubular plastic shower head, Shah quickly wet her body and her hair. Just Jake's nearness made her feel safer. Then all conversation ceased for the next fifteen minutes as she cleaned and scrubbed away the horror of the night before.

Jake sat down on another log and clasped his hands between his thighs. The muddy Amazon was so wide that it boggled his mind. If Americans could see this mighty river, they'd think the Mississippi was a stream in comparison. A grizzled smile touched his mouth. Oddly, he felt happier than he could recall feeling in a very long time. Maybe it was because of Shah.

Keying his hearing to Shah, who was showering behind his back, Jake continued to peruse the Amazon and its banks. There was tension in the air, thick enough to cut with a machete blade. The Tucanos were fearful, but Jake had helped to allay some of that fear by setting up a watch by guards who would switch every two hours tonight to prevent another surprise attack. The old chief had been grateful for Jake's suggestions, and Jake was glad he could offer these gentle people a plan. Pai Jose, who had slept only a little, then come down to survey the needs of the village, was also grateful for Jake's ideas. He'd backed Jake's efforts enthusiastically, which had helped convince the Tucanos that it was the right way to protect themselves from Hernandez.

When he heard the shower shut off, Jake straightened. "Feel a little better?" he called over his shoulder.

Shah towel-dried her hair. "Yes, much better, thanks." She pulled on the slacks and tank top. Hanging the towel on a branch, she emerged moments later, brush and comb in hand.

"I feel a hundred percent better," she told Jake. He was sitting on the log that she usually sat on to pull on her socks and hiking boots. Shah sat down at the other end. The hungry look that suddenly gleamed in Jake's eyes sent a tremor of fear rippling through her. He quickly looked away, and she felt heat flood her neck and face. With trembling hands, she quickly moved her thick, heavy hair across her shoulder and began to ease the snarls out of it with the brush.

Jake berated himself. He'd stared at Shah like a slavering wolf—and he'd seen the instant terror in her eyes. Cursing his own weakness, and upset at frightening her, Jake moodily stared at the Amazon's quiet surface. He cast around for a safe topic of conversation, because the invisible tension had risen between them once again.

"Things have quieted down and more or less gotten back on track," he said, giving her a quick glance. It was his undoing. Shah sat combing her thick, luxuriant hair, looking fresher and more beautiful than he ever could have imagined. She wore no makeup, yet her skin had a golden glow and her cheeks a heightened rosiness. He stared, mesmerized, as she combed her hair, the sunlight glancing off it, bringing out blue and black highlights. He swallowed convulsively and quickly looked away, his heart pounding like a freight train.

Shah saw surprise, tenderness and then desire in Jake's eyes as he watched her comb her hair. She continued to ease the knots and snarls out, taming half her hair into a braid. Looking toward the village, she saw the Indians working to clean up the area where the five huts had been burned to the ground. A lump formed in her throat, and she tried to swallow it. This was all her fault.

"When I get done here, I'm going to leave," she said shakily.

Jake's head snapped up, and he turned, disbelief in his eyes. "What?"

Shah eyed him grimly. "Hernandez wants me out of here. It's obvious now that he'll do anything to accomplish his goal. I'll leave so that these people can get on with their lives. I've caused them enough pain."

Jake held her level gaze and saw that her mouth was set in stubborn determination. "Where will you go?" He knew enough about Shah already to recognize that arguing with her was a useless exercise.

With a sigh, Shah tied off a braid with a rubber band. "I'm going to take my canoe and load it with my video camera and tapes." She pointed down the Amazon. "Hernandez's parcel is three miles down the river. I intend to go down there, set up camp and begin secretly filming his operation."

Jake held on to his patience. "You'd be walking right into the lion's mouth by doing that."

"I didn't come here to turn tail and run, Jake."

"Parking in his backyard isn't cowardly, it's foolhardy."

Shah ignored the low fury in his voice. "Well, it's not your problem, is it?"

"Why the hell isn't it?"

"Because you don't believe in what I'm trying to do, that's why! You're not committed to anything."

Anger frayed his patience, but Jake remained sitting on the log. He knew that if he got up and towered over Shah, it would only make her more defensive. "You don't know me well enough to say that," he answered, struggling to keep his tone even. "In fact, you've gone out of your way to pretend I don't exist."

Shah quickly braided the rest of her hair. Her fingers were trembling, and she wondered if Jake saw just how much he affected her. She knew for a fact that if not for Jake's shadowy presence in all their lives, more people might have died last night—during the attack, or later, in the hospital. Still, she couldn't admit it.

"I came down here to get proof that these land barons are destroying our rain forest," she insisted. "Not only that, I *know* that Hernandez is illegally using chain saws to cut down those trees. That's against Brazilian law, you know." She glared at Jake. "I want to nail that slimy bastard's hide to the wall with his own country's laws. I want him taken off the board as a player. But I need proof. All of these barons use illegal chain saws instead of axes or hand-held saws. My plan is to seek them out, videotape them and land them in jail. I may not be able to single-handedly stop the destruction of this basin, but I sure can slow it down."

Jake assimilated Shah's impassioned explanation, forcing himself not to speak for several minutes, allowing the tension to dissolve. She'd finished braiding her hair and was putting on her white cotton socks when he finally spoke.

"I didn't know it was against Brazilian law for these guys to use chain saws. In the U.S., all the loggers use them."

Shah jerked laces through the eyelets of her hiking boot. "Brazil is caught between a rock and a hard place, Jake. They've got millions of poor in the cities, and they're hurting. To try and ease the situation, the government gives them small parcels of farmland. These people can cut down trees with axes or saws, to clear the land for farming. That might be all right, but greedy businessmen have been buying up the small plots from the poor and contracting countries like Japan to buy the trees. It's a very big, *very* profitable business."

Shah quickly finished lacing up her boots. With a frustrated sound, she faced Jake. "Brazil is taking a lot of heat from the world scientific community and from ecological groups. But they've got runaway inflation, and the people are in turmoil. Brazil is getting squeezed inside and out by groups and factions. I see myself as a stopgap measure, Jake. I can help buy time for the rain forest in hopes that more pressure and education will make the Brazilian government realize they've got to stop destroying the Amazon Basin. I did it before on the Rio Negro, with another Brazilian realtor who was out to rape Mother Earth. He's in jail right now in Rio."

Jake's eyes narrowed. "Does Hernandez know about this?"

"Kind of obvious he does, don't you think?" Shah gestured toward the village. "Why else would he have attacked?"

With a nod, Jake rested his hands against his chin. "I think you're right."

"I know I am."

Jake glanced at her out of the corner of his eye. "You're a pretty courageous woman."

"I'm a warrior, Jake. I've always been one. It doesn't mean I'm not afraid. I live with fear daily. All kinds of fear. The difference is, despite my fear, I'll move forward and act on my beliefs. I won't allow it to stop me." She made a helpless gesture with her hand, her voice filled with frustration. "Ever since I was born, I've been in hot water of one kind or another. First, it was with my father, who is a closet alcoholic. He'd never admit he's got a problem, but my mother and I sure know he does." Shah stood suddenly, realizing she'd said too much. To reveal the pain she carried to a near stranger—who was in the employ of her father!—was dangerous, to say the least.

"Wait!" Jake leaped to his feet and covered the distance between them. He reached out and drew her to a halt. "Wait," he entreated her softly. "Tell me more about your father."

His touch was branding. The ache it sent through Shah was like a raw, unsettling current of longing combined with desperation. She pulled out of his grasp and looked up into his gray eyes, trying to ferret out whether he was sincere in his request.

"Why should I?" she asked challengingly.

"Because you know I care."

"I don't know that."

Jake smiled slightly and relaxed. Shah stood rigidly, as if she were going to run at any moment. "Yes," he said softly, "you *do* know that."

Shah took several steps away from him, unable to hold his burning gray gaze or accept the tenderness he seemed to offer. "It doesn't matter," she said waspishly.

"You matter, Shah."

A tremor passed through her, and she closed her eyes briefly, then turned away. "Words, just words. You men are so good with words. It's actions that count with me, not your damnable words."

He felt a rift in the tension, and seized the moment. Approaching Shah slowly, he kept his hands at his sides—the last place he wanted them to be. Shah was openly suffering. He could hear the anguish in her husky voice.

"My actions of the past twenty-four hours should prove something to you," he began, his voice raw. "It sounds as if you've been fighting pitched battles by yourself all your life, Shah." His eyes darkened. "This time you don't have to fight alone."

The gritty sound of his voice wrapped around Shah like a protective blanket. She drew in a shuddering sigh and slowly raised her head. She met and held the gaze from his narrowed gray eyes, eyes that were banked with some heated, indefinable emotion. "What are you talking about?"

His smile became grimmer. "I'll go with you down the Amazon. We'll find a good place to make camp, then we'll get that tape you want."

Stunned, Shah gasped. Her mind spun with questions, but her heart told her that Jake Randolph was more sincere than any man she'd ever met.

"Why would you do that?"

"Because I believe in your cause. I believe in you."

She frowned. "My father is paying you."

"So?" Jake shrugged. "My orders were to be a body-guard if you decided to stay down here, and that's ful-filling my assignment as far as Travers is concerned. He didn't tell me what to do with my time. If I want to help you, I will."

"If he knew what you wanted to do, he'd hit the ceil-ing," Shah growled. "He wants me out of this place permanently."

"Guess he won't get his way, will he?"

Jake's teasing broke the terrible tension she carried in her shoulders. Shah searched his harsh features ruth-lessly for any sign that he was lying. Men had always lied to her.

"I don't trust men," she warned him throatily.

"Why?" Jake asked the question so softly that he wasn't sure she'd heard him at first.

Her mouth compressed, Shah wrapped her arms across her chest and looked out at the river. "I never talk about my past."

"Most kids who come from alcoholic families feel that way," Jake said gently.

Shah's eyes narrowed. "I suppose you've got a degree in psychology, too, besides philosophy?"

Grinning bashfully, Jake shook his head. "I got trained a long time ago to be more aware of other peo-ple's feelings and motivations." Memories of Bess pooled in his heart, and he shrugged. "An incredible woman with a heart as big as yours helped me open up and see a lot more than most men do about people and their prob-lems."

Curiosity stalked Shah. For just a moment, she'd seen Jake's face lose its harsh cast. Underneath, she'd seen a man of immense sensitivity. Then that cloak of grief had surrounded him again. She swallowed hard. "You're married?"

Jake was wrestling with real, unresolved pain. "I was...but that was a long time ago." It hurt to breathe in that moment, and hot, unexpected tears momentarily blurred his vision, dissolving Shah's taut features. Blinking them back, he tried to steer the conversation back to her. When he spoke, his voice was rough. "So how long did your mother tolerate your father's alcohol problem?"

Caught off guard by the tears she saw in Jake's eyes, Shah stood very still. She felt her way through the ravaged, haunted look on his face. She'd never seen tears in a man's eyes before. The only tears she knew were ones shed in hurt and pain by women and children. Were Jake's tears due to some memory, a past he couldn't put to rest? His features remained open and accessible, and the words, the feelings, tumbled out of Shah's mouth before she could stop them. "My mother was very young—and very beautiful—when my father met her. She was waiting tables at the best hotel in Rapid City, South Dakota, and he fell in love with her. My mother was a medicine woman in training at the time, and she tried to explain that to my father. She lived in the traditional ways of our people, but he didn't care or want to know about my mother's beliefs.

"My father shrugged off her explanations, dazzled her with beautiful gifts, fine food at the best restaurants, and within days they were married. I guess I was conceived the first night. But when my father wanted my mother to move away from the Rosebud reservation, where our family has land and homes, my mother said no. Her medicine teacher was there, as she'd tried to tell him days earlier. One day she'd be a medicine woman helping her people, and she couldn't leave the reservation."

"Your mother is a healer?" Jake asked, seeing all too clearly the suffering that speaking about her past was causing Shah.

"Yes, but that didn't matter to him. My father started drinking, flew into a rage and beat my mother senseless. When she came to, they were driving to Denver, where he lived." Shah's voice died in her throat, and she shook her head. "My mother was a virtual prisoner at my father's estate. He was jealous and guarded her. She could never go anywhere without a private detective in plain sight. He was a Jekyll-and-Hyde personality, and when he drank, he beat her."

Jake shut his eyes, buffeted by her pain. When he opened them again, he stared grimly into her distraught features. "I'm sorry," he rasped. It took every bit of Jake's control not to reach out and touch Shah in a gesture of humanity, but he knew that, given her distrust, she might wrongly interpret his action. The ache in his heart for her, for the tragedy that surrounded her, grew.

Shah pushed the grayish-white sand around with the toe of her boot. So much misery was surfacing as she spoke. "My mother convinced my father to let her give birth to me on the reservation. Living with him for nine months, she'd figured out how to manipulate him without making him angry enough to beat her. I was born in my grandmother's cabin at Rosebud, and three days later we were taken back to our prison in Denver.

"I don't have a lot of memories until I was about six years old. I do remember this huge, cold estate that was like a fortress. My father hated me. He told my mother to keep me out of his sight, to keep me quiet because he hated to hear a child crying. I remember being held by my mother, her hand pressed to my mouth if I started to cry. She used to press my face against her breast, hold me very tightly and pray that father didn't hear me."

Biting back a curse, Jake stood helplessly. Shah's lower lip was trembling. It tore heavily at his own grieving heart to hear how much abuse she had endured.

"Until I was twelve years old, I remember living in a nightmare war at his house. I went to school, came home and went to my room. I had my meals served there, I did my homework there, and I played with my dog out in the big yard, which was enclosed by a black wrought-iron fence." Shah wearily touched her brow. "As I got older, I became aware that sometimes my mother would have terrible bruises all over her. One time... one time I saw my father beating her in a drunken rage. I flew down the staircase, screaming and shouting at him to leave her alone...." Shah made a strangled sound and fell silent.

Jake moved over to her and slid his hand along her slumped shoulder. His mouth moved into a thin line as he thought of the daily suffering Shah had lived with. The anger he felt toward Travers ballooned tenfold. No wonder Shah was combative. "What happened? What did he do to you?" he asked, his voice cracking.

Shah felt Jake's fingers tighten on her shoulder, and gathered the strength to go on. "I— Well, I was like a wild animal attacking him, I guess. I don't really remember what happened, to tell you the truth. Mom told me about it later—after I woke up in the hospital with a severe concussion."

"My God," Jake choked out, reeling with shock.

She gave him a cutting look. "In those days, hospitals didn't question a child being beaten. My mother took me to the emergency room. She was in tears when she told them that I'd fallen down the stairs. I was in the hospital for three days. On the third day, my mom came and got me. I found out later she'd stolen money from my father's wallet and bought two bus tickets for Rosebud. We escaped. I remember being wrapped up in a nice, warm star quilt that my grandmother had made for me when I was younger. I was still dizzy, and I couldn't walk straight, but it was sure nice to be held in her arms on that bus trip. I was so happy to be going home, I cried most of the time. My grandmother ... well, she's a wonderful woman. She loved me and my mother with a fierceness that defies description."

Unconsciously Jake slid his hand back and forth along Shah's shoulder. He forced out a question that he didn't want to ask—because he wasn't sure if he could handle hearing the answer. "Did it end there?"

"No." She sighed. "Once we got on the res, we were legally safe from my father. He tried to get the tribal council to give him permission to take us back to Denver, but a reservation is like a foreign country, Jake. We have our own laws and ways of doing things. My mother filed for a divorce the day she arrived, and the tribal council supported her decision to stay at Rosebud. From the age of twelve until I was eighteen, I never left the res, for fear that one of father's hired detectives might try to kidnap me. I went to the missionary school over in St. Francis, about fifteen miles from where we lived."

"At least your mother protected you," he said, his voice raspy with emotion. "What did Travers do next?"

"After he got over the initial rage that his money couldn't buy us back, I guess my father started feeling guilty about what he'd done to me and my mom, so he sent money for me to go to college. By that time, I didn't fear him trying to kidnap me, so I took his money and went to Stanford. I got a master's degree in biology, because I wanted to serve Mother Earth and her people as my mother continues to do in her capacity as a healer at the res.''

Jake allowed his hand to drop, because he was afraid that if he didn't he would fold Shah in his arms and hold her, try to protect her against the pain that was clearly etched on her face. When she lifted her chin and stared up at him, he saw the extent of the devastation her father had wreaked upon her.

"Saying I'm sorry seems useless in the face of what you went through,'' he whispered roughly. Travers better hope he never crossed his path again, he thought grimly.

Shah's mouth pulled into a slight, pained smile. "Men feel it's their right to beat women,'' she told him bitterly. "When I was at Stanford, I got mixed up in politics. I met my husband, Robert, who's half Lakota. He'd been raised over at the Pine Ridge reservation. I was so lonely for my people and for our way of life that I let the infatuation go to my head. I married Robert in my third year.''

"Are you still married?''

"No.'' Shah shook her head sadly. "I repeated my mother's mistakes. Can you believe that? Robert was an alcoholic, too. At first he used to manipulate me mentally and emotionally. He tried to make me feel unworthy because I was a woman. He thought I should be serving him. Well, that didn't go over too well with me. By then my mother was a full-fledged medicine woman, and she'd taught me that women are sacred to the Great Spirit.

"Robert tried to demean me over the next two years. When I wouldn't break and become a victim, he finally attacked me. The moment he laid a hand on me, I was out of there. I filed for divorce the next day. I wasn't about to get beat up the way my mother had. Enough was enough."

Jake nodded, a bitter taste in his mouth. "Now I understand why you don't trust men."

Shah pulled back and gave him a measuring look. "I have a bad track record," she agreed. "And I've still got a lot of anger toward men that I'm trying to work out," she warned.

"Rightfully so," Jake conceded. He was dying inside, for Shah, for the brutal way she'd been treated.

Shah weighed his words, the sincerity of them. "I'd like to believe you, but I can't, Jake." She gave a helpless shrug. "Too much water under the bridge between me and men. I'll pack up and leave in about an hour. I don't want to be a noose around Pai Jose's neck here. You go home. This isn't your battle—it's mine." With a sad little smile, she added, "After hearing about my life, no man in his right mind would stay around me, anyway."

For the first time since his family's death, Jake felt the numbness leave his heart, all of it. In its wake came a vibrant, living mass of emotions bubbling through him, emotions that were both good and bad. He stared at Shah, unable to put his tangled feelings into words. She'd suffered just as grievously as he had, he realized. Perhaps even more so, because she'd been a child, caught in a trap, with no safe place to hide, and no escape.

Clearing his throat, he said, "Well, this time you aren't alone, Shah. We'll take care of Hernandez together, whether you can trust in me or not." He wanted to add, You're too special, Shah, too important, to be putting your neck on the line by yourself. Jake held up his hand when she began to protest. "No argument on this," he told her firmly. "You're stuck with me, whether you like it or not."

Chapter Six

"What is this nonsense about you leaving, Shah?" Pai Jose demanded as he halted on the dock next to her.

Shah looked guiltily up at the old priest. She stopped packing the canoe and got up off her hands and knees. Rubbing her hands against her trousers, she said, "I can't stay here, *Pai*. I've caused all of this." She gestured toward the village. "Hernandez wanted to scare me off."

The priest gave a sorrowful shake of his head, resting a thin hand on Shah's shoulder. "No, child. Don't go. You've been here three months. The people love you. You belong here, doing your work on the medical herbs with the shamans."

Shah saw Jake coming down the bank. Had he told Pai Jose she was leaving? Still wrung out from last night's ordeal, she patted the priest's hand and captured it between her own.

"*Pai,* I love you and the Tucanos people enough to keep you safe from Hernandez. Please try to understand that."

Pai Jose frowned, his silvery, caterpillarlike eyebrows moving downward. He gripped Shah's hand. "I can see your mind is made up. We'll pray for you, my child."

Prayer, no matter who did it—or from what religious or spiritual base—was not only good, but powerful, in Shah's opinion. "That's wonderful. Thank you," she answered softly.

"Father, did you talk her out of going?" Jake asked as he drew to a halt. He had an olive green canvas knapsack slung across his shoulder. Glancing at Shah, he saw her staring accusingly in his direction.

"No, my son, I didn't." Pai Jose turned to him. "At least you're going along."

Shah snorted softly and knelt down to finish her packing. "My father hired him, *Pai,* so don't be so sure he isn't waiting to jump me from behind, drag me off to Manaus and throw me on a plane bound for North America."

Pai Jose chuckled indulgently as he stood there, his hands clasped against his body. "I would think that after Mr. Randolph's magnificent work helping us save lives you would see him in a kinder light."

Shah gave a sharp, derisive laugh. "*Pai,* you're a man, therefore you trust other men. I'm a woman, and I don't."

Making the sign of the cross, Pai Jose blessed each of them. "God be with you, my children. Will you be coming back here once you've gotten the film you want?"

Shah, who was wrapping her camcorder tightly in plastic for the trip down the Amazon, paused for a moment. "I don't know, *Pai* . . ."

"We'll probably stop here for supplies," Jake said.

"If you get into trouble," Pai Jose told Shah seriously, wagging his finger in her direction, "you come home. You come here."

Home. The word formed a lump in Shah's throat. She blinked back the tears and got to her feet. Wordlessly she stepped over to the priest and embraced him.

"No promises, but we'll try," she whispered, her voice cracking.

Jake smiled to himself. Shah had used the word *we* instead of *I.* Good. Unconsciously she was accepting his presence on this foolhardy expedition. Jake wouldn't have had it any other way. It was obvious to him that Shah did trust the old priest, even if he was a man. That gave him renewed hope as he watched her turn away to wipe the tears from her eyes. If she trusted Pai Jose, she might trust him. *Let it be so,* Jake prayed. *Let it be so.*

"Ready?" Jake asked when he saw that Shah had completed her packing. The sun was heading for the western horizon, and it was nearly 4:00 p.m. Shah had planned to use the two hours of light that remained to get down the Amazon, dock the canoe and make camp. Three miles downstream wouldn't be a problem; but coming back would be more difficult. They would have to paddle the canoe by hand, since it didn't have a motor.

Shah nodded. She put the valuable camcorder and some extra videotapes in a small knapsack that she shrugged over her shoulders. Waving goodbye to the many Tucanos who stood on the bank silently watching, Shah felt like crying all over again. These people had openly accepted her as one of their own. Jake moved beside her and sat on the edge of the dock, removing his boots. He placed them inside his knapsack.

"I learned the hard way that wearing boots in a canoe is a stupid idea, when I got dumped in the Orinoco," he told her ruefully.

Shah moved beside him to sit in the rear of the canoe.

"Wait," he said. "You move to the bow and paddle. I'll sit in the rear and be the rudder."

Shah hesitated. "I suppose you know how to paddle this kind of canoe, too?"

"A little," he admitted sheepishly. Shah's features were dark and wary. "Hey," he told her playfully, trying to ease her worry about his presence, "the biggest, strongest guy always sits in the stern to paddle and be the rudder. You know that. I outweigh you by a lot."

Wasn't that the truth? Shah said nothing as she slipped carefully into the canoe, her bare feet touching the bottom's roughly hewn wood. Kneeling in the stern, Jake handed her one of the two paddles. Her heart was in utter turmoil, and so was her head. Jake was acting as if he were going along with her on some kind of picnic. Did he realize the danger they would be in? Hernandez had proved himself capable of murder. And he wanted her dead. A part of her that she was trying desperately to ignore didn't want Jake in the line of fire. Not that he couldn't take care of himself, she admitted grudgingly. Still, she was agitated by the possibility that he could be hurt on her account. She couldn't bear that thought.

"Cast off," Jake called as he unhitched the loop of rope that tethered the canoe to the dock. He saw Shah turn and give him a questioning look, then straighten to face the bow of the canoe. He saw the shadows in the recesses of her eyes, but said nothing. Raising his hand, he waved to the people on the shore, then picked up his own paddle.

Jake used his paddle as a rudder, maneuvering the twenty-foot-long dugout only a little way offshore to avoid the swift currents that lurked beneath the seeming calm surface of the Amazon. The bank curved, the lush rain forest like a lumpy green velvet ribbon bracketing the huge river. His ears were keyed for any out-of-place sounds, because he didn't trust Hernandez in the least. Ahead of them, an osprey wheeled, looking for unsuspecting prey swimming close to the surface.

Shah did little paddling, because the canoe moved slowly but surely along with the flow of the river. Jake admired her straight, long back, wondering what it would be like to glide his fingers down that proud spine and feel her respond. Jake frowned, castigating himself. Where was all this wishful thinking coming from? In four years, he'd been around plenty of other women, but none of them had engaged his heated imagination. Until now.

Jake watched her graceful movements as she moved the paddle from one side of the canoe to the other. She reminded him of a long-limbed ballerina, her every economical movement gliding into the next.

"You ever take ballet lessons?"

Startled, Shah twisted a look across her shoulder at Jake. "What?"

He flushed. "I just wondered if you'd ever taken ballet lessons?"

With a soft laugh, Shah returned to her paddling. "No."

Jake's paddle dipped into the water. Suddenly an image of Katie, his ten-year-old daughter, flashed before him. She was running toward him in her pink tutu. She was laughing, excited about the plans for a recital. The memory hit Jake like a punch to the gut. Kneeling there in the stern, he paddled for a long time without speaking as deeply closeted emotions from the past overwhelmed him. He'd pushed away so much about his family, because it had been too painful to remember. Now his past seemed to be surfacing, and he didn't know what was going on.

Shah relaxed as the first mile slipped behind them. The scents of the rain forest were many and complex. Sometimes she'd get a whiff of an orchid, or the odor of decaying leaves on the sandy soil of the forest floor. Brightly colored blue-and-yellow parrots hid in the tall, stately pau trees that hung over the bank, their dark green leaves like an umbrella over the muddy Amazon. The vines were numerous, varying from thin snakelike ones to some as thick as Jake's muscular arms.

Shah remained hyperaware of Jake's silent presence behind her. Sometimes she could almost feel his eyes boring into her—but then she would shake off the silly feeling. But no matter what she did, she couldn't completely ignore him. What was it that drew her to him? Frowning, Shah tried to figure it out. His size, at first, had frightened her, bringing back memories of the violence done to her by her father and then her husband. Jake's hand alone was nearly twice the size of her own.

Yet he didn't swagger like most males. He didn't have that shallow arrogance she'd seen too often. Shah swallowed and remembered the sadness in Jake's eyes when he'd seen her hold the little Tucanos girl in her arms. She recalled the frantic emotion in his voice last night when he'd charged into her hut to see if she was safe. Shah rested the paddle across the canoe, in front of her, deep in thought. Yes, Jake had shown his feelings to her—in many ways. The only feelings she'd ever seen from a man on a consistent basis were such negative ones as anger, envy and jealousy—until now.

Jake was different, her heart whispered. Shah closed her eyes and hung her head momentarily, feeling the impact of that realization, absorbing it. Jake scared her. Badly. He *was* different from most men she'd met, in ways she had absolutely no experience with. She'd never realized someone like Jake even existed! A small part of her still questioned his motives for being here. She felt torn apart inside. Time would be the true test of Jake's intentions, the only test. A frisson of panic shot through Shah. To make matters worse, she acknowledged, her heart was responding of its own accord to Jake, and there didn't seem to be anything she could do to stop it. Jake's vulnerability was like a magical key able to unlock Shah's closely guarded heart, and it made her feel as exposed as a deer caught in the cross hairs of a hunter's lethal rifle.

"Shah?"

Her head snapping up, Shah jumped at the unexpected sound of Jake's lowered voice. Her hand moving to her pounding heart, she twisted around. "What?"

"I didn't mean to scare you...." Jake said apologetically.

"I'm just naturally jumpy when a man's behind me," she said. Shah saw darkness in Jake's gray eyes, but he quickly hid his reaction. "I got jumped by my husband from behind, and some part of me has never forgotten it," she explained, realizing he was upset for her, not with her. That was another new discovery—a man caring about her.

"I understand," Jake said, noticing how Shah's face had paled, her eyes widening enormously. He could see not only her fear, but, even more moving, her vulnerability, as well. "You were deep in thought."

She tried to smile, but didn't succeed. Her hand was still pressed to her heart. "Yes..."

The overwhelming desire to blanket Shah in all the warmth and tenderness he possessed threatened to be Jake's undoing. He understood Shah's fragility where men were concerned, now that he knew where it had originated. His mouth curved slightly. "Maybe canoe rides invite people to think long and hard," he offered.

"They always do for me," Shah admitted. She purposely kept her voice low for fear of discovery—just in case some of Hernandez's men were nearby, invisible in the thick jungle.

"How do you want to approach this area where Hernandez is being allowed to cut down trees? Is it on this side of the river or the other?"

"This side. I tied a piece of red cloth to a bush hanging near the edge of the water. Once we see that, we can make camp anywhere nearby."

"Don't you feel it would be wiser to camp outside of Hernandez's area and hike in? He could have sentries patrolling the river where that parcel's located."

Shah shook her head. "If you've been in Brazil before, you know that this jungle—" she pointed to the trees with her finger "—is thick with vegetation. It would slow us down too much. I want to be as close as possible to the area where he's going to be cutting."

Jake conceded to her reasoning. Most of the rain forest was overrun with vines that hung like giant pieces of spaghetti off trees that towered well over a hundred feet above them. Add to that many gnarled roots of bushes and trees, exposed by six months of rain on sandy soil—ready to quickly trip a person. Jungle hiking was slow and tedious, requiring the utmost focus. "Okay," he said, "we'll land when you spot that red cloth."

Jake didn't like hugging the bank of the river. When the hair on the back of his neck began to stand up in warning, he used the paddle as a rudder to guide the canoe about a hundred feet farther into the river.

"What are you doing?"

"We're too close to the bank."

Shah frowned. She could feel the current begin to snag and pull the canoe farther out. "It's dangerous to get out too far, Jake! The Amazon makes huge whirlpools. If we're caught in one, we could be killed! We might not be able to paddle hard enough to break the hold of the current. I know the river looks calm and safe on the surface, but it's not, believe me."

"I know that, darlin'. Now, just relax. I'll get us safely back to shore."

Shah couldn't shake her sudden tension. The truth was, she wasn't a good swimmer. Believing that each living thing had a spirit, she never entered the Amazon without offering it a gift of tobacco to ask for safe transit. She gripped the sides of the canoe, her knuckles whitening as Jake continued to guide the canoe farther from shore.

"I'm a lousy swimmer, Jake! If we tip over, I'll be a liability." Shah turned around. "I could never make it to shore from here."

Jake felt bad for having frightened her. "This is for our safety, Shah," he explained, keeping his voice low and calm. "What if Hernandez has his goons along the bank where we want to land? Do you think they're going to welcome us with open arms? My bet is they'll draw a bead on us and kill us."

Shah lowered her head, biting nervously on her lower lip. "I— Okay, it makes sense. I don't know what I'm more scared of—bullets, or trying to survive being dumped in this river. A lot of people have drowned here.

The current's just too swift. It pulls you down. You don't have a chance, Jake."

"Take it easy," he said soothingly, reading the panic in her voice. Shah was gripping the sides of the canoe like a person who was sure she was going to drown. "I'm an ace swimmer," he told her, trying to get her to relax. "In the recons, I had to swim a mile with a forty-pound pack strapped on my back, wearing combat boots. So don't worry. I don't trust Hernandez. I'd rather face this river than hot lead. We can survive this river, but if we get wounded, we could die. There's no medical help out here if we get hurt, Shah."

Jake was right—again. Embarrassed by her sudden display of weakness, Shah whispered, "So much for me being a warrior."

Jake laughed pleasantly, using the paddle expertly in the swift, powerful current. "A smart warrior admits his or her fear. I've been afraid plenty of times."

Shah nodded jerkily. "I've always found that no matter how bad the fear, it's important to keep moving ahead."

"That's right," he agreed. "Recognize it, make it your friend, but for God's sakes, keep moving forward."

With a tight little laugh, Shah felt some of her terror drain away. "That's what the Lakota believe. You'd make a good warrior among them, Jake." She made a conscious effort to stop digging her fingers into the rough sides of the dugout. It was obvious from the way he deftly maneuvered the canoe through the water that he knew how to deal with the lethal currents. His adventures must have taught him a lot.

Jake said, "There's an old Moorish proverb that says, 'He who fears something gives it power over him.'"

"I like an Irish saying better," Shah responded. Maybe talking would help ease her fear of the current turning the canoe over. " 'Fear is a fine spur, so is rage.' "

"You've known both," Jake murmured, his heart reaching out to Shah. He watched her battle her very real fear of the water, and admired her ability to stay level-headed despite it, not giving away her power. In fact, the discovery that Shah had an Achilles' heel only made him respect and desire her more.

With a dip of her head, Shah nervously touched her paddle. "A spur makes a horse jump forward to avoid the pain of it. I guess I grew up like that horse. I guess that's why I'm so jumpy now...."

"Well," Jake said, "maybe in the next week or so I can help you change your view of men as spurs in your side." When he saw her twist her head to give him a look, he added, "Hey, I'm not such a bad specimen of a male. I kinda pride myself on being a little more sensitive toward women than most guys—even if I was in the Marine Corps for sixteen years. We're not all ogres, you know."

No, Jake was far from an ogre, Shah admitted silently. Belatedly she realized that he was teasing her, trying to get her to trust his judgment of the situation. Grimly she said, "I want you to know this is the first time I've ever let a man call the shots." She jabbed her finger down at the milky brown water. "And I can't swim worth a damn!"

Jake chuckled indulgently, then smiled. "You're doing just fine, darlin'. Didn't you know? A good relationship always requires give-and-take by both partners." Now where the hell had that come from? Jake chastised himself. What relationship? And why had he used the word *partners?* Unconsciously he saw Shah as his partner, he grudgingly admitted. If only these unexpected feelings would stop surfacing. If only he would think before he inserted his foot in his mouth. Shah gave him a strange look, but turned around and said nothing. The humidity had frayed her hair along her temples, giving her angular face a softer look.

Jake studied Shah's clean profile as she looked across the water toward the bank. She opened her mouth to say something, then seemed to think better of it, and turned away without saying a word. Had she been about to deny that she was his partner? Jake thought so. Every moment spent with Shah was tearing down those defensive walls she hid behind to protect herself. Jake wished mightily that she would reach out and try trusting him. He wouldn't take advantage of her. Well . . .

Laughing harshly to himself, Jake forced an honest appraisal. Shah was a beautiful woman, and suddenly his body was behaving like that of an unruly sixteen-year-old. He liked Shah's independent streak, her vitality and unapologetic passion for life. There weren't many people, man or woman, who would knowingly put their life on the line for their ideals. That was true courage, in Jake's estimation—something badly needed in this world today.

Nightfall stalked them as they neared the boundary of Hernandez's land. The sun had set long ago, leaving only a lavender strip of color on the horizon above the silhouetted jungle. Howler monkeys could be heard here and there, their cries mingling with the songs of night birds. A chill worked its way up Jake's spine as he began guiding the canoe closer to shore—a powerful warning that shook him into renewed alertness. He tried to penetrate the misty dusk toward the darkened bank of the river. Was he allowing his imagination to get the best of him? he wondered. He almost thought he saw the shapes of several men with submachine guns standing there, waiting for them.

Shaking his head, Jake chastised his overactive imagination and kept searching the jungle as he paddled strongly to break the current's hold on the canoe. Then a noise coming from far away caught his attention.

Shah whirled around. "Do you hear that?" Her voice was high, off-key.

"Yeah? What is it?"

Shah frantically searched the dusk sky. "It's a helicopter! Hernandez has one."

Jake cursed under his breath. That was it. That was the sound. The noise drew closer. An ugly feeling snaked through Jake.

"Shah—"

The sound of gunfire erupted from the shore. Jake jerked his head to the left. He saw the winking of the submachine guns, heard the popping sounds filtering and echoing across the river toward them.

"Duck!" he yelled, and leaned down, moving the canoe sharply out toward the center of the river again.

Too late! Bullets whined and whizzed around them. Bark flew and exploded as several slugs slammed into the hull of the dugout. He realized with horror that these weren't ordinary bullets—they were dumdums, the type of bullet that expanded as they struck their quarry, tearing huge holes as they wreaked their damage. Jake heard Shah give a sharp cry as she flattened down in the canoe for protection. Had she been hit?

From the darkening sky above the jungle a small helicopter suddenly loomed. The sound of its rotor blades cut thickly through the humidity, pounding heavily against Jake's ears. The dugout was rapidly filling with water. Gaping holes had been torn in the sides by the bullets. They were sinking! Realizing it as Jake did, Shah frantically began using her hands to bail out the canoe, exposing herself too much to gunfire from the nearest bank.

Jake's eyes narrowed on the approaching helicopter. His heart ached in his throat. No! He saw light machine guns mounted on both of the aircraft's skids. "Shah! Jump! Jump!"

Gunfire erupted from the helicopter as it swept thirty feet above the surface of the river, coming straight at them. Jake saw Shah hesitate. Bullets were marching in two lines, right for them, making explosive geysers rise from the surface of the water. If they didn't jump now, they'd be killed!

With a grunt, Jake lunged forward, grabbing Shah and throwing her over the side. The bullets whipped closer. Jake jumped, too, diving deep into the river.

Shah's scream was cut short as the powerful current caught her legs, yanking her downward. With the heavy camcorder in her knapsack on her back, she flailed frantically, her nose and mouth filling with water, her breath cut off. For several seconds, she panicked, swallowing water. Then a large, strong arm grabbed her and wrenched her upward. Shah shot upward breaking the surface, choking and coughing.

"Hang on!" Jake gasped. He clutched Shah to him as she blindly threw out her arms in terror. He maneuvered her away from his neck where she threatened to cut off his own air with her death grip. Kicking out strongly, he saw the helicopter sink the canoe with a withering hail of bullets. Three men ran along the edge of the bank, continuing to fire in their direction.

"H-help!"

"Shah," Jake gasped, "don't panic!" Keeping them both afloat in the arms of the current, he tugged at Shah's knapsack until it came off her shoulders, then fastened the snap of the camcorder to the side strap of the knapsack he wore. His mind was working like a steel trap now, because he knew that if it didn't they were going to die. The thought of Shah being killed by these bastards shattered Jake with anger. And the anger gave him the necessary strength to keep them afloat in the powerful, deadly current.

Shah gripped at Jake's neck, and she felt him trying to loosen her fingers. What was he doing? She gave a little cry, panic seizing her again, water funneling into her nose and mouth. No! She was going to drown!

Grimly Jake transferred Shah's clawing hands to his shoulders. The current kept trying to suck them downward. He kicked hard with his bare feet, grateful that he'd had the intelligence to take off his boots. His recon training was going to come in handy.

"Hold on to my knapsack, Shah!" he croaked. "Hold on and I'll get us to shore!"

Trying desperately to contain her panic, Shah clung to Jake's shoulders. She twisted her head, hearing the helicopter turning around to come after them again.

"Oh, no!" she cried. The helicopter was bearing down on them, barely twenty feet off the water. She saw a floodlight on the nose of the aircraft flash on, the glaring white light skimming the surface of the water.

Jake's eyes widened. The bastards had a spotlight, and they were hunting for them! He stopped moving and began to tread water.

"Shah, we're going to have to dive when that light gets near. Take a deep breath and hold on!"

"But—"

"If we don't, they'll find us and kill us!" he yelled.

She didn't have time to argue, with the helicopter roaring down upon them. The water's surface lifted in a huge circle of fine spray ahead of the approaching aircraft. Her eyes widening, Shah took a huge gulp of air, digging her fingers frantically into the knapsack on Jake's back. Jake dived deep and fast, and she was jerked along, the raw, physical power of his dive overwhelming her as they spiraled downward. Her eyes closed, she buried her head against the knapsack, clinging wildly to him.

The current tugged and played with them. Shah heard pinging sounds all around them. Bullets! Jake was still diving, and she wondered if she had managed to gulp enough air to last for the duration.

A minute later, they broke the surface with a gasp, both choking on the brackish water.

"Shah?" Jake gasped, his voice cracking. He reached frantically for her. "Shah! You all right?" The helicopter was moving farther downstream, away from them, the floodlight still searching the dark water.

"I... Yes..." She clung to the knapsack, coughing violently, retching up the water she'd swallowed.

"Hang on," Jake ordered. He knew it would be impossible to land nearby with Hernandez's henchmen waiting for them on the shore.

"What—what are you doing?" Shah couldn't believe it. Jake was striking out toward the center of the wide river!

"We can't land now," he gasped. "We're gonna have to let the current carry us a mile or two downstream before we go ashore."

Fear clawed at Shah. The darkness was complete now, except for the dazzling light from the helicopter, now a good half mile away from them. "C-can you make it?"

"I think so. Don't struggle anymore. Kick your feet and help me."

Her panic subsided, replaced with the very real fear of drowning. The river was filled with schools of piranha that, if they caught the scent of blood, would descend upon them in a feeding frenzy and strip the flesh from their bones. Shah wondered bleakly if Jake was wounded. Was she? There was no way to know. The current was frighteningly potent—but so was Jake's constant, seemingly tireless swimming stroke.

The dreaded jacare, the Amazonian crocodile that could grow to more than twenty feet in length, prowled near the shores. Any kind of splashing would alert the reptile to their presence. The jacare had no fear of man. It didn't even fear the dreaded jaguar, lord of the rain forest. Gulping convulsively, Shah tried to do as Jake instructed, kicking with her feet.

Her thoughts were clashing with her heart. How long was Jake going to stay in the center of the river? How long could he remain afloat? She prayed fiercely to the Great Spirit and begged the spirit of the river to have mercy on them, to let them get safely to shore.

In the ensuing minutes, as Shah clung to Jake's knapsack, she slowly began to realize just how strong he really was. The current was deadly, constantly moving around their legs and trying to pull them under. But each powerful stroke of his arms and legs kept their heads above the water's surface. And each stroke gave Shah a little more hope. But then, up ahead, she saw the helicopter stop and hover at the bend in the Amazon.

"Oh, no!" she cried. "They're coming back toward us!"

Chapter Seven

Relief coursed through Shah as Hernandez's helicopter missed them completely on its second pass. Instead of searching the center of the Amazon, the pilot flew low near the left bank. As the aircraft swept past them, Jake grunted and struck out strongly toward the same shore.

Shah's panic eased as she felt his steady strokes begin to pull them out of the grip of the current. And their luck changed markedly when a six-foot-long log drifted by them.

"Grab it!" Jake gasped.

Shah trusted him with her life now, and without thinking she lunged toward the log, which was as thick as a man's middle. Instantly she was buoyed upward by the floating log. Jake followed, maneuvering the log so that he gripped the end of it. With forceful kicks of his legs and feet, he was quickly able to guide them toward shore.

Light was fading fast, and Shah clung to the log, her teeth chattering. At night, the temperature in the forest dipped, and it actually got cold—at least by the standards of the thin-blooded natives. She'd lived here long enough to have become acclimated to the steamy Amazon weather, so she knew she was going to be terribly chilled once they got to shore. *If* they got to shore.

"Jake!" she croaked. "When we get near the bank, look out for crocodiles. They're around this time of night, hunting for food."

"Yeah...okay..." Exhaustion was pulling at Jake. The adrenaline charge that had helped him remain afloat with Shah clinging to him had begun to dissolve. With a nod, he blinked, the water running in rivulets down his face. His fingers were numb from holding and guiding the stubborn log. The current was tricky, trying to lure the log back toward the center of the river, and he had to kick damn hard. But with each kick, the current's grasp seemed to grow weaker.

Glancing upstream, Jake saw the helicopter bank and move back over the rain forest. Soon it disappeared from view, and the sound of the blades faded. Even straining his eyes, he could barely make out the shore. They had less than three hundred yards to go. Every muscle in his body screamed in protest. He knew he needed to rest, but if he tried, the current would snag him and haul them back out. And if that happened, they would surely die, because he knew he didn't have the necessary strength left to fight the Amazon's power all over again. Jake also knew about the fierce, aggressive jacare that plied the waters of the Amazon. He knew about the piranha, which often numbered in feeding schools of a hundred or more. He had no idea if he or Shah was cut and bleeding. The smell of blood could draw the savage little silver-and-red fish with their razor-sharp teeth.

Drawing huge gulps of air into his lungs, Jake concentrated on making it to shore. He'd worry about the local jacare once they got there. His main concern was for Shah. Had she been hit by a bullet? Broken a bone? She clung to the log, her face contorted in silent terror. At least she wasn't panicking, and for that Jake was grateful.

As they got close to shore, Jake stopped making large, loud kicks that spewed water high into the air. The jacare were drawn to churning water, honing in on the splashes like radar. Instead, he made scissorlike kicks beneath the water, making no sound at all. Suddenly his feet hit the sandy bottom, and he stood up. His knees wobbly, he used his upper-body weight to send the log toward the bank. As he staggered out into the shallows, he felt all his joints burning with pain from overexertion.

Stooping down, he hooked his arms beneath Shah's armpits and helped her to stand. She was shaking badly.

"It's all right," he said, turning her around and bringing her tightly against him to keep her from falling. His knees were none too steady, but hers were like jelly. Jake couldn't blame her for her reaction; a weak swimmer had every right to fear the Amazon. It crossed his groggy mind that Shah might rebel and push his arms away, but he needed her in that moment. He'd almost lost her. The instant she sank against him, her arms moving around his waist, her head against his chest, Jake released a low groan. How right Shah felt against him. He held her with all of his remaining strength.

Closing his eyes, he rested his head against her wet hair. He could feel Shah's heart pounding against his chest, her breathing coming in ragged sobs. Unconsciously he pressed a kiss to her tangled hair and moved one hand down across her back in an effort to soothe away her terror.

"We're safe...safe..." he said unsteadily. She was so slender. Slender and strong. He felt her woman's strength renew itself in his arms, in his protective embrace. Nothing in the past four years had felt so right to him.

Gradually, the minutes flowing by as they stood in the ankle-deep water getting their second wind, Shah felt strength returning to her shaking knees. With each trembling stroke of Jake's hand up and down her spine, she felt him giving her renewed energy. She understood better than most the transfer of energy, because that was what a healer did for a sick patient—transferred the vitality of life. Jake was doing the same thing for her, whether he realized it or not. Her shorted-out mind awed by the discovery, Shah could only humbly receive the warmth that flowed from him to her, receive it with unspoken gratitude.

Jake forced himself to lift his head. He wanted to kiss her lips, to taste and feel her life mingling with his as his mouth met hers. Against his bulk, she was like a slender arrow. In that moment, Jake realized that Shah presented a powerful presence to the world because of her height and the way she carried herself. But holding her in his arms, he had discovered her fragility, and the discovery made his heart open like petals on a flower. Despite being a warrior for Mother Earth, Shah was decidedly human, and that gave him hope. No matter how strong someone appeared, how invincible, Jake knew from personal experience that everyone had faults and weaknesses. He was glad Shah was able to share her weaknesses with him, as well as her strengths.

"Better?" he asked, leaning down, his mouth inches from her ear. Jake felt Shah nod. He gave her a small squeeze, wanting to feed her hope that they would be safe now. Purposely he kept his voice very low, fearing discovery by Hernandez's roving henchmen. He had no idea if they were still on Hernandez's parcel of land.

The light was sparse as Jake lifted his head to survey the place where they'd come ashore. He felt Shah pull away, and he opened his embrace so that she could step out of his arms if she wanted. However, still not convinced she could stand, he kept his hand around her waist—just in case. If Shah minded his action, she didn't show it, and Jake savored the soaring joy that swept through him. To his surprise, Shah kept her arm around his waist and rested against him as they faced the rain forest together.

Shah tried to grapple with her receding terror. They had survived the Amazon River unscathed, and she sent a prayer to the spirit of the river in thanks for its having spared them. Looking up into Jake's harsh, shadowed features, she met his turbulent gray gaze.

"We need to find a tree," she told him, her voice scratchy. "We'll have to sleep up in one, or the jacare will find us. It's not safe to sleep on the ground."

With a nod, Jake pointed to a rubber tree about fifty feet inland. With proper pruning and shaping, rubber trees grew straight and tall. However, in the wilds of the rain forest, the trees spread their smooth-barked limbs in all directions, often looking like grotesque, twisted caricatures of octopuses.

"What about that one?" Jake asked. The trunk of the tree rose a good eight feet straight up, then its limbs flowed outward like tentacles. Jake thought it looked like a candelabra.

"Yes." Shah hated to leave Jake's embrace, but she knew that now that they were on land it was her responsibility to help. Jake hadn't lived in the rain forest, as she had. Or had he? They climbed the riverbank together. As Jake shed the heavy knapsack, Shah asked, "What do you know about survival in a rain forest?"

"Probably not as much as you," Jake admitted. Shah's hair, once braided, was coming undone, sheets of the drying strands like a dark cloak against the curve of her small breasts.

"The Tucanos have taught me a lot about this place, Jake." Shah turned. "That rubber tree is a good place to sleep tonight." She frowned, flexing her hands. Her fingers were stiff from the death grip she'd had on the log. "The only thing we've got to worry about is the jaguar. She's the only tree-climber."

"We've got a pistol and a knife," Jake said. "We'll be safe enough."

Shah moved carefully through the knee-deep vegetation. Transferring all her focus to her feet, she felt for vines and exposed roots that might trip them on their way to the tree. Shivering as the night became cooler by the minute, Shah wrapped her arms around herself. She had no change of clothes. And with the high humidity, the wet clothes they wore would dry only slowly, and probably not completely. Trying to stop her teeth from chattering, she halted at the base of the rubber tree.

When Jake joined her, Shah pointed upward. "We're in luck. See those two branches that criss-cross like a large loop on a high-backed chair?"

Squinting, Jake could barely make out the thick branches that tangled together. "Yeah . . ."

"That's like a cradle, Jake. It's strong enough and wide enough to hold you. All you have to do is ease back into the tree's branches like a hammock. You'll be able to sleep comfortably, and you won't fall."

"What about you?" he asked. Searching the rest of the tree, he could find no limbs that would give Shah that kind of guaranteed safety. And, more than anything, they needed a good night's sleep to ready them for the trials that lay ahead tomorrow.

"I'll just find a branch and lean up against the main trunk," Shah assured him.

"Like hell you will," Jake growled. He shrugged out of the knapsack and tied it to an overhanging limb. Taking Shah's, he tied it next to his. "Come on, I'll boost you up," he ordered.

Surprised at Jake's sudden authoritative tone, Shah allowed him to lift her into the rubber tree. She watched as he gracefully hefted himself up on the opposite limb.

"Follow me," he said, and began the climb toward the cradle of limbs.

Perplexed, Shah followed him. The rubber tree's bark was smooth, and the oval leaves were large and waxy. The cacophony of night sounds surrounded them like a swelling orchestra. Her teeth chattering uncontrollably now, Shah watched as Jake settled gingerly back into the limbs that would hold him safe for the night. He tested the makeshift bed for strength, satisfying himself that the limbs weren't going to break.

"Come here," he said.

Shah was transfixed. "What?"

"I said, come here."

She frowned as he held out a hand to her. "Jake, I can't stay with you!"

"Sure you can." He gestured for her to come over to him. "I don't want you falling thirty feet and breaking something, Shah. If you fall asleep, you're liable to lose your balance against the trunk.''

A new kind of panic struck at Shah. Her mouth grew dry. "Jake...I can't!"

"No arguments, Shah. Now come on.''

The grimness in his eyes and mouth warned her not to debate his decision. Her heart beating wildly in her breast, Shah hesitated. "How am I going to sleep with you?" she demanded in a high, off-pitch tone.

"In my arms." Jake patted the smooth, thick limb beside him. "I'll be your mattress. My arms will be around you, so you won't fall."

"But—"

Jake held on to his patience. The alarm in Shah's voice was real. He understood her hesitancy, but under the circumstances he couldn't be swayed by it. "I'll hold you," he said patiently, "and we'll sleep. I'm not going to hurt you, Shah.''

She moved toward him and gripped his hand. "This isn't right!"

"It will be okay," Jake told her. In his heart, he knew it was the right thing to do. Hadn't he wanted to hold Shah, sleep with her? Taking her hand, he guided Shah toward him. "Now, turn around and sit down in my lap," he instructed her. The crisscrossed branches behind his back supported him completely.

Shah's heart was beating so loudly that she thought Jake must surely hear it as she settled stiffly on his broad thighs. His hands gripped her upper arms to steady her. A different fear raced through Shah—the fear of herself and her response to Jake as a man. He must have sensed her tension, because he squeezed her arms.

"You're safe," he murmured, pulling her toward him until her back rested against him. She was stiff in his arms. "Here, turn on your side. Just think of me as a big, lumpy mattress, with my shoulder as a pillow for your head . . ."

His teasing broke through her panic. She slowly turned so that her left side was ensconced against Jake's body.

"I'm afraid the limbs will break!" she protested. "We could fall and be killed!"

Reaching out, Jake stroked her damp hair. "You're so wild and untamed," he murmured. "We're not going to fall, Shah. This tree is old and strong, like me." He chuckled softly at his own joke.

Just the touch of his fingers against her head, caressing her as if she were an animal caught in a snare, calmed Shah to a degree. Her teeth chattered, and she had to admit she was freezing, and in need of shared body heat. Physical exhaustion stalked her in earnest now, and she had no choice but to lay her head against his broad, capable shoulder and press her brow to the column of his neck.

"Old?" she muttered. "How old are you?"

"Thirty-eight. And you?"

"Thirty."

He smiled. "You're young."

"And you aren't?" Her voice was softening as the fight went out of her.

"That's it," Jake whispered, and he groaned inwardly as Shah finally capitulated and eased against him. Her arm moved hesitantly around his waist. "You're cold," he whispered, wrapping his arms around her for warmth.

Shah shut her eyes and surrendered to Jake. This was the second time in her life that she'd truly trusted a man. The first time had been with her husband, who had proven quickly that he wasn't worthy of her trust. A shiver raced through her, and Shah felt her legs jerk of their own accord.

"Just lie here. I'll warm you up a little," Jake soothed, and he took his hand and began vigorously rubbing her wet trousers across her thigh and hip. Despite the danger they were in, Jake had to admit that nothing had ever felt more right than the weight of Shah nestled deep in his arms.

"Wh-why aren't you cold?" she chattered.

With a rumbling chuckle, Jake said, "I've got you in my arms, darlin'. The right woman always makes a man feel warm."

Shah's eyes flew open. He was teasing her, wasn't he? She moaned a little as his hand created warmth across her thigh and hip. He had to be teasing! Pursing her lips, she muttered, "I'm not any man's woman!"

"You can be."

"No one would want someone like me, Jake Randolph! I'm mean-tempered, defensive, and in general I don't care for men!"

"You're such a wildcat, Shah." Jake stopped rubbing her, because she'd ceased shivering. Wrapping his arms around her, he gave her a light squeeze. "You've got a lot of fine points about you," he whispered close to her ear. "And not every man is going to be scared off by your past or that tough-broad act you put on."

Confused and exhausted, Shah couldn't decide whether Jake was teasing or serious. She closed her eyes and pressed against him, absorbing his heat. How he could be so warm when she was freezing was beyond her. "I've been wounded too many times, Jake," Shah warned him, realizing her words were slightly slurred. "I don't trust men."

Jake smiled in the darkness and slowly began to undo the rest of her braid so that her thick, silky hair could cover her. It was one more way to keep her warm. "Darlin'," he said softly, "we've all been wounded one way or another by love."

She stubbornly shook her head. "I suppose that's a quote from some famous philosopher."

His teeth were white against the darkness. "Yeah, a hell of a guy said it. I think Jake Randolph was his name."

All the tension Shah had been holding within her snapped. She giggled a little, and covered her mouth with her hand so that the sound wouldn't carry far. Just the simple act of Jake unbraiding her hair and allowing it to flow across her like a coverlet had been her undoing.

"What?" he asked teasingly. "You're not familiar with that famous philosopher?"

The darkness was complete now, and Shah allowed herself the luxury of enjoying Jake's embrace. She lifted her hand and rested it against the column of his neck. "You're good for morale," she murmured, "and I'm not going to comment one way or another about your philosophy."

Chuckling indulgently, Jake sighed and rested his head against the tree. "We've all been wounded," he told her softly. "But wounds should be allowed to heal, Shah."

"They still leave scars," she muttered with a frown.

"Nothing wrong with that. Scars are memories, but they shouldn't stop you from trying to reach out and live again." Jake laughed harshly at himself. Had he thought he'd ever laugh again? Ever love again? After his family had been taken from him, Jake had truly known the bleakness of a future without hope. Not until he'd met Shah, not until he'd held her in his arms, had he found

hope again. She fit against his length like a missing piece
of a puzzle. A piece he had never envisioned finding.

Warmth was beginning to seep back into Shah. Jake
was like a huge furnace, and surrendering to him had
been right. She laughed at herself for having thought
she'd never trust a man again. Jake's rumbling voice
flowed across her, bringing an unfamiliar ache to her
heart. In some way, he was able to get through her complex defenses to touch her—gently, without engaging her
fear. Yet Shah did fear the future. At some point, would
Jake, like all the rest of the men in her life, turn on her?
Abuse her? Take advantage of her?

Shah squeezed her eyes shut. She didn't know the answer, and not knowing left a helpless feeling in her heart.
Jake absently stroked her arm, as if it were the most natural thing in the world. His touch, unlike any other man's
that she'd known, was quieting and healing, and that
amazed her.

Wearily Shah nuzzled against Jake's neck, and felt an
instant response, his arm tightening around her just
enough to let her know he liked her trust in him. "I'm so
tired, Jake...."

"Go to sleep," he urged her huskily. "I'll hold you safe
and warm tonight."

A soft smile tugged at Shah's mouth. "I can't believe
a man could make me feel this safe...."

Those last words chased around in Jake's head most of
the night. Sleep, though badly needed, wasn't on his list
of priorities tonight. The need to stay alert, not only for
four-legged predators, but for two-legged ones, as well,
kept him thoroughly awake. The Amazon was like a lover
in some ways, Jake thought as he lay there through the
hours of darkness, experiencing the rich sounds of insects and animals and the heady fragrance of nearby or-

chids. His body throbbed with the knowledge that he wanted to make love with Shah. She slept deeply, like a lost child in his arms, her hand curled against his chest, over his heart.

Jake's attention was torn between keeping watch and succumbing to Shah's presence. The thrill of her trust was keeping him awake on another, more physical level. The ache deep within him surprised him even as it made him hungry in a way he'd thought he would never know again. He absorbed each soft, moist breath she released, felt her breasts lightly rise and fall, and devoured the sensation of her body resting against his. He almost laughed aloud at the thought that if she could read his mind she'd fly out of his arms.

A quarter moon rose silently in the sky, lending a misty luminescence to the landscape. Jake marveled at the hazy beauty of the rain forest, which seemed to be more magical than real. He watched wisps of mist twist slowly, like graceful hands and arms, through the branches overhead. The Amazon, now a wide black ribbon, shone like an ebony mirror in the moonlight. Several times he saw the sleek, dark shapes of dolphins as they leaped out of the river, made a quick splash and dived beneath the surface again. Never had Jake felt as fulfilled as he did at this moment.

Somewhere near dawn, Jake dropped off to sleep, his head tipped back against the tree, his arms wrapped around Shah. But his dreams were torrid and heated, instead of being filled with his usual cutting feelings of loneliness and grief.

Shah awoke slowly, feeling warm and safe. The scent of a man entered her nostrils, and she inhaled it as if it were some forgotten perfume that only her heart recognized. The bristles of Jake's beard chafed pleasantly against her brow, and she released a sigh of pleasure. The weight of his arms made her feel secure. The entire length of her body followed his, and as she flexed and moved her fingers, which lay against his powerful chest, she felt the smooth flow of muscles beneath his damp shirt. Jake had a hidden power, she decided groggily, and she didn't want to wake up, wanting instead to stay contained in the safe haven of his arms.

Jake's broken snoring made her smile softly. At some point in the night he had shifted just enough to allow his head to rest against her hair, and now his moist breath was flowing down across her. Forcing her eyes open, Shah blinked and allowed her senses to open up to the sounds and smells surrounding her. A huge part of her wanted to lift her head and explore Jake's mouth. What would it be like to kiss him? Would he overwhelm her with his superior strength? Or would he be tender and sharing with her? Shah tried to berate herself for her idealism. Her mind told her that men had no capacity for sharing, but her heart argued that Jake had already shown her his tenderness in many small, meaningful ways.

Ribbons of mist lay across the Amazon, and transparent, gauzy clouds of humidity floated just above the triple-canopied rain forest. The mist darkened the trees so that everywhere she looked the jungle seemed ethereal— as if it were a floating, moving mirage that could, at any moment, disappear before her very eyes. This was what she loved about the Amazon—its mysteriousness, the way it appeared and disappeared in these haunting white mists that reminded her of ever-moving curtains. Trees were silhouetted, then blotted out by a thick cloud moving silently across them, only to reappear later. Sounds were muted by the humidity and mist moving sensuously through the trees.

Shah heard a loud hiss from beneath the tree. Instantly she froze.

Jake jerked awake, his embrace tightening around Shah. "What?" he muttered, startled.

"Don't move," Shah breathed, craning her neck. "There's a huge jacare right under the tree, Jake."

At the base of the tree was a fifteen-foot jacare, its jaws open, the pink of its mouth and rows of white, pointed teeth showing. The reptile hissed again and whipped its tail, thumping it hard against the jungle floor.

Jake sat up, holding Shah hard against him. Sleep was torn from him as he stared down at the nasty-looking creature. They were safe. There was no way the jacare could climb the tree. He shifted his awareness to Shah, who was leaning forward.

"Don't fall," he warned.

"I won't." Shah gulped and decided it was time to get out of Jake's embrace. If she stayed, the temptation to kiss him, to explore his mouth, would overwhelm her. "Let me go."

Jake released her, scowling. "What are you doing?"

Shah moved slowly to the opposite side of the tree. "Trying to get rid of the jacare," she muttered. The jacare followed her movement, sluggishly turning in a half circle as she moved out onto another, smaller limb.

"Dammit, Shah, get back here!" Jake launched himself upward and gripped an overhead limb. What was she doing?

"Stay there," Shah ordered. She retrieved a hefty piece of limb that had fallen from a pau tree and lodged in the rubber tree. "Do you want to stay up here all day with him waiting for his meal to come down to him, or do you want him to leave?"

"Just tell me what you've got planned," he growled.

"I'm going to get rid of him. You can't shoot him. The noise will tell Hernandez we're alive and in his territory." She twisted her head toward Jake, who had a thundercloud look of disapproval on his darkly bearded face. Didn't he think she could help?

Retrieving the four-foot limb, Shah whispered, "Give me your knife."

Jake grudgingly handed it to her, butt first. Her logic was faultless.

Leaning down, Shah pricked two of her fingers with the tip of it.

"What the hell are you doing?" Jake demanded, alarmed.

"Relax." Shah allowed the blood to drip over the end of the limb. Then, satisfied that there was enough, she wiped her fingers on her trousers and handed Jake his knife. He was glaring at her.

"Jacare have lousy eyesight," she informed him testily, "but they've got noses like bloodhounds." She held up the limb. "They can smell blood half a mile away in the water. Unless you want to get down and wrestle this guy, this is the best way to get rid of him! The Tucanos showed me this trick."

Disgruntled, Jake watched as Shah clambered down to the lowest limb of the tree. The jacare heard her and whipped around with amazing speed for such an unwieldy creature. Shah took the limb and poked it down toward the hissing jacare, waving it back and forth in front of him. The crocodile tested the air with his long, thin snout, making several loud whuffing sounds. Shah chuckled.

"He's got the scent," she whispered excitedly. Then, with all her strength, she hurled the limb toward the bank of the river. Scowling, Jake watched Shah sit down on the limb and wait. Within a few minutes, the jacare lifted its dark green snout again, sniffed the air and slowly trundled toward where the limb lay on the bank.

Shah grinned expectantly as the jacare got within a few feet of the limb and attacked it, scooping it up in his massive jaws. Within moments, the reptile made a waddling run for the river and slid back into the muddy Amazon waters, disappearing beneath the surface with the limb. She tossed a triumphant look up at Jake.

"That jacare is going to have one heck of a bellyache after he eats that wood," she said with a chuckle.

Admiration for Shah flowed through Jake. He forced himself to stop scowling. "That's a pretty neat trick," he congratulated her. "How are your fingers?" It had hurt him as much to see her prick them as if they'd been his own.

She held them up and smiled. "Fine." Standing gingerly, Shah looked around, then back at him. Her smile faded. "Well, I guess we'd better start planning our day." She pointed to the north. "Hernandez's land is that way. If my camcorder isn't ruined, we'll be in luck."

A scowl instantly formed on Jake's brow. "What the hell are you talking about, Shah?"

She eased out of the tree and lowered herself to the ground. "You're sure grouchy when you first wake up, you know that? Are you always like that? Or is this something special for my benefit? Maybe you need a cup of good, thick Brazilian coffee..." Shah retrieved Jake's knapsack and laid it on the ground. To her delight, the camcorder was not only undamaged, but dry, as well.

Jake dropped to the ground next to her. "I only get grouchy when I think someone's going to make a fool out of herself." He hunkered down opposite Shah. "You aren't still planning to film Hernandez cutting down those trees, are you?"

Glancing up as she gently pulled the plastic wrap aside, Shah said, "Of course I am."

Jake stared at her in shock. "After what he's done?"

Heaving a sigh, Shah held his gaze. "Especially after what he's done," she said grimly. "I know the score with him, Jake. I know he'll try to kill me."

"Us."

"You don't have to go. I'm not asking that of you."

He held on to his thinning patience. "You nearly drowned yesterday!"

"Don't shout, Jake."

He frowned. "I'm shouting because I care, Shah. I care about your neck. Okay? It's too dangerous to go after Hernandez now. The smartest thing we can do is get our butts out of this sling, get back to Pai Jose's mission, make a radio call for police help and have them arrest Hernandez for attempted murder."

Shah tried to placate Jake. "Yesterday, I was on your turf, the water. Today—" she looked around the rain forest "—you're on my turf, Jake. I've been trained by the Tucanos. I know how to survive here. Look, you don't have to go along with me. I know the way back to the mission from here. I've got an excellent sense of direction, and I never get lost."

"That's not the point," Jake gritted out, feeling completely helpless beneath her stubborn determination. On one hand, his protective instincts were getting the best of him. On the other, he respected Shah's knowledge of the area. What he didn't want to deal with any more than was necessary was Shah's life being in danger again. "Dammit, Shah, I care about you! I want you safe!"

His words cut through Shah, and she slowly stood. Jake cared for her. His gray eyes were turbulent with feeling, and she heard the undisguised emotion in his voice. "Don't," she pleaded. "Don't care about me, Jake. It's no good. I'm not a good bet. Don't you understand?"

Jake rose, towering over her. How beautiful Shah looked with her long, loose hair flowing across her shoulders like an ebony cape. Her mouth was soft and parted, and her lovely golden eyes were filled with pain. He reached out, just barely grazing her cheek. "I don't have a choice," he rasped. "I don't want a choice, Shah."

She stood there looking up at him, stunned by his low, trembling admission. She looked around helplessly, then took a step away from his presence. "I— No, Jake. This isn't good—"

"That's what your head is telling you. What does your heart say, Shah?"

Stunned by Jake's insight, Shah felt nakedly vulnerable as never before. How could he read her true thoughts so easily? Panicking, she cried out softly, "It doesn't matter how I feel! Just go home, Jake! Go home to America and leave me here! This isn't your battle, it's mine!"

The tears in her eyes tore at him. Shah was frightened of him—of the connection he was offering her. Jake didn't have time to analyze why he'd said what he'd said. He wanted to take back the words, but it was too late. Shah wasn't ready to hear the depth of his feelings. Her fear regarding men was well-founded, and he was a man. It was that simple—and that complex.

"I'm not leaving you out here alone," he told her grimly.

"Because my father paid you?"

"Your father doesn't have a thing to do with this now, and you know it!"

Angry and frightened, Shah tensed. "I'm a lousy risk, Jake. So just—"

"You're a risk I want to take," he snapped. "And that's my decision, Shah." He jabbed a finger at her and instantly regretted the action. "You're stuck with me. Don't be bullheaded about this. Let's go to the mission first and report the incident."

"No," Shah said firmly. "No. Hernandez thinks he's killed us. Now he'll bring out those chain saws and let his men use them because he thinks we're not around to catch him on tape." She knelt again by her knapsack and pulled the last of the plastic away so that she could thoroughly examine the video equipment.

With a growl, Jake leaned down and gripped her by the shoulder. He used very little real strength, because of her fear of violence from men. "Then we'll do this together," he rasped.

Jake's hand was like a hot, searing iron against her flesh. Shah looked up, lost in the thundercloud blackness of his eyes, surrounded by his emotions. *Together.* Tears pricked her eyes, and she lowered her lashes. "You don't deserve this, Jake," she said, her voice wavering. "You're a good man. One of the best I've ever met. Please, just go home."

"No way, Shah," he whispered as he straightened. Jake had seen her tears and understood them. A part of her wanted him to stay; he'd seen it mirrored in her topaz eyes. Another part of her was so frightened of him and her feelings for him that she would rather risk her neck alone against Hernandez than have him around. Jake felt helpless and angry. But he was damned if he was going to abandon Shah. She'd been betrayed by men too many times before and for once he was going to show her that a man could be counted on to stick it out with her— even under threat of death.

Chapter Eight

"Look!" Shah whispered excitedly. "There's Hernandez!" Hidden deep in the shoulder-high bushes, she glanced over as Jake quietly crept up beside her. To her surprise, trekking through the rain forest hadn't been as bad as she'd thought. There was comparatively little underbrush, because smaller plants had difficulty surviving in the shade of the triple canopy of the trees overhead.

Shah pointed toward an area a quarter-mile down the slight hill they were kneeling on. Jake nodded but said nothing as he intently studied the situation. Shah could see three bulldozers and at least forty workers. Already the tall and the medium-sized trees had been taken down, leaving only the shortest trees still to fall to the buzzing chain saws wielded by the workers. The hillside looked stripped, and soon would be bare. Shah wondered if any of them realized that with the root system no longer holding the soil the earth would flow into the Amazon when the summertime rainy season began. Losing the foot-and-a-half layer of topsoil that had accumulated in the past million years would have dire consequences. Once upon a time, in a prehistoric era, the Amazon Basin had been a vast desert wasteland. Now, only that precious layer of decayed leaves and trees on top of the sand base created the fragile barrier between life and death. If the destruction of the rain forest was allowed to continue unabated, the Amazon Basin would once again be a desert, incapable of sustaining life.

Without thinking, Shah gripped Jake's arm. "Chain saws!" The air rang with their sound; at least thirty of the men were using them against the last of the standing trees.

Looking around, Jake realized that daylight was slipping away from them. They had hiked at least three miles to the northeast, and there was no doubt that they were now on Hernandez's parcel of land.

"Yeah, but look," he growled, pointing out three men walking along the periphery of the work detail. All three were carrying submachine guns.

With a nod, Shah took off her knapsack, which contained the camcorder. "I promise we'll get the photos and get out, Jake. I don't want to get shot at again any more than you do." She kept her voice low so that they wouldn't be detected by the guards.

Edgy, Jake said nothing, but helped Shah prepare the camcorder for recording Hernandez and his men illegally using chain saws. Sweat ran down his face, and he wiped it away with the back of his arm. Shah seemed impervious to the steamy heat, but then, Jake reminded himself sourly, she had already become accustomed to the demands of the tropics.

"Ready?" he asked.

With a nod, Shah slowly stood, the camcorder balanced on her left shoulder. She moved to a nearby araba tree whose five-foot-tall roots resembled flying buttresses. Each root was less than an inch thick at the top, with a wedge shape that thickened to sometimes two to three feet in width as it breached the ground. Shah hid herself behind one of the dark brownish-gray barriers, just her head and the video camera visible above it. Leaning against the root's stability, Shah began to tape, her heart pounding a steady, heavy beat of triumph.

Jake remained alert, scanning the area for any sign of trouble as Shah continued to shoot the necessary footage. He tried to ignore the carnage that Hernandez's men were wreaking below them. He wondered what animal species were being displaced and, worse, what potentially life-saving medicinal plants were being destroyed before they could ever be discovered.

The sunlight was almost gone now, brief beams cutting through the rain forest only occasionally. In another two hours it would be dark, and Jake wanted to be a long way from this particular area. Detection by Hernandez's guards was still a very real possibility.

After forty minutes of taping the timber cutting operation, Shah knelt down behind the buttress root and shut off the camcorder. Jake joined her and took the videotape she proffered. Slipping it into an airtight plastic bag, he made sure the tape was well protected, hidden deep within his knapsack.

"We've gotta hightail it out of here," he muttered near her ear. "It's getting dark, and we've got to find a safe place to sleep before nightfall."

"No argument," Shah said, giddy with excitement, with the knowledge that she could put Hernandez behind bars with the tape. She looked up and met Jake's darkened gaze. He'd been testy and grouchy all day, and she couldn't blame him—this was dangerous work. "You've been wonderful!" she said, and spontaneously threw her arms around him and gave him a quick, hard embrace.

Surprised, Jake had no time to react—at least not the way he would have liked to. The glow in Shah's eyes told him of her joy, and he smiled crookedly.

"Glad to see there's a little of the child left in you," he said teasingly as he rewrapped the camcorder in protective plastic.

Years of weight seemed to lift off Shah's shoulders as she stared up at Jake. His smile was that of a bashful boy, and if her eyes weren't deceiving her, there was a new ruddiness in his cheeks. "Jake, you aren't blushing, are you?" She laughed softly with delight at her discovery.

"Hey," he muttered, "it's been a long time since a beautiful lady hugged me." Jake felt the heat nettling his bearded cheeks. He was thankful that the darkness of his two-day beard probably hid the worst of the flush, but he still felt vulnerable to Shah's observation. When had he last blushed like a teenager? Jake couldn't even recall. His neck and shoulders still tingled where Shah had touched him. The ache to love her, to make her his, nearly overwhelmed him. But the feelings he held for her, though heated, were tender. He smiled into her dancing gold eyes, losing himself in her happiness.

The danger of their situation was still very real, and Shah was well aware that they couldn't sit and chat. Within moments they were slipping out of the area, undetected. Their plan called for heading back to the banks of the Amazon, then simply walking along it to shorten their journey back to the mission, instead of moving inland and fighting the rain forest all the way back. The inland route would be safer, but they'd weighed that against the time factor and decided that speed was their best asset, so they'd chosen the river route.

Grateful that Jake was ahead of her, Shah made a mental note to ask him about his past sometime. He'd once referred obliquely to not being married. Why had he blushed? He was a thirty-eight-year-old man with obvious experience with women. Dividing her attention between where she was placing her feet and the sounds around her, Shah decided to ask her questions tonight, after they made camp.

To Shah's delight, they came upon a mango tree, the fruit ripe and edible. She had already collected edible berries that had dropped to the damp jungle floor, and she knew they'd eat well once they camped. Jake remained tense, and Shah had to admit that she had no idea whether they were still on Hernandez's land.

Again she selected a rubber tree with grotesque limbs to support them during sleep, and Jake nodded at her choice. Was he disappointed that she wouldn't sleep in his arms tonight? Last night had been one of the best nights of sleep Shah had ever experienced. Confused, she tried not to think about it—or Jake. She watched as he moved like a shadow upstream through the rain forest while she made camp for them in the tree. The trunk rose almost ten feet straight up, and then began to spread out its twisted, gnarled limbs.

Standing on a nearby log to tie both knapsacks high in the tree, Shah looked up to see the pale pink sunset along the western horizon. The color was softened and muted by the ever-present mist, which was beginning to return in earnest now that the sun had set.

Near dark, she sensed Jake nearby from her tree perch and strained to see him. Or was it Jake? Shah wasn't sure, and remained parallel to the trunk so that she took on the shape of the tree as camouflage.

Jake appeared silently. He looked up and raised his hand without a word.

Relieved, Shah sighed and returned his gesture. She watched as he jumped to grip the lowest-hanging limb, then moved easily up into the tree. Jake's face had a dangerous look to it with his two-day growth of beard. His gray eyes looked darker, and more lethal, and the harsh planes of his face were emphasized. Shah smiled happily when he sat down on the limb opposite her, the tree trunk between them.

"Anything?" she asked in a whisper as she handed him a mango to eat.

"No, it's quiet." Jake sank his teeth into the juicy flesh of the mango. They'd lost their food pack when the canoe overturned. If not for Shah's knowledge of the rain forest, they'd have starved today. Jake was trained to live off the land, but the rain forest had many deadly forms of plants and berries, not to mention the multitude of poisonous mushrooms that grew in the dampness of the jungle floor. Shah had learned her lessons well from the Tucanos shaman she had worked with finding the medicinal plants. Throughout the day, she'd gathered berries or nuts that had fallen from last year and lay partly hidden by the damp leaves.

They ate in silence, watching as the sunset turned a bloodred, then slowly dissolved into the swiftly approaching cloak of darkness. Shah shared the last of the berries with Jake. The night sounds of insects rose around them, and she felt a good kind of tiredness. She was still on a high from getting the video of Hernandez's illegal operation.

"A penny for your thoughts," Jake said. He wiped his long, strong fingers across his thighs. Shah was positively glowing with happiness, and he felt fortunate to see this side of her. He'd never realized how beautiful she really was until she'd smiled; now he'd never forget it. More than anything, he wanted to be the one to make her smile like that again.

"Oh..." Shah sighed softly, resting her head against the trunk. "I'm just so happy, Jake. I think I'm floating on air."

He grinned. "I like seeing you happy."

She lifted her chin and held his searching gaze. "You've been wonderful today, too. I couldn't have done it without you."

"Can I get that in writing?" He chuckled indulgently. He liked Shah's thoughtfulness and ability to share. She made him feel a part of her team effort. Yes, she was a good leader.

Shah reached out and slapped his hand lightly. "Jake, you're such a tease!"

He relaxed a little, wanting badly to devote all his attention to Shah. Jake estimated it would take roughly a day and a half, maybe two days, of walking to reach the mission. He desperately wanted this time alone with Shah. There was a natural, powerful intimacy that sprang up between them, and he wanted more of these moments with her. He caught Shah's hand in midair and held it for just a moment. The surprise in her eyes wasn't fueled by fear, he realized, but by desire. Hope beat strongly in his chest. Was it a desire for him?

Shah's hand tingled where Jake had touched it. "Jake?"

"Hmm?"

"Are you tired?"

"Yeah. You?"

"No, not really. I guess I'm too excited."

Jake felt exhaustion pulling at him. Tonight he'd have to sleep in spurts if he was going to maintain security around them. "Do you always get like this?"

"What?"

"Excited when you get what you want?"

Her smile was large. "Yes." The seconds fled by, the silence lengthening. Shah sobered a bit. "Jake, may I ask you a personal question?"

Jake suddenly grew very alert, the exhaustion torn from him. He'd hoped beyond hope that Shah would reach out and establish a more personal relationship with him. Maybe this was his opportunity. "Sure," he mumbled, trying not to sound too eager.

Shah sat nervously for a long moment and stared down at her clasped hands in her lap. Torn, she finally offered, "I have a terrible case of curiosity. It always gets me in trouble. If you think I'm getting too personal—"

"I'm an open book to you," Jake said, and he meant it.

Shah glanced over at his shadowy features. "I don't see how you can be so vulnerable. It scares me to open up."

"That's because you've been hurt every time you did it," Jake offered gently.

"I guess . . ." Shah said. Then she made an exasperated sound. "You're so trusting and open, Jake. I've never met a man like you. Sometimes I feel you're from another planet."

Chuckling, Jake said, "Believe me, I'm no alien. I'm very male. You just haven't run into my bad side yet."

"I think you're bluffing, Jake. Somewhere along the line, you learned that manipulation and control of a woman wasn't right. I guess that's what I wanted to know. You said you aren't married now. Are you divorced?"

Of all the questions Shah could have asked, this was the most unexpected. He felt his gut tighten, as if someone had sucker-punched him. For a moment, it was hard for him to breathe, much less talk.

Shah watched Jake wrestle with a multitude of emotions plainly etched on his grim features. She saw the torture appear in his eyes, and, too late, she realized that she had stepped into a very painful topic for him. "Jake, I—"

"No," he said, his voice raw, "I'll tell you, Shah." He swallowed back a lump that threatened to shut off his breathing. "I want to tell you."

The words were charged with emotion, and Shah felt uneasy. Unconsciously she reached over and touched the hand that he'd clenched into a fist against his powerful thigh. "I'm sorry...."

Jake turned his hand and gripped her long, slender fingers. How small Shah's hand was in comparison to his. He expected her to pull out of his grasp, but, to his surprise, she didn't. He was heartened by that. Jake needed Shah's compassion and understanding in that moment in order to answer her question honestly. He knew what it had cost Shah to make this overture to him, and he owed it to her to be just as brave.

"Four years ago," he croaked, "I was married. But I have to go back to the beginning, I guess. I went into the Marine Corps when I was eighteen. I was a real hell-raiser then, footloose and fancy-free. I never wanted to be married or tied down." Jake studied Shah's hand, barely able to see it in the darkness. Soon the moon would rise and he'd be able to see her better. Still, the darkness gave him the courage to go on. He didn't want Shah to see his face as he related his past.

"Five years later I met Bess at a USO club in Los Angeles. At the time, I was stationed at Camp Pendleton, and a couple of the guys and I decided to go up there for a change of pace." Jake shut his eyes. "I walked into that place and felt like lightning had struck me. Bess was a 'donut dolly,' one of the girls who serve food to the servicemen and women. She was twenty-three also, fresh out of college, and beautiful—with light brown hair, brown eyes, and a pretty smile that made me feel ten feet tall."

Shah felt Jake's pain. Something had happened to Jake and his wife. Automatically she clasped his hand a little more tightly.

Jake began to move his fingers back and forth across the top of Shah's hand, lost in the bittersweet memories, caught up in the old pain and grief. "Bess had a degree in economics, and she was sharp as hell. I courted her for a year before she'd marry me. At the time, I was getting my college degree, even though I was still an enlisted marine." Jake shook his head as the memories swiftly welled up. "Bess was a lot like you," he went on in a hushed tone. "She had the love of the land, of nature, and she wanted children more than anything. Nine months to the day after we got married, Bess had Katie..."

Wrestling with a gamut of new emotions, Jake hung his head and clung to Shah's hand. "Katie," he choked out, "looked a lot like that Tucanos girl you held in your arms a few days ago. She had my dark hair and her mother's pretty brown eyes and smile." Taking a deep breath, Jake plunged on. "Two years later, we had Mandy, and she had her mother's light brown hair and my gray eyes. Things were going well for us, and we were happy. I eventually got my degree, went to Marine Officer's Candidate School and came out a lieutenant.

"To make a long story real short, after almost eleven years of marriage, Bess and the girls were in the wrong place at the wrong time." Anger, white-hot and suffocating, flowed through Jake. "I was stationed near Miami, part of a multiservice drug enforcement team that worked closely with the Coast Guard. We'd made a couple of big busts, and the boys down in Colombia were plenty angry. Somehow," Jake said bleakly, "information was leaked on all of us, our names, our addresses, where we lived...."

"Oh, no," Shah cried softly.

Jake bowed his head, holding Shah's hand as if to release it would be to lose control of himself and his violent, grief-stricken emotions. "A drug lord down in Peru had his men come up to the States to even the score. He had the bastards plant a bomb under my car," he rasped. "I was sick at home that day with the flu, and Bess had to take both girls for ballet lessons, so she took my car, because it was parked outside the garage." Tears dampened Jake's eyes, and he shut them. When he spoke again, his voice was trembling. "I was asleep up in the bedroom.... The next thing I knew, the whole damn side of the house was blown off in the explosion. I— It was a nightmare...."

With a little cry, Shah withdrew her hand and stood up. She couldn't endure the anguish in Jake's voice, and she knew he needed to be held. Carefully she moved around the tree until she could sit down beside him, her back supported by another branch so that she couldn't fall.

"Come here," she choked out, and gently drew her arms around Jake's broad shoulders. Her eyes blinded by tears, she felt Jake's arms slide around her waist, and she felt the air rush out of her lungs as he held her tightly against him. As he buried his head next to hers, Shah whispered brokenly, "I'm so sorry, Jake. So sorry..." The rest of the words died in her throat as it closed up with tears, and she sobbed.

Shah's unexpected compassion broke Jake's hold on his grief. He'd cried off and on throughout the years since losing his family, but there had remained a stubborn part of his grief that he'd never been able to reach. Shah's simple act, placing her slender arms around him, holding him with her woman's strength, shattered that last bastion of grief. Her hair was like a silken curtain that he could bury his face in. Somewhere in his cartwheeling mind, he realized how much courage it had taken Shah to come to him, to hold him.

The first sob, like a fist shoving violently upward through the center of him, slammed into his throat and lodged there. He tried to fight it, but Shah's trembling, soothing hand across his hair broke through his control. Jake had always cried alone. Cried when no one was around. The Marine Corps didn't see tears as strong or good—only as a sign of weakness.

"Cry," Shah whispered near his ear. "Cry for all you've lost, Jake. I'll hold you.... I'll just hold you...." And she did, with all her strength and all her love. Shah felt another sob rack Jake's body, and she held him even more tightly. This bear of a man she'd been so afraid of, so distrusting of, before, was hauntingly human now as she held him in her arms. As she sat rocking him ever so slightly, much as a mother would a hurt child, she cried with him. She cried for his terrible loss, unable to imagine how much it must continue to hurt him. The closest comparison Shah could imagine was her mother being torn brutally and suddenly out of her life. She thought how terrible that loss would be, and she was able to transfer that understanding to Jake. But only he knew the full emotional impact of losing his family.

The moments melted into one another. The darkness was so complete that Shah couldn't see anything. It didn't matter, anyway, because the tears flowing from her eyes were blinding her. She continued to stroke Jake's head, shoulders and back. If only she could take away some of his grief. And then she laughed softly to herself as Jake expended his heartache within her arms. Amazingly, all her fear of him as a man had dissolved. As she sat there in the aftermath, a half hour after the storm had broken within Jake, Shah watched the moon rise in the east. She saw the soft, luminescent light silently spreading across the dark, silhouetted rain forest, as the symbolic light of a new day.

Intuitively Shah understood that she had been a catalyst in Jake's healing process. The moon was a woman's symbol, a feminine one, and the light from the silvery sphere was always gentle and nonintrusive. She prayed to the Great Spirit that her questions hadn't been damaging to Jake, but had served instead as a catharsis for further healing.

Leaning down, she pressed a kiss against his heavily bearded cheek. Jake's scent entered her nostrils, and she inhaled it deep into her lungs. The bristles of his beard were wet from his tears. Or were they her tears, too? Shah was lost in the textures, scents and awareness of Jake as a vulnerable human being. As she pressed a second kiss to his cheek to console him, she felt his hands frame her face.

A soft breath escaped Shah as Jake opened his eyes and looked deep into her soul. Her breathing suspended, she felt her world tilt out of control. Vividly she recalled that her ex-husband had always called her cold, unable to respond. Hesitating fractionally, she wondered if she had anything to offer Jake. Another part of her urged her to try, despite that knowledge. Her lips parting, she leaned forward to meet and touch Jake's mouth. Never in all her life had anything felt so right.

Shah's entire existence centered on Jake's questing mouth, touching her lips, sliding gently against them. The bristles of his beard were a counterpoint to the strength of his mouth as it molded and captured hers. With a moan, she melted against him, drowning in the splendor of his mouth as it moved with a reverence that made tears squeeze beneath her lashes. His hands, large, scarred and rough, held her gently as he touched, cajoled and silently asked Shah to participate in the beautiful dance of life their kiss was creating. It was life, she realized hazily, all her senses moving in a rainbow of vibrant feelings as she hesitantly returned his kiss.

The steamy Amazon jungle caressed them like a lover, and Shah's breathing increased as she felt his tongue move across her lower lip. There was such a ribbon of pleasure beneath each touch. Jake proceeded to explore her slowly, deliberately—as if each contact were an exquisite gift. And to Shah it was. Her mind was no longer functioning. She was aware only of Jake, of his tenderness and his coaxing. With each small kiss, each nip, each touch with his tongue, she yielded, like a flower opening for the first time. Reality mingled with euphoria, with the fragrance of the orchids that surrounded them, with the singing sounds of the night that embraced them, and with Jake's ragged breath flowing moistly across her face.

How long Shah clung to his mouth, allowing him to explore her fully, to kiss her reverently, she had no idea. She felt bereft when Jake drew inches away, his breathing uneven, his hands still framing her uplifted face. Slowly opening her eyes, Shah lost herself in the silver glitter of his narrowed ones. Her body felt on fire, a bubbling volcano ready to explode, and it left her trembling and anticipating. Anticipating what? She had no idea. All she knew was that Jake had made her feel more alive, more of a woman, with that single kiss, than in all her experience with her ex-husband combined.

Gently Jake leaned down and brushed Shah's parted lips one more time. He knew he'd reached the limit of his control. If he continued to kiss her, continued to teach her that love, real love, was not painful, but something so beautiful it could make a man cry, he'd take her to the jungle floor and make love to her there. Shah's eyes were lustrous with desire, and the moonlight was radiant and lovely on her upturned features. With her hair loose, she looked like a magical part of this rain forest—a goddess, perhaps, flowing like the silent mists through the jungle.

Jake felt as if someone had taken a bottle brush to his insides, leaving him miraculously lighter. The load he'd unconsciously carried for so long was gone. Blinking away the last of his tears, he smiled down at Shah, who clung to him as if she might fall out of the tree. There was such beauty in her dazed-looking eyes, and Jake knew that the kiss they'd shared had been wonderful—for both of them. Caressing her high cheekbones with his thumbs, he erased the last of her tears there. More tears were beaded on her thick lashes, and Jake felt such a fierce love for Shah that it left him stunned in its wake.

As he sat with Shah resting against him, her hands pressed against his chest as she looked up at him, Jake assimilated the discovery. He loved Shah. And then he realized that from the moment he'd met her he'd been falling in love with her. There wasn't anything not to love about her, Jake decided as he continued to dry her cheeks with his thumbs. Weren't they both terribly scarred by past battles with life? Was it possible not only to feel like living again, but to want to love again? Shocked by the prospect—a silly dream he'd never envisioned coming true—Jake could do nothing but lose himself in Shah's golden eyes, eyes that spoke of her love for him. Was she aware of it? Jake, humbled by the realization that they could have shared so much in such a short space of time, had no answers.

There were no words he could say, so Jake took the ultimate risk and folded his arms around Shah. They would sleep here, together, with him leaning against the trunk of the tree, holding her safe in his arms. Shah could lean against him. To his surprise, she eased into his arms, her body meeting his, molding against it. He shut his eyes, and a low sound, like a groan, escaped his lips. As her arm went around his waist and she nestled her head in the crook of his shoulder, Jake knew he was the luckiest man alive.

Too shaken by the grief he'd expressed, Jake's mind refused to work coherently. Exhaustion and lack of sleep overtook him, and in minutes he slept. A nagging thought flitted through his spongy senses as he surrendered to sleep. How would Shah react to him tomorrow morning? Would she run away from him because he was a man? He loved her with a fierceness that defied description. As he rested there, with Shah secure in his

arms, he knew that he was being given a second chance—
and nothing short of dying was going to keep him from
taking the risk of loving Shah without reservation. But
did she love him? Could she ever fall in love again?

Chapter Nine

Shah awoke first, wrapped in a warm, secure feeling she'd never felt anywhere except in Jake's arms. It was barely dawn, not light enough yet to travel, so she relaxed and absorbed the moment at his side.

The mists moved slowly and sensuously through the rain forest's branches, seeming to symbolize Shah's own life: the twists and turns she'd taken, some of them by her own choice, most of them not, and where they had led her at this moment. The kiss Jake had branded her lips with lingered hotly in her body, like a fever that refused to subside. It was a new and unfamiliar sensation, one that Shah basked in. There was a gnawing ache within her, and she didn't know where it was coming from, or why it was there. The entire lower region of her body felt like a simmering cauldron ready to overflow. Because Shah was Native American, she had grown up seeing life in terms of symbols, and understanding that everything was connected to everything else. This new and wonderful yet disturbing feeling in her triggered her curiosity. Would Jake know what it was? What she was feeling? She had long since recognized his perceptiveness about human beings in general. If anyone would know, Jake would, she decided.

The sky, a veil of thick and thin curtains of mist, took on an ethereal glow as the night eased its grip on the rain forest. The horizon, covered with magnificent pau trees stretching for the sky with their arms, became a panorama of golden hues and darker tones. Shah lay there, her head pressed to Jake's chest, the slow beating of his heart soothing the chaotic feelings that were moving through her like a wild, unmanageable river that had escaped its banks.

She felt Jake jerk awake. Lifting her head, she sat up and brushed the hair away from her face. Never had she felt more vulnerable than in the moments before she forced herself to meet and hold Jake's gaze.

Jake reached over, laid his hand on her arm. He saw the terrible uncertainty in Shah's face. "Don't go," he rasped, and his fingers closed gently around her arm.

"I—" Shah gulped unsteadily as she anxiously searched Jake's sleep-clouded eyes. His raw voice had sent a shiver of need through Shah that tore at her fear of rejection. "No... I'm not going anywhere...." she whispered.

Fighting to regain wakefulness, Jake hungrily absorbed Shah's innocent gestures. Her lips were still slightly swollen, proof of his need of her. All his focus, his world, narrowed on her as he eased into a sitting position. The bluish sheets of her hair moved in a rippling wave, and he captured some of the thick strands and tucked them behind her shoulder so that he could have a good look at her profile. Shah's nervousness touched him deeply.

"It's all right," he assured her, sliding his hand along her arm and capturing her fingers.

Shah shrugged and looked down at his large hand. The hand that had been so incredibly gentle with her the night before. The hand that had wiped the tears from her face. "I feel mixed up inside, Jake," she admitted hoarsely. "I'm sorry I asked you about Bess...about your family." She risked a glance up at him. "I don't understand how you survived with that happening to you. I—I'd go crazy. I'd kill the bastards. I'd do something...."

He sighed and nodded. "What I didn't tell you was that I left the Marine Corps shortly after it happened. I wanted to kill the men responsible for my family's murders. The only place I could go was Perseus, the company I work for now. Morgan Trayhern, who runs it, let me take assignments having to do with drug dealers here in South America. I'd been in Peru and Columbia on a number of missions, putting the bastards out of commission, usually in jail. I had one assignment that put me on the Orinoco River, close to the Brazilian border. For the past four years I've been waging a one-man war against the drug dealers. It's helped me settle past debts."

Shah gauged him in silence. "A one-man war." She laughed, a little self-consciously, glad that Jake was holding her hand. "I've always seen myself as waging a one-woman war down here with a different kind of criminal—an ecological one."

"I know," Jake whispered, and managed a lopsided smile. "We have a lot more in common than you first thought."

"Yes..." Shah bit down on her lower lip. "What I don't understand is why you took my father's assignment. This has nothing to do with drug dealers, Jake."

He held her shimmering golden gaze, touched as never before, because Shah was completely open to him, without any of her old defenses in place. Had their kiss been the reason? Jake didn't know, and he desperately wanted to find out. Caution made him move slowly, however, because he sensed that so much of what Shah had experienced last night was new to her. How could it be? She was thirty years old—a grown woman with experience. *Patience,* he ordered himself. *Be patient with her.*

"I just happened to have come off an assignment for Perseus and was in the office when your father and Morgan were talking. Morgan called me in because I was the only available agent who spoke Portuguese and had South American experience." Jake watched Shah's expressive features, his gaze centered hotly on her parted lips. The kiss they'd shared had been unlike any other. "I didn't like your father or his attitude, and neither did Morgan. At first, because of your father, I wasn't going to take the assignment. Besides, I needed a rest, and I didn't want to get sent out this soon after my last mission."

Shah frowned. "What changed your mind?"

He smiled gently. "I saw the photo your father had of you. Morgan isn't stupid. He knew I wasn't going to take the mission, because of your father's abrasive attitude. Neither of us could figure out why he was angry with you. We could understand why he'd be concerned and worried, but not angry. Pieces of the puzzle didn't fit. Of course, when I got down here and found out your father had botched two other attempts to have you kidnapped, then I figured it out."

"Chances are," Shah whispered bitterly, "that my father has stock in some Brazilian lumber company or something. It would be just like him. He always wants to make a quick buck at the expense of Mother Earth and all her relatives. He doesn't care."

"I know," Jake said soothingly, sliding his fingers across the back of her hand. Shah's pain was no less real than his. "I still have questions I want to ask him when I get back. When I get to Manaus, I'm going to call Morgan and get him to check on your father's business interests. Then we'll see what cards he's holding. I feel that will explain the rest of the missing pieces to us."

Shah cringed inwardly. Jake was leaving for Manaus? When? She was afraid to ask. She was afraid of her own feelings for him. "So my photo convinced you to take this mission?"

Jake nodded. "Yeah. Morgan's like a brother to me, and he knows me pretty well. All he had to do was slide that photo of you into my hands, and he knew I'd take the mission, no questions asked."

She smiled hesitantly. "Morgan sounds like a decent human being."

"Even if he is a man?" Jake teased gently.

"I guess I had that coming, didn't I?"

"Don't ever apologize for how you feel, Shah," Jake told her in a low, vibrating tone. "What happened to you has shaped your life and your actions."

"I'm trying to get rid of my anger toward men," Shah admitted, looking away from Jake's burning gray gaze. "I really am. I know it doesn't seem like it most of the time...."

"Listen to me." Jake took Shah by the arms and made her look at him. "No one knows better than me what pain can do to a person. It's taken me four years to crawl out from beneath all that grief over losing my family. I tried, the other night, to put myself in your shoes, to try and feel what it might be like to be a kid growing up in that kind of brutal, violent environment.''

"I walked on eggshells," Shah admitted. "Mother did, too. We tried to find out what kind of mood Father was in as soon as possible so we could plan how we were going to behave for the rest of the day."

Jake shook his head. "Sweetheart, you're a survivor of a war. I don't know if you realize that or not, but you are. You were in a dangerous war zone for twelve of your most formative years." He gave her a small smile of encouragement. "From my vantage point, I'd say you've made something worthwhile out of your life, despite the lousy start you had. There are lots of kids who come out of that same kind of environment and end up on drugs or in prison. Look at you. Look at how you're helping the world. I'm proud of you."

Shah turned her head away to wipe her eyes free of the tears that had gathered unexpectedly.

"No, you don't," Jake rasped, and he captured her chin, forcing her to meet his gaze. "Don't ever be ashamed to cry in front of me, Shah. How can you feel that way after I cried in your arms last night?"

He was right, Shah acknowledged. "Jake... You—all of this—it's so new to me. I'm so confused."

"What do you mean?" He gently wiped the tears from her cheeks. There was such hope burning in Shah's eyes; this was a look he'd never seen in them before. Perhaps sharing that load he'd carried alone for so many years had been the most right thing he'd ever done.

"It's you!" When Shah realized she'd raised her voice above a whisper, she clapped her hand over her lips and sent Jake a silent apology. She looked around, and when she was finally convinced there were no humans nearby to hear her, she said, in a strained undertone, "It's you, Jake. You're different. You aren't like the men I've known."

"All you've known are the violent bastards, the ones who would strip your soul from you because you're a woman." He grimly held her wavering stare. "I know all about that type, Shah. They're weak little men with low self-esteem, and the only way they feel powerful is to keep a woman or a child under their thumb. That makes them feel powerful when nothing else does. Men know they've got more physical strength than a woman, and so they'll use it to keep you captive, to keep you docile."

"But by hurting a woman they are hurting them-selves!" Shah whispered, her voice choked with emotion. "The Lakota believe that within each of us is the spirit of both man and woman." She touched her breast. "If a man despises and fears women, he despises his own gentleness, his ability to cry, to reach out and nurture someone other than himself."

"That's right," Jake agreed. "Our society has sup-pressed women's feelings and strengths."

"But why?" she asked, her voice cracking. "Women know how to cry, how to be creative, how to be in touch with Mother Earth."

He saw the terrible sense of loss in Shah's eyes, and he understood her pain. "Listen." he said. "I don't have all the answers, Shah. Each woman is going to have to find the courage within herself to stand up and say that she will no longer be controlled. Each man has to have the courage to allow women to be their true selves."

She shook her head in awe. "Jake, before meeting you, I never realized any man could understand what we women see so clearly." Then she corrected herself. "Well, some women see it. Others are just starting to awaken to the imbalance and unfairness of it all."

"Yes, and still others are asleep," Jake agreed.

"Or," Shah said softly, "too frightened to make the change, even though they're aware of the unfairness."

"As I've always said," Jake told her grimly, "it doesn't take much just to exist a day at a time, but it sure as hell takes the rawest, purest kind of courage to *live* your life. Living life means changing and growing. And change is frightening to most people."

"I just wish women would realize that the unknown future will be a better one than they're in right now," Shah said. "My mother was like that, you know. At first she was so afraid of my father that she cowered like a dog. Over the years, she never grew less afraid of him, but she began to put my safety and welfare ahead of her own."

"Yes, your mother thought she couldn't help herself, but she felt you were worth saving."

"It's called being a victim," Shah rattled. "I know—I used to be one myself, in my marriage with Robert."

Jake stroked her hair in an effort to take away her obvious shame over her lack of fearlessness. "But you chose to grow instead of becoming trapped like your mother. That took real courage, Shah. The rarest kind."

"My marriage was a travesty," she admitted painfully. "I let Robert beat me down, and I started to believe I was as worthless as he said I was. Talk about brainwashing." She smiled bitterly, not feeling very proud of herself. "I swallowed everything he said to me. It never occurred to me he might be wrong."

Jake wanted to tread carefully, but he had to know the truth regarding Shah's marriage. "Did you love Robert?"

"Yes and no. At first I did, but, Jake, it was a stupid infatuation, that's all. I woke up one morning six months later realizing Robert and I had very little in common." And then she muttered, "I wasn't any good in bed, either."

Jake's eyes narrowed. "Who told you that?"

Shah refused to look at him, too humiliated by the admission. Once Jake had cried in her arms, she'd become helpless to erect defenses against his questions, and now she was blathering like the village idiot. But she couldn't help herself—the words just came tumbling out in a hurtful torrent.

"I was a virgin when I married Robert. I guess he'd been around a lot, and he—" Shah swallowed, because the words were sticking in her throat "—he said I was lousy in bed. I didn't know what I was doing, and he said I was too stupid to learn. He said I was cold...."

Jake stared at her in disbelief. He remembered hotly how her mouth had opened to his. He'd tasted her sweetness and felt her passionate response to his kiss. "What?" The word escaped before he could take it back.

"Frigid," Shah said in a strangled voice. She cast a glance over at Jake and saw the thundercloud blackness in his eyes. Was it aimed at her? Had her kiss been that bad? Had Robert been right?

"Answer me something," Jake demanded heavily. He forced Shah to hold his gaze. "After you divorced Robert, did you have any lovers?"

Blinking, Shah said, "No."

Jake's hands tightened around Shah's upper arms. "The bastard. The lowlife bastard." He snapped his mouth shut. He saw the confusion in Shah's eyes and realized she wasn't sure if he was angry at her or at her ex-husband. Getting hold of his escaping emotions, he whispered tautly, "Robert is wrong, Shah. Do you hear me? He's wrong."

"I— Well, how would you know?"

He smiled grimly. "Sweetheart, anyone who kisses like you do, who makes me feel like I'm melting in a hot fire, isn't frigid—believe me."

"Oh . . ." Shah sat looking up at Jake in the moments that followed. The heat of a blush stung her cheeks, and she gave a little laugh of embarrassment, placing her hands against her face. "Look at me! I'm blushing like a girl!"

Jake allowed his hands to drop away. "Every woman should have a bit of girl in her," he whispered. "It makes you beautiful, Shah." He savored the mixture of embarrassment and sudden hope he saw burning in Shah's eyes. If he never did anything else for her in this lifetime, he'd at least given her back a piece of her soul, her womanhood, by helping her realize how wrong her ex-husband had been. He ached to teach her about love between a man and a woman. He ached to feel her open and blossom beneath his hands and body, like a lovely, fragrant orchid opening to the misty Amazonian sunlight for the first time. But those were all dreams, Jake realized sadly. And dreams, as he well knew, could shatter unexpectedly and be destroyed before one's very eyes. It had happened once. It could happen again.

It took long minutes for Shah to gather her strewn composure. The dawn brightened, light gliding silently across the rain forest. Birds began to sing, the sound echoing the song in Shah's heart. Jake's arm remained around her shoulders as she sat, her hands pressed to her cheeks.

"Talk to me," Jake urged her finally as he saw her drop her hands to her lap and clasp them nervously. "What are you feeling?"

She gave a startled little laugh. "Feeling? Everything! I feel like I'm in chaos, Jake."

"Happy? Sad?" He held his breath, cherishing the intimacy strung gently between them.

"Both," she admitted, and she glanced over at him, a sad smile pulling at the corners of her mouth. "I feel sorrow for myself, because once again I fell for Robert's lies." She frowned and stared down at her hands. "There were a couple of times—not many—when other men walked into my life. They weren't bad men, and I got interested in them. But the moment they tried to take me to bed, I froze." Shah frowned and admitted, "That was when I was younger, and I ran."

Gently he rubbed her shoulders. "That's over now. You're more mature and settled."

With a nod, Shah said, "Yes."

"What are you happy about?"

She hesitated. "*Scared* would be a better word."

"About?"

Uncomfortable, Shah finally said, "Us."

His hand remained still on her shoulder, the thick silk of her hair beneath his fingers. He yearned to take her into his arms and kiss her until she melted like sweet nectar in his hands, his body. "What about 'us'?"

"Well," Shah mumbled, "it's probably just me, not you. I have no right to assume anything. Especially when we haven't known each other that long, and—"

Jake grimaced. "Shah, you can tell me anything. I'm not like Robert. I'm not going to judge how you feel."

Closing her eyes, Shah remained silent. The words got stuck in her throat and congealed there. She was struggling to say them, and she could feel Jake's tension, too. Finally she rubbed her temples in a nervous gesture. "I—I didn't want to like you, Jake. At first, I thought you were like all the men I've known."

He studied her intently, praying for her to tell him that she liked him even half as much as he loved her. Jake couldn't stand the tension, but he realized Shah was genuinely struggling to overcome her fear. Robert had taken advantage of Shah's innocence. He'd placed her in a cage and nearly broken her magnificent spirit.

Gently Jake smoothed the damp fabric across her back. "Look," he told her huskily, "don't force anything, Shah. Let's you and I take it one day at a time."

Touching her throat, Shah gave him a pleading look. "I—I just can't say the words, Jake. I'm afraid. Afraid . . ."

So was he. Just as much as she was, and maybe more. "It takes guts to admit even as much as you already have," he murmured. Glancing up, he said, "It's light enough to travel. What do you say we finish off those last two mangos for breakfast and hightail it back to the mission? When you feel like talking, you can. In the meantime, we've got work to do, darlin'."

Grateful for Jake's understanding, Shah fought the desire to throw her arms around his neck and embrace him. Would that one heated kiss he'd shared with her ever be repeated? She couldn't tear her gaze from his strong, mobile mouth, which was drawn into a wry smile. If Jake realized she was gawking at him, he didn't say anything. Instead, he eased off the limb and dropped to the jungle floor below.

He held his hands open to her. "Come on."

* * *

The day fled swiftly, as far as Shah was concerned. They had made good progress toward the mission. With each hour, Jake relaxed, feeling that Hernandez and his henchmen were far behind them. However, he cautioned Shah to speak in low tones and not make any undue noise.

Sometimes, to Shah's delight, Jake would drop back and capture her hand, and they'd walk beside each other. It was as if he had read her mind, understanding her doubts about the kiss they'd shared last night—as if he were silently trying to convince her that his feelings toward her weren't short-term. Jake's hand was warm and reassuring, and Shah savored those moments when he'd look down at her with such warmth that she felt as if she were walking on air.

Water was a problem in the forest—drinking from the Amazon would have given them parasites and germs—so Shah showed Jake the liana vines, about one inch in diameter. Whenever they needed water, they would carefully cut a vine open and drink from the water stored within it. He praised her knowledge of survival, and she felt like a true team member, not just some bothersome burden to Jake.

Jake's own jungle training came in handy when he spotted a certain type of palm that, when stripped of leaves, yielded a sweet inner core that supplied them with lunch. Heart of palm was a delicacy in Brazil, often pickled and sold for a high price in the cities. They sat hidden in the rain forest, eating the sweet, juicy heart of palm and exchanging smiles over the pleasure of sharing such a stolen moment together. As the day began fading and dusk set in, they looked for another tree to act as bed and security against the denizens of the Amazon night.

Jake spotted a rubber tree about a hundred feet inland from the bank of the Amazon. Taking off his pistol and laying it on a stump next to Shah, who was shelling some nuts she'd found, he went in search of the makings of a better bed for them tonight. Moving around the immediate area, Jake found a number of broken limbs that had probably been torn off in the sudden thunderstorms that constantly occurred in the Amazon Basin.

Satisfied with the platform he'd made out of the branches, Jake cut a number of palm leaves to create a mattress. If they had to spend another night in a tree, it might as well be in relative comfort, he rationalized. Satisfied with his handiwork, he leaped off the finished platform and dusted off his hands.

Shah was sitting by the tree stump, having just finished dividing their larder, when she heard a sharp squeal. Her eyes widened enormously.

"Jake!" she screamed, and leaped to her feet, pointing behind where he stood.

Startled, Jake whirled and crouched. He'd heard the almost human squeal, too, and he was expecting an attack from a man. Instead, the green vegetation thirty feet away shook and trembled, and a brown, furry boar with long, curved white tusks exploded out of the jungle, charging him. Jake started to move, but the fifty-pound boar, with small red eyes and a long snout, shifted course, aiming directly for him.

Time slowed down to a painful, crawling clarity. Jake knew his only safety was the tree, which was a mere ten feet away. He saw the boar's mouth open, froth spilling from the corners of it, his lethal, razor-sharp tusks glinting with saliva. What about Shah? She was even more vulnerable to attack by the angered beast. The moment's hesitation cost Jake. He could have turned and made it to the safety of the tree in three strides. But he'd have left Shah defenseless. Grimly he stood his ground.

The boar smashed into him, knocking him down. With a shrieking squeal, the animal whirled around and charged into him again, then again. Each angry movement of his tusks slashed long, deep cuts through Jake's torn pant legs. Floundering, he tried to keep the boar at bay by using his feet to kick out at the animal. Jake yelled for Shah, but the squeals of the furious boar drowned out his cry.

Shah jerked the Beretta out of its holster. She watched in horror as the boar ruthlessly attacked Jake. She saw blood staining his legs, and she rushed forward. The boar whuffed and grunted as he butted Jake's feet, pushing them aside to again attack his extremities. Shah aimed the pistol, praying she wouldn't hit Jake. The Beretta jerked once, twice, three times. The roar of the pistol shattered her eardrums. And then there was silence.

Sobbing, Shah allowed the pistol to drop from her hands. "Jake!" she cried. "Jake!"

Chapter Ten

A cry tore from Shah as she raced to Jake. The boar lay dead near his boots. Falling to her knees, her mouth contorted in a silent cry, she touched his shoulder. At first she thought he must be dead, but then she saw Jake's eyes flutter open.

Pain was beginning to replace the initial numbness Jake had felt during the savage boar's attack. He forced himself to focus on speaking. "I'm okay," he choked out, and made an effort to rise. Shah helped him sit up. He watched as she moved toward his legs. The boar had cut his pants to ribbons and Jake realized with a sinking feeling that the fabric was stained with blood. His blood.

"Jake, you're hemorrhaging!" Shah barely touched the surface of his trousers with her shaking fingertips. The boar had opened some thirty wounds in Jake's legs. If Jake hadn't had the coolness to use his heavily protected feet to keep the boar from getting to other, less protected parts of his body, he might be dead.

"Take my knife," he ordered Shah sternly, "and cut my trousers off at the knee." Leaning to one side, Jake unsnapped the knife from his belt and handed it, butt first, to Shah. Her face was pale, and her eyes were dark with shock. Jake knew he was in shock himself, because he was acting too calmly. They had to act fast, before the initial shock wore off. "Cut off my trousers," he repeated to Shah, and she took the knife with shaking hands.

"The wounds...they're terrible, terrible..." Shah whispered as she surveyed the damage to Jake's legs.

"I'm alive," Jake said, supporting himself with his arms behind him. He tried to prepare himself for how badly damaged his legs were as Shah cut away the fabric to expose the extent of his wounds. His mouth turned downward as he realized that it looked as if someone had taken a razor blade and slashed indiscriminately at his flesh from his ankles to his knees. He saw Shah trying not to cry, trying to be brave.

"You're doing fine," Jake told her in an unsteady voice. He was starting to feel light-headed, the first effects of the adrenaline charge in his bloodstream beginning to wear off. "Shah," he called as he lay down, "put something, anything, under my feet. Get the blood back to my head. I'm feeling faint...."

Those were the last words he spoke. Before Shah could get off her knees, Jake passed out. Alarmed, she made sure his head was tipped back enough to allow air to flow in and out of his lungs. Blood was soaking into the decomposed leaves all around his legs. Shah shoved her own unraveling feelings aside. She had to think swiftly and clearly now. She had to think for both of them, or Jake might bleed to death.

Getting to her feet, she found a small log and placed it beneath his ankles, elevating his legs by six inches so that the blood would begin to flow back toward his upper body and to his head. Then she ran to their knapsacks, wondering what, if any, first-aid kit she'd find in Jake's pack. Because he had been a recon marine and a paramedic, she thought he might have packed medical items; she'd packed only aspirin and Band-Aids in her own pack.

She tore at the buckles and the leather straps, her breath coming out in sobs. Where had that boar come from? Why hadn't she remembered how dangerous the wild boars of the Amazon Basin were? And, worse, why hadn't she warned Jake about them? They were the only animals she'd failed to tell him about.

Tears blurred Shah's eyes as she rummaged quickly through the pack, throwing things out in a desperate search for a first-aid kit. The wild pigs lived in small and large groups, always lorded over by a huge older boar, and they were feared by the Indians for their savagery and their willingness to attack anyone who entered their foraging territory. Oh, why hadn't she told Jake about them?

Her fingers closed over a large metal container. Shah froze for an instant. She was down to the bottom of Jake's pack, and there was nothing else left in it. If this wasn't a first-aid kit, they were in trouble. Gulping, she yanked the rectangular box out of the knapsack. Her eyes widened when she saw that it was white, with a large red cross painted on its smooth surface.

Trying to talk herself out of her panic, Shah set the kit down on the ground and unlatched it. To her relief, she found huge rolls of gauze, ace bandages, scissors, iodine and adhesive tape. Shutting her eyes, she hung her head and sent a prayer of thanks to the Great Spirit.

Getting up on unsteady legs, Shah forced herself to calm down and try to think coherently. It was almost impossible, because in those horrifying moments when the boar had attacked Jake, she had realized something that she knew would change her world. Dropping to her knees, she quickly examined the wounds that criss-crossed Jake's exposed extremities. The curved slashes scored his flesh, but as Shah looked closely at them, relief began to trickle back and give her hope.

She hadn't had much medical training—all she knew was what Pai Jose had taught her over the past three months, when she'd helped him at the mission hospital—but she knew that Jake's loss of blood wasn't life-threatening. He would need a great many stitches—perhaps a hundred or more on each leg—and she couldn't do that. Taking the iodine, she poured it liberally into the wounds on both legs and hoped that Jake remained unconscious during her efforts to bandage them.

Shah's head spun with options. She had no idea how badly the boar had cut into Jake's legs, or if his muscles had been damaged. If they had, he wouldn't be able to walk, and she'd have to leave him here to rush back to the mission for help. But the mission was still maybe half a day away. Unrolling the thick gauze, Shah reassured herself that Jake's wounds, while serious, wouldn't be fatal. What was potentially life-threatening was the fact that she had no antibiotics to stop any infection that would occur as a result of the attack.

She glanced down at Jake's booted feet, then studied the boar's bloodied tusks. Dirt and stains marred their curved length, and she was convinced that bacteria must have been transferred to Jake's many wounds. Urgency thrummed through her as she quickly wrapped his legs in swaths of gauze. The pristine whiteness of the dressing stood out starkly against the dark, damp leaves on the floor of the jungle.

Rubbing her brow with the back of her hand, Shah stood up. She went to the river and quickly washed her hands. As she hurried back to Jake's side, she heard him groan and watched him weakly raise his hand. Kneeling and placing her fingers against his shoulder to orient him, Shah realized with a clarity that frightened her that she loved Jake Randolph. The boar's attack had ripped away all her defenses against her feelings. Now, as she watched him slowly become conscious, Shah felt her heart contract beneath the weight of the discovery. Jake could die before she could get him to the mission. If she left him here and went alone, a jaguar or jacare could find Jake, because of the powerful smell of blood. Infection would set in quickly, due to the humid climate, and could make him feverish and delirious within the next twelve hours. Worst of all, Jake could have blood poisoning, which would mean a race against time before the lethal bacteria reached his heart and caused it to stop beating forever.

Her fingers tightened on Jake's shoulder as his lashes lifted to expose his bewildered gray eyes.

"Jake, you're all right," Shah told him, her voice shaking. "You're safe, and the boar's dead."

Fighting the faintness rimming his blurred vision, Jake homed in on Shah's husky voice. He felt her strong, slender hand on his shoulder. Weakly he captured her hand and held it. Flashes of the boar coming out of the jungle and attacking him forced him to recall why he was lying on the ground feeling light-headed. As the minutes crawled by, the pain drifting up from his legs forced him into full consciousness. The smarting, jabbing pains were like thousands of hot needles being poked into his flesh.

Jake looked up into Shah's anguished face. Her eyes were huge and dark with suffering, and her lips were compressed as if she were about to burst into tears. His mouth stretched, but the smile twisted into a grimace. Squeezing her fingers, he rasped, "I'm alive."

"Y-yes."

He frowned and lifted his head. "How bad?"

"Maybe thirty or so cuts on each leg, Jake. The boar's tusks were like razors."

"How much blood did I lose?" he asked, craning to look at his bandaged legs. The effort was too much for him, and he sank back to the ground.

Shah glanced anxiously down at him. For Jake's sake, she wanted to sound calm. She didn't want to alarm him. "I don't know. Maybe half a pint, a full pint. I'm not a nurse. I don't know."

With a nod, Jake clung to her hand. "If I'd lost a lot, I'd be feeling a hell of a lot more light-headed than I do," he muttered. "I'm in shock right now."

"I know...."

"Just let me lie here for another half hour, Shah, and I'll start coming out of it."

"Are—are you cold?"

He was, but he knew there were no blankets to put over him. "A little, but I'll be okay." He heard the terror in Shah's voice, although it was obvious she was trying to hide her panic. He loved her fiercely for her courage.

"That was one hell of a pig," he joked wearily. "I think I'd rather see my pork all nicely wrapped in a package in a grocery store. What do you think?"

Shah wiped the tears off her face. "This isn't funny, Jake. He must weigh close to sixty pounds," Shah told him. "Old and big. Oh, Jake, I'm sorry I didn't tell you about the wild pigs. If I had—"

Forcing his eyes open, Jake met and held her tearful gaze. "Honey, even if you had, it couldn't have prepared me for his charge. I didn't know he was there, and neither did you."

"But you hesitated!" Shah cried. "Why? You could have jumped up in the tree and been safe! Why didn't you?"

A loose, pained smile crossed Jake's mouth. He squeezed her fingers. "Because he'd have gone after you with me out of the way. There was no place for you to go, Shah. I didn't have my pistol on me, or I could've shot the bastard. I didn't want to jump into the tree and leave you the target."

Shah digested his logic. It was true: she'd had absolutely nowhere to go to escape the boar's charge. The animal could have outrun her easily—and boars were strong swimmers, too, so it wouldn't have helped to jump in the river. Jake had made a conscious decision to be the boar's target to save her from his attack. Kneeling next to him, she held his warm gaze. It was marred by pain.

"You should have saved yourself," she whispered.

"I'm your bodyguard, remember? It's my job to keep you safe," he joked wearily. Then he sighed heavily. "You've been a target all your life, Shah. I was damned if I was going to be like every other man in your life and leave you open for attack. No way."

Shaken, Shah hung her head and forced back the tears that threatened to fall. Her love for him welled up fiercely within her, and she fought the urge to tell him exactly that. Several minutes passed before she was able to control the feelings rampaging through her.

Jake watched Shah's reaction to his reasoning, seeing disbelief then confusion in her eyes. Didn't she realize she was worth saving? There had been such damage done to Shah by her father and her ex-husband. Little men with brittle egos who had used her as a scapegoat for their own shortcomings. He lifted her hand toward his mouth and kissed her fingers.

"We need to plan what we're going to do," he said with an effort. Night was beginning to fall, turning the Amazon a misty gray and making the rain forest a dark silhouette against the sky.

With a jerky nod of her head, Shah agreed. Jake's lips upon her fingers sent a ribbon of warmth through her pounding heart. Despite the pain he must be in, he was trying to soothe her! Shah knew she had to be strong for both of them if she was going to get Jake back to the mission alive. Time was the enemy now.

"We've got to get you up on that tree platform," Shah said, her low voice off-key. She wondered if the pistol shots she'd fired had been heard by Hernandez's men. The rain forest was thick and absorbed sounds quickly, so it was unlikely. Still, there was always a possibility of further threat from the land baron.

Jake agreed. "Take the limb out from under my feet and help me get up," he said.

Shah removed the limb and gently placed his booted feet on the ground. She watched Jake's face carefully, realizing that he had an extraordinary ability to master pain. Perhaps it was because he'd been a recon marine.

"I'll help you sit up," she whispered, placing her arm beneath his neck and pulling him up.

Biting back a groan, Jake sat up. Dizziness assailed him, and he leaned forward, resting his brow on his knees to draw the blood back to his head. He felt Shah's hands on his shoulders, steadying him.

"Put your arm around my shoulders," she told him as she crouched next to him. "You can lean on me as we get you to your feet."

Jake didn't know the extent of his injuries. If that old boar had slashed deeply enough into his legs, his Achilles tendon might be cut, leaving him unable to walk. Bothered, but keeping that knowledge to himself, Jake did as she instructed. He knew she wasn't strong enough to support his full bulk and weight. No, he had to use his own inner fortitude to stand up.

But as Shah straightened, Jake realized that he'd underestimated her strength. Despite her slenderness, she was like a steel cable supporting him as he rose to a standing position. Dizziness might have felled him if not for Shah holding him steady.

"You're stronger than I thought," he rasped, his head resting against her hair.

Shah nearly blurted out, *My love for you has made me strong.* The discovery that she loved Jake was so new, so overwhelming, that she hadn't had time to react to the knowledge. Too many more important things had to be addressed before she could sit quietly and examine her feelings. "How do your legs feel?" she asked.

Jake slowly raised his head and leaned heavily against Shah until he got his bearings. "They smart like hell, but I need to see if I can walk."

Her fear magnified, as she silently agreed with his judgment. She knew he was aware of the ramifications if he couldn't walk. "Take just a small step," she pleaded hoarsely, praying that he wouldn't fall.

His mouth tight against the pain that attacked him in ever-growing waves, Jake gripped her shoulder and moved his right foot. Biting back a groan, he lifted his leg and took that first step.

"Okay?" Shah demanded breathlessly, watching his rugged profile anxiously.

"Yeah...sore but usable," he rasped. "Let me try the left one." He lifted it and then slowly placed his full weight on it. His leg didn't buckle beneath him. Jake released a long-held breath. "No muscle damage. Or, if there is, it isn't going to cripple me."

The words were sweet to Shah's ears. "Thank the Great Spirit," she murmured. Their next challenge was to get Jake up on the platform for the night. With each step, Jake seemed to grow a little bit stronger, a little more stabilized. As they passed the dead boar, Jake stopped and looked down at the animal.

"Three shots?" He looked at Shah.

"Yes. I fired three times." She gulped. "I was so worried I'd hit you instead of the boar."

He squeezed her shoulder. "Who taught you to shoot like that?"

"I used to belong to the pistol team at Stanford," Shah muttered.

Impressed, Jake smiled slightly. "With the way that boar was moving around, there was every chance you could have nailed me instead."

With a shake of her head, Shah said unsteadily, "I know...."

"The tree's next," Jake said, and they began a slow walk toward the platform.

Shah's admiration for Jake soared in the next few minutes. She watched him heft himself onto the platform with his powerful arms. The pain he must be feeling didn't stop him from lifting his legs high into the air and landing with a thunk on the platform of palms and branches he'd built earlier. Unable to assist him, she stood on the ground, watching him maneuver himself around until he lay down.

"You okay?" she called, amazed.

"Yeah," Jake grunted. His legs were hurting like hell, but he wasn't about to let Shah know it. She was shaken enough by the incident. "Just get the knapsacks, the pistol and our food. It's getting dark." Then he said weakly, "You don't need to be jaguar bait." He lay down, dizziness forcing him to close his eyes and lie still. He'd probably lost close to a pint of blood, he thought. But if he could sleep tonight, his body should revitalize enough for the trek back to the mission tomorrow morning. His mind spun with options. The worst, Jake knew, would be if his legs were infected. Iodine would kill a certain amount of bacteria, but not all of it. No, he needed powerful third-generation antibiotics, or he'd more than likely be a dead man within the next day or two.

As he lay in the gathering darkness, contemplating the gloomy limbs and leaves above him, Jake knew he didn't want to die. Not this way, and not now. He loved Shah. For a long time, he'd walked numbly through life, not really caring whether he lived or died. Now, for the first time since his family had been torn from him, Jake desperately wanted to live.

As Shah climbed up to the platform with the knapsacks, he studied her in the growing dusk. There was such determination written on her features. Jake saw the guilt and anguish in her eyes and realized she felt responsible for his wounds. With time, he told himself as he threw his arm against his sweaty brow, he could ease Shah out of the overresponsible attitude she had toward people in her life. There was so much he wanted to share with her, to teach her—and have her teach him—he thought as she left the platform to retrieve their food.

Night fell rapidly after Shah climbed up on the platform with their cache of food. She had cut several liana vines, knowing that Jake would grow thirsty throughout the night, as a fever was sure to set in soon. Placing the vines against the trunk of the tree, she moved over to him.

"How are you feeling?" she asked in a low voice, touching his shoulder.

"Better," Jake said. It was a lie.

"Really?"

He heard relief and surprise in Shah's voice. Jake believed in white lies, lies that hurt no one and sometimes kept the damaging hurt of truth at bay—if only for a little while. "Yeah, I'm dizzy, but that's about all. A good night's sleep will set me up for tomorrow's hike."

A gasp escaped Shah. "Jake, do you really think you can walk back to the mission?"

"Do I have a choice?" he asked wryly.

"You could stay here," she began hesitantly, "and I could run back and get help."

Jake shook his head. "It wouldn't work, sweetheart." He reached out and gripped her hand, which was resting lightly against his chest. Barely able to make out her features now, Jake said, "One thing recons are taught is that no matter how much pain you're in you can walk. My wounds aren't life-threatening, Shah. Another thing they taught us is that you go in as a team, and you come out as a team. A marine never leaves a squadmate behind. No, we'll go back together." That was partly a white lie. He knew his wounds could very well be life-threatening.

"You did a hell of a good job wrapping my legs. It was smart putting the ace bandages over the dressing. They'll hold everything in place until we get back to the mission."

Shah didn't have the courage to mention the possibility of infection. It scared her too much to speak about it. "You have enough courage for ten men," she said, and placed her hand against his broad forehead. His flesh was damp, but Shah didn't know whether it was the first sign of fever or just the normal humidity and temperature that was causing Jake to sweat.

"You're the reason I want to make it back to the mission, Shah." He absorbed the light, cool touch of her hand on his brow. Just that simple connection stabilized his out-of-control world. She possessed a serenity that calmed him no matter how much danger swirled around them. She was checking for fever, and he knew it. Jake loved her even more for trying to protect him against the worst that might happen. He watched her grow quiet over his statement.

Stunned by Jake's whispered admission, Shah could say nothing. Taking her hand away, she said, "I want you to eat the two mangos—and no argument, Jake. You've lost a lot of fluids, and we need to replace as much as we can before we start back. I've got plenty of liana vines for water for you."

Exhaustion stalked Jake as they ate and then settled down for the night. Shah insisted on keeping the pistol and taking the watch, for fear of a jaguar getting the scent of his blood and coming to investigate. Jake didn't argue. He obediently took two aspirin with a little water. So far, he wasn't feeling feverish, but he knew it was only a matter of time. Neither of them broached the subject, but he could feel the tension in Shah. Her worry was like a tangible thing.

As the aspirin dulled some of his pain, Jake fell asleep. He couldn't roll on his side the way he wanted; his legs were too badly cut up for him to stand them touching each other. The last thing he saw was Shah leaning against the tree, her knees drawn upward toward her body, the pistol nearby.

Jake was jerked out of his sleep at dawn by a shattering, screaming cry that rocked the forest around them. Sitting up, he saw Shah leap to her feet, the pistol in hand. Her attention was riveted on the rain forest behind them.

"What—?" he mumbled groggily.

"Jaguar," Shah breathed. "It's the jaguar...."

Shaken, Jake froze. "How close?"

"N-not far," she stammered. Shah's eyes burned. She hadn't slept at all. Trying to steady her hammering heart, she whispered, "She's been around most of the night. I've heard her from time to time." Licking her dry lips, Shah tried to penetrate the shadowy darkness of the rain forest. If only there were more light! "She's close, Jake. Very close."

Feeling helpless, Jake took his knife from its scabbard and held it firmly in his hand. His eyes wouldn't adjust to the darkness so that he could try to spot the cat. "Will she attack?"

"I don't know," Shah said, holding the pistol ready. Now and then throughout the night she'd felt her back crawl with shivers. Intuitively she'd sensed the jaguar's presence. The cat's scream unnerved her, but she knew she mustn't panic. She glanced over at Jake. His face was pasty, with a sheen of sweat across it. Her heart dropped when she realized that he was looking feverish.

"Tell me about jaguars," Jake demanded, trying to sit up in a position that wasn't so painful for him.

"They hunt at night and sleep during the day. That's what we have going for us," she told him. "It's going to be daylight soon, and maybe she'll go home to her tree and sleep."

"Unless she's really hungry and sees me hobbling along the riverbank," Jake muttered.

Shah nodded wearily, gazing hard at the vegetation. "I hope she's not that hungry."

Jake sat there another fifteen minutes, tense and alert. The dawn grew brighter, and the birds began singing in the distance, but not near them—a strong indication that the jaguar was still close by. "Maybe," he joked weakly, "if we give her this platform, she'll stay here instead of tailing us."

Her arms tired and heavy, Shah slowly allowed the pistol to drop to her side. Pushing her hair away from her face, she realized how tangled it had become. She glanced over at Jake. Forcing a slight smile, she said, "Why don't we try it?"

Staying here might mean their demise, and Jake knew it. "Okay, partner, let's saddle up and blow this joint. What do you say?"

Shah avoided his feverish gaze. Jake had such courage. He was the one who could die, and yet he was trying to lift her spirits by teasing her. As she silently gathered the items to put into the knapsacks, Shah allowed the word *partner* to touch her heart. Oh, if only she could be! Throughout the hours of darkness, Shah had ruthlessly examined the contents of her heart. For thirty years she'd experienced only the negative side of men. Now, when she'd least expected it, Jake had come along, epitomizing the positive male. He'd walked into her life and turned it upside down.

Shah made a silent promise to Jake that if they both survived this journey she would find the courage to tell him she loved him—regardless of his reaction. She didn't know if Jake loved her. She knew he liked her, but for Shah that wasn't enough. From the moment the boar had attacked Jake, her heart had belonged to Jake forever. She knew with a certainty that shook her soul there would never be another man for her. Jake was a gift from the Great Spirit—a second chance to live life happily.

Avoiding Jake's red-rimmed eyes, Shah busied herself with the preparations for their journey. She left the camcorder behind to lighten their load, along with everything else except the first-aid kit, the pistol, and the videotape that incriminated Hernandez.

"Good move," Jake praised her. "Bare essentials."

Shah forced a grin. "I'm not lugging you *and* the knapsacks. Something had to go."

Rallying beneath her indefatigable courage, Jake took hope. Fever was stalking him in earnest now, and he had realized earlier that his legs were puffy and swollen—a sure sign of infection. "Nice to know I'm more important than what's going to be left behind," he teased.

Shah moved over to the edge of the platform. "Jake Randolph, I'd never hear the end of it if I left you behind. Knowing you, you'd haunt me from the other world. Come on, we've got some hiking to do today—together."

Chapter Eleven

"*Pai*, is he going to be all right?" Shah stood anxiously next to the priest as he injected Jake's limp arm with a hefty dose of antibiotics. Jake lay unconscious on a gurney. Night was falling, and a nun who had been a surgical nurse, Sister Bernadette, stood opposite them. Despite her exhaustion, Shah's gaze moved from the priest to the sister. Jake had collapsed a quarter of a mile from the Tucanos village, falling unconscious from a high fever and delirium. Luckily, several Indians fishing nearby had spotted them from their canoes. The short trip back to the mission had brought Jake safely home. *Home.*

"It's too early to tell, child," Pai Jose whispered as he handed the empty syringe to the sister. "Sister Bernadette will change his dressings, scrub out all his wounds and then dress them again." The priest placed his hand gently on Shah's shoulder. "Come, you're nearly ready to fall over. How long has it been since you ate any food or drank any water?''

Blearily Shah answered, ''I made Jake eat the food and drink the water.'' She touched her brow, on the verge of tears. Jake's face was pale, frighteningly pale. Had she gotten him to the mission in time? The sister, a pleasant-faced woman in her sixties who wore a gray-and-white habit, took up a pair of surgical scissors and began to cut off the blood-soaked dressings on one of Jake's legs. Unable to stand the sight of the festered wounds, Shah turned away. His infected legs had turned puffy, and the smell made her gag.

''Come,'' the priest told her, more firmly this time, and he guided her out of the ward and toward his small residence. ''First, you must eat. Then I want you to take a shower, change clothes and sleep.''

Tears stung Shah's eyes. ''*Pai,* I'll eat, shower and change. But after that I'm coming back here. Jake needs me.'' *And I need him.* Throughout the day, Shah had seen the raw courage that Jake possessed. He had grown delirious toward afternoon, but he had clung to her voice, leaning heavily on her and trusting her implicitly. They'd kept going despite the overwhelming odds against them. The jaguar had stalked them—quietly, out of sight, but Shah had known the cat was never more than a few hundred yards away at any given time. Twice she'd fired the pistol in hopes of scaring the hungry cat away. Afterward Shah could feel that the cat had left, but then, a little later, her back would crawl with cold shivers of warning and she knew the jaguar had returned to stalk them.

''You need sleep, child,'' the priest murmured.

Shah knew she hadn't slept for thirty-six hours, but it didn't matter. She felt anything but sleepy. The possibil-

ity that Jake could die, that the antibiotics had been given
to him too late, shook her as nothing else ever could have.
"Pai," she whispered, her voice cracking, "I love Jake.
I want to be at his side. He could die. Don't deny it. I
know enough about this rain forest. I've seen a small cut
become so infected that it caused blood poisoning. No, I
want to be with him, pray for him . . ."

"We'll all pray for him." Pai Jose patted her shoulder
gently. "I'm sure Sister Bernadette will be finished with
her duties with Jake by the time you get back to the
ward."

"If blood poisoning doesn't get him, gangrene could.
He could lose his legs," Shah whispered as she halted in
front of the priest's small room.

Pai Jose barely nodded his silvery head. "If blood
poisoning has set in, that's a possibility," he agreed
somberly. Placing his hands on her slumped shoulders,
he added, "He could die, too. Losing his legs to gangrene would be terrible, but not fatal."

"We don't even have the capacity to get him to a hospital from here," Shah said, blinking back the tears. The
radio, old and worn, wasn't working at the moment—
their only tie with the outside world.

"Now, now, child. I've already sent Red Feather upstream to where the tugs dock with a message to bring a
boat down here to transport Jake back to Manaus."

Shah threw her arms around the old priest. "Oh, thank
you!" she cried, swallowing against a sob.

The priest patted her consolingly. "You pray to your
Great Spirit," he told her, "and I'll pray to God. Between our prayers, Jake will make it."

The dim night light outlined Jake's sweaty, harsh features. Shah numbly wrung out a cloth again from the

nearby bowl of water and gently wiped down his face, neck and shoulders. It was nearly midnight, and she was fighting back tears of terror. The rest of the ward was quiet; a few snores of the Tucanos still recovering from their wounds and the chirping of crickets were the only sounds to soothe her fear. Moving the damp cloth across Jake's powerful chest, she prayed steadily.

Sister Bernadette had confirmed her worst fears. Jake had blood poisoning. Now he wore only boxer shorts, the rest of his body unclothed to try to cool him from the fever's effects. Shah could see those dangerous red lines moving up his long, powerful thighs. It was only a matter of hours, perhaps a day at the most, before they would reach his magnificent, giving heart and stop it from beating.

The sister had given Jake the largest dosage of antibiotics allowed—any more, and that could kill him, too, she had warned Shah earlier. Shah gripped Jake's hot, sweaty arm and stared at his face. She understood as never before why Jake's face was lined, with brackets carved deep around his partly opened mouth and furrows across his brow. There were many laugh lines at the corners of his eyes, too. She wondered if she'd ever see him smile again, or hear that booming laughter rumbling up out of his chest like thunder.

Jake's temperature hovered at 104 degrees, and since their return to the mission it hadn't moved downward, not even with all the antibiotics he'd been given to combat his massive infection. There was no ice available, so all Shah could do was continue to use a damp cloth to wipe the sweat from him—and pray. Luckily, they had IVs, and two of them were replacing the necessary liquids Jake was losing via sweat due to his high fever.

"Fight," Shah whispered to him. She gathered up his hand and pressed his limp fingers to her lips. "Jake, fight for yourself. Fight—" she choked "—for me. Jake, I love you. Do you hear me? I love you!" Her raspy voice flowed into the silence. Shah pressed her fingertips against Jake's massive wrist. His pulse was fast and hard, symbolizing the fight his body was valiantly waging against the blood poisoning.

Pressing her brow against Jake's damp, naked shoulder and clinging to his hand, Shah released a shuddering sigh. She was beyond exhaustion, beyond any sense of time. The only thing she felt was her heart bursting with an agony she'd never encountered in her life. She alternately prayed, cooled Jake down and caught brief snatches of sleep.

Toward morning, Shah jerked upright. She was disoriented for a moment, but then she realized that Jake was moaning and muttering. Her hands shaking, she touched his glistening chest. Beads of sweat stood out all over his skin as she pressed her hands against him. His skin was cooler! Gasping, Shah turned and took the thermometer from the glass of alcohol on the bedside stand and slipped it beneath Jake's armpit. It was the longest three minutes of her life. All of Shah's awareness narrowed on that thermometer. Jake was muttering and turning his head slowly from one side to the other. The IVs would soon need to be replaced, Shah noted, for they were nearly empty of their lifesaving contents.

Taking the thermometer from his armpit, Shah stood up and held it under the night-light at the head of the bed to read it. Her blurry eyes stung with the effort. Blinking several times, frustrated by the tiny markings, Shah tried to steady her trembling hands. A gasp tore from her.

The thermometer read 102! She gave a little cry and lurched back to her chair. She had to sit down before she fell down. Jake's fever had broken! The antibiotics had done their job, turning back the raging poisons that had threatened to overwhelm his body's defenses. Quickly, Shah rinsed out the cloth and wiped the sweat from Jake's body. Euphoria raced through Shah. Tears streamed down her cheeks, but she didn't care. All those prayers had helped turn the tide and she knew it.

A hand settled on her shoulder, and Shah twisted a look upward. Sister Bernadette's sharp but kindly features came into view.

"And how is our patient?" she asked.

Sniffing, Shah showed her the thermometer. "Look," she said, her voice the merest quaver, "Jake's going to live. He's going to live. . . ."

Jake heard Shah's voice, low and husky, near his ear. Was he dreaming again, or was it real? He wasn't sure. Thirst vied with his focus on her lovely voice. The darkness he rested within was comfortable, and he felt no pain. Flashes of the boar attacking him, of Shah screaming, raced across his closed eyelids. He felt a woman's hand in his, her fingers interlaced with his own. Shah. It had to be Shah! His heart galloped at the revelation. Jake fought the darkness, fought against the unconsciousness that tried to hold him prisoner.

Shah sat tensely as she watched Jake struggle to become conscious. She sat now on a metal chair next to Jake's hospital bed. Did he have any idea that two days ago he'd been transported by tug and then by ambulance to the best hospital in Manaus? Probably not. The urgency to see Jake open his eyes, to talk with him, nearly overwhelmed her.

"Jake? Can you hear me? It's Shah. Come on, it's okay to wake up. You're safe...." She bit back the need to speak of her love to him. His lashes fluttered, dark brown spikes against his pasty complexion, and she felt his fingers move weakly in her hands. Breaking into a smile of relief, Shah stood up and placed a hand on his damp brow. She hated the sterile smell that inhabited the hospital room, but was grateful for the cleanliness that surrounded them. Leaning down, she pressed one small kiss after another on Jake's brow. He desperately needed a shave; his dark beard accentuated his harsh looks.

"Jake?" she whispered, and, following her heart's bidding, she lightly placed a kiss on his stubbly cheek and then on his mouth. His lips were slightly parted, dry and cool to her touch. Shah couldn't help herself; she pressed her lips more firmly against Jake's mouth, breathing her life, her love, into him. There was such fragility to life, Shah realized as she shared her sweetness with him. When she felt him respond, his mouth moving weakly against her own, her heart soared with joy. Caught in the web of love created by his courage, her defenses gone, she drowned in the returning strength of Jake's mouth as he took hers.

As his hand lifted to caress her neck and then her cheek, Shah sighed against his mouth and eased inches away. She smiled down into his dark gray eyes and pressed her hand against his. The words *I love you* begged to be spoken. But she was too emotional, too grateful for Jake's life, to speak.

Jake sighed and closed his eyes. He savored Shah's kiss; her lips were soft and beckoning, pulling him out of the darkness. He felt her velvety flesh beneath the palm of his hand and felt her cool hand upon his. "I love you," he whispered, his voice rusty from disuse. "God,

I love you, Shah.'' And then he sank back into semiconsciousness, aware of her presence, her touch, never happier.

Shah felt Jake's hand begin to slip from her cheek, and she caught it and gently placed it across his belly. Had she heard right? Had Jake whispered that he loved her? Or had it been her exhausted, starved imagination? She stood there, holding his hand, unsure. She'd slept very little—only snatches here and there over the past four days. She touched her brow, and her mind coldly informed her that she was imagining Jake's words. Simultaneously her heart cried that she'd heard him correctly.

Torn, Shah could do nothing but watch Jake float in his semiconscious state. The doctors had warned her that it would take a long time for him to become completely conscious after his close brush with death. He would drift in and out of consciousness, muttering and perhaps not very coherent. She held his hand, moving her fingers slowly up and down his forearm, caressing him, letting him know in the silent language of touch how much she loved him.

The door to the private room opened, and she turned her head. A man with neat black hair, wearing a dark gray pinstripe suit, stood hesitantly at the entrance. Shah felt the power around him, met his hard, intelligent gaze, and knew that it must be Morgan Trayhern, Jake's boss. He was a tall man, powerfully built. Despite the veneer of civilization provided by the expensive clothes he wore, Shah knew him for what he was—a warrior. She offered a slight smile of welcome.

''Mr. Trayhern?'' Her voice was charged with emotion, with relief that Jake was going to live.

"Yes." He entered the room and quietly shut the door behind him, giving her a slight, strained smile. "You must be Shah Travers." He held out his hand to her.

For a moment, Shah was on guard against Trayhern, but then his eyes thawed, and the same kind of warmth that Jake possessed surrounded her. She released Jake's hand and turned. "Yes, I'm Shah Sungilo Travers. I'm the one who called you." She returned to Jake's side and picked up his hand again. "When they gave me Jake's clothes and belongings, a business card fell out of his wallet. Your name and phone number were on it. I knew Jake worked for you, and I figured you'd want to know his condition."

Morgan nodded. "I'm glad you did." He frowned and moved around to the opposite side of Jake's bed. His dark brows drew down in worry as he studied his friend. "How is he?"

"Have you talked to his doctors?"

"I don't speak Portuguese," Morgan said.

"Oh, of course. Well, he tangled with a wild boar four days ago, as I told you on the phone. The doctors didn't know at first whether Jake would lose his legs or not. That's when I called you." Shah gave a shrug. "I'm sure I must have sounded like a blithering idiot, but I was worried..."

Morgan smiled gently. "You made perfect sense to me on the phone, Shah. I'm just grateful you called."

"He needs the best medical attention possible," she went on quickly. "The doctors say he will recover, but I worry..." She bit down on her lower lip, unable to finish.

Morgan gazed around the spare, clean room. "When one of my people gets hurt out in the field, we always try to bring them back home for treatment and recuperation, Shah. I've brought the company jet. With your help, we'll get Jake out of here today and flown stateside to Bethesda Naval Hospital, in Maryland. It's one of the best, and they have an extensive knowledge of tropical infections, thanks to the Vietnam War."

Shah gasped. She had hoped for help, but she had never imagined that Morgan Trayhern had this kind of power and influence. She saw his smile deepen, his eyes warm and thoughtful, as he held her gaze.

"Will you act as my interpreter? I'll need help getting the release from his doctors and clearance from the airport authorities to place Jake in our charge."

Our charge. Shah blinked belatedly. "But—"

"I've got a doctor, one of my employees, standing by in the jet. She's fully qualified to take care of him on the trip back to Andrews Air Force Base. I don't leave my people stranded on a mission if I can help it."

Overwhelmed by the sudden turn in events, Shah was speechless. Jake as going to be taken home. He was going to be torn from her. She couldn't possibly afford the thousand-dollar one-way fare to the States to follow him. All her money—what little there was of it—had been donated to the fund to save the rain forest, because Shah had needed so little to live at the Tucanos village. She stood, stunned, unable to think of a way to go home with Jake. Her mother was poor and always gave away most of her money to those on the reservation who were in greater need than she was. And she would never call her father and beg for money. *Never.*

"Well, I— Yes, of course I'll help," she whispered, her heart breaking into a thousand pieces. "Jake needs the best medical attention he can get. He almost died." She turned away so that Morgan couldn't see the tears in her eyes.

Her emotions had been brutalized over the past four days, but from somewhere Shah gathered the strength to force herself to fulfill her promised obligation, despite her pain. Blindly heading for the door, she whispered, "I'll go find his doctors and get things started, Mr. Trayhern."

"Fine. Thank you."

Shah didn't return for nearly forty-five minutes. She didn't dare. After getting the release signed by the doctors, Shah went to the nurse's station and used the phone to call the American embassy in Brazilia, the capital city. The embassy official she spoke to told her there should be no problems with the Brazilian authorities, and promised to call the Manaus airport immediately to explain the situation and make sure Jake could be placed on the jet as soon as he arrived from the hospital. Shah then saw to it that an ambulance was available to transport Jake to the airport. That done, she walked slowly down the highly polished hall toward Jake's room, weaving slightly with exhaustion. She knew she needed sleep, long, uninterrupted sleep, in order to throw off her dizziness, her confusion in her mind, and see the situation with some clarity.

A lump formed in her throat, and she fought the urge to cry. Jake was leaving within the hour, conscious or not. She loved him, and now he was being torn from her. But he needed the care that an American hospital could give him if he was to make a complete recovery. She wasn't angry at Morgan Trayhern—just the opposite. There weren't many businessmen who would spend corporate money to rescue one of their employees.

Slowly opening the door, Shah tried to prepare herself emotionally. But it was impossible. When she entered, she saw Morgan standing next to Jake's bed. And Jake was awake. Shah let go of the door, stunned. Jake's ravaged face looked angry, and his gray eyes were flashing with thunderstorm darkness. Her heart sank.

"What's wrong?" Shah managed, standing tensely.

Morgan moved aside, looking uncomfortable. "I think I'll come back in about fifteen minutes," he said, and left the room.

In shock, Shah watched Morgan leave, as quietly as he'd come. Slowly she turned to Jake, who sat up in bed, the white sheet draped haphazardly around his waist. His fists were wrapped in the bedding. Joy clashed with fear as she met and held his dark eyes. "Jake, what's wrong?"

He winced. "Come here," he ordered gruffly, his voice sounding like sandpaper. As weak as he was, he lifted his hand, his fingers stretched outward. "Come here, Shah...."

Numbly Shah walked toward him. She realized the effort it cost Jake to lift his hand. Her fingers outstretched, she caught and held it. She swallowed the lump in her throat. "Why are you so upset? Are you in pain?"

"Pain's the right word," Jake muttered, closing his fingers around Shah's hand. "I just woke up, and Morgan said you were getting authorization to send me stateside."

"Well... he has a jet standing by, with a doctor on board, and—"

"Dammit, I don't want to go!" He looked up at her drawn, pale face and saw her lower lip tremble. "I told Morgan to shove his plane and his doctor." His hand tightened on hers. "I'm not leaving you behind, Shah. I can heal here just fine. I'm not letting you go. Do you understand that?"

She stared at him, her mouth dropping open. As weak as he'd become, Jake still had the strength to hold her hand in a painful grip. Clearing her throat, she tried to control her wildly fluctuating emotions. "Don't I have anything to say about this?"

"What the hell are you talking about?" Jake demanded, breathing hard.

"Morgan came in here and told me what he was going to do. He's right, Jake. You stand a better chance of full recovery at a hospital that knows how to treat wounds like yours."

"Morgan told me I've been unconscious for four days. Is that so?"

"Y-yes."

"Tell me what happened. I don't remember."

For the next five minutes, Shah outlined the series of events that had brought him to the hospital in Manaus. He was glaring at her, his chest rising and falling with exertion, and she couldn't understand why he was so upset. He was going home. Wasn't that what he wanted?

Jake ruthlessly examined Shah's suffering features. Hadn't she heard him say he loved her? He knew he'd spoken the words, and he knew she must have heard them. Why was she behaving like this? Why was she acting so unsure? That last day, as they'd hiked toward the mission, their closeness had melted into a oneness Jake had never before experienced. His anger was ballooning, and so was his frustration, and his fear of losing her.

"Did Morgan ask you to come with us?"

"No. Why should he?"

"Shah, don't turn away. Look at me, dammit. Look at me!"

She turned and sniffed, her eyes filling with tears. "What do you want?" she cried. "What have I done wrong?"

Her cry tore at his heart. Jake pulled her closer, until she stood next to his bed. Tears blurred his vision. "I'm not leaving you behind, Shah." His fingers tightened painfully around her hand as he tried to steel himself against the answer she might give to the question he was going to ask. "Will you come home with me? Back to America?" His heart aching, Jake held his breath as he anxiously searched her distraught features. He hadn't meant to make Shah cry. Tears dripped into the corners of her mouth, and she sniffed.

"Home?" she asked scratchily. "With you?" She saw his reddened eyes fill with tears. Afraid to ask why, she saw him nod once.

"Too much has happened too fast," he told her, in a rough, emotional tone. "We need time, Shah. You've got the proof against Hernandez you wanted. You can send a copy of the video to the Brazilian embassy in Washington. I know Morgan will help you." He took a deep, ragged breath, wanting so badly to tell her again that he loved her. But he'd told her before, and it was obvious to him that he needed her more than she needed him. "Please," he said, his voice hoarse, "just see me home. That's all I ask. I know it's more than I deserve, but I need you, Shah."

Need. She took a deep, halting breath and covered his hand with hers. Didn't Jake realize how much she needed him? Perhaps even more than he did? "Yes," she murmured, "I'll fly back with you."

Shaken by her soft, anguished tone, Jake closed his eyes, relief flowing through him. "Thank you," he said unsteadily.

* * *

Jake was agitated. He lay on a comfortable, clean gurney on the corporate jet, which was being flown by two Perseus pilots. Morgan was sitting at a small desk just behind the cockpit, phone in hand, talking to someone stateside. To Jake's left was the medical doctor, Anne Parsons, a woman in her early thirties with short black hair and blue eyes. She had offered a warm, welcoming smile when they'd come aboard earlier at the Manaus airport.

Jake twisted his head and tried to look back toward the rear of the cabin. Dr. Parsons raised her head from a report she was filling out on Jake's medical condition.

"May I get you something, Mr. Randolph?"

"No." Jake craned to catch a glimpse of Shah, who had moved to the rear of the plane after takeoff. "Is Shah okay?"

Dr. Parsons smiled and nodded. "She's asleep, Mr. Randolph." Putting her clipboard aside, she rose. "Matter of fact, I think I'll put a blanket over her. It's a little chilly in the cabin. Are you cold?"

Jake grunted a "No" and turned around. Both his arms had IVs in them, and he felt like a fly caught in a spiderweb. He was agitated because Shah had appeared not to really want to come along. He'd whispered his love to her, but she hadn't responded. Heartsick, frustrated, Jake lay back, his mouth compressed against pain much worse than that in his legs.

He knew he was going to live now. Shah had told him on the way to the airport how close he'd come to dying. Jake knew the prayers of many people had pulled him through, but he also knew that his love for Shah was a powerful part of his will to survive. Shutting his eyes, eaten up by frustration and anger over his medical condition, he tried to fall asleep. As he spiraled downward, somewhere in that twilight zone between sleep and wakefulness, Jake felt Shah's lips tenderly touching his own, felt her moist breath fanning across his face, felt the gossamer touch of her mouth sliding across his. He dreamed of Shah, of loving her, sharing laughter with her and helping her birth their babies. They were such powerful dreams, wishes, hopes, that Jake fell into a deep, healing sleep.

Shah awoke slowly, the slight vibration of the corporate jet surrounding her, the low growl of the engines at the tail of the aircraft filtering into her consciousness. As she sat up, the blanket slid off her shoulders and pooled around her waist. The cabin was dimly lit and gloomy. Looking out the small window, she saw it was pitch black outside. What time was it? How long had she slept?

The watch on her wrist read 4:00 a.m. They had been in the air for a long time. On a commercial flight, it took nine hours for a jet to fly from Miami to Rio de Janeiro. Morgan's jet, because it was much smaller, couldn't hold that sort of fuel load and had to fly back via the long route, up through Brazil and Mexico and then into the U.S. Had they landed and taken on fuel that she hadn't been aware of? More than likely. That told Shah just how deep her sleep had been.

All of Shah's awakening attention shifted to the gurney that bore Jake in the center of the cabin. Directly across the aisle Dr. Parsons was curled up in a chair that had been pulled out into a reclining position. Everyone was asleep, except the two pilots up in the cockpit.

Lying back down, Shah sighed and closed her eyes again. The vibration of the plane gave her a faint sense of security, though she felt none in her heart. Why had

Jake asked her to come along? Shah refused to believe that she'd heard him whisper that he loved her after she'd kissed him. Her spongy mind, after having gone without sleep for days, had merely made it up. She turned on her side, gripping the blanket, and curled into a fetal position. If only Jake did love her. She loved him. He had nearly given his life for her by standing in the way of that charging boar.

Shah was confused, and she realized that she was still in desperate need of sleep. And what she needed even more was to sit down and have a long, uninterrupted talk with Jake. But she knew that wouldn't happen soon. According to Dr. Parsons, Jake would need immediate surgery. At least six of the boar's slashes had torn into leg muscles, and they would all have to be repaired. How Jake had managed to overcome the terrible suffering he must have felt with every step, Shah didn't know. She was in awe of Jake's ability to master his pain. Maybe, she thought, losing his family had been the worst possible pain in the world for Jake to survive, and physical agony was nothing in comparison.

Snuggling down into the pillow—the blanket a poor substitute for Jake's nearness—Shah fell asleep, dreaming of Jake, of his kisses, of his incredible tenderness....

Chapter Twelve

Shah stood uncertainly at the nurse's desk on the surgical floor of Bethesda Naval Hospital. Morgan had called at her hotel room at eight o'clock this morning. She'd still been asleep. Jake had come through the leg operation just fine and wanted to see her now that he was out of recovery and in his private room. Gripping the bouquet of flowers that she'd bought downstairs, Shah found out Jake's room number and slowly walked down the white tiled hall. Nurses and doctors and a few patients and visitors passed her, but she barely saw them.

Last night they'd landed at Andrews Air Force Base, outside Washington, D.C. Shah had accompanied Jake by military ambulance to the prestigious hospital in Maryland, not far from the air force base. They'd held hands all the way to the hospital, few words exchanged between them because of the presence of Dr. Parsons and a military paramedic.

Trying to gather her strewn emotions, Shah slowed her step even more after she spotted Jake's room. She had entered the emergency room with Jake last night, only to be shuffled quickly out of the way as Jake's gurney was surrounded by medical personnel. Jake had tried to call to her, but Shah had moved out the doors and into the visitors' lobby, reeling with emotional stress and exhaustion. Morgan had come by half an hour later in a rented car, gotten her a posh hotel room near the hospital and taken her there. He'd told her that since Jake would be going directly into surgery there was no use waiting for him at the hospital. What she needed, he'd said, was a shower and sleep, in that order.

Everyone seemed to know what was best for her, and Shah was too numb to fight back. She'd surrendered to Morgan's assessment of the situation and allowed him to take over. The only clothes she had were the ones she wore, inappropriate for the cold, snowy East Coast.

Morgan had tactfully asked if she had money, and, when Shah had shown him the ten dollars she had in her pocket, he'd slipped three hundred-dollar bills into her hand and told her to buy some clothes at one of the boutiques in the hotel lobby. Shah had protested at first, but Morgan had patiently explained that Jake would want him to help her.

A terrible uncertainty haunted her waking and sleeping hours. This morning, she'd gone to the hotel lobby and purchased a pair of dark brown wool slacks, a camel-colored turtleneck sweater and sensible brown socks and shoes. Luckily, the hotel provided shampoo and conditioner for her hair, and beneath a scaldingly hot shower she had cleansed her hair and her body until she was free of the damp smell of the Amazon.

Now her hair hung in ebony sheets, loose and flowing across the lightweight red nylon jacket she'd also purchased. The paper around the flowers crinkled under the tight grip of her nervous fingers. She lifted her hand to knock, hesitated, then lightly struck the door with her knuckles. Hearing no sound from within, Shah thought Jake might be asleep. Pushing the door open, she peeked around the edge of it.

"Shah?"

She froze. Jake was propped up in bed, a breakfast tray nearby. She tried shakily to smile, and forced herself to move into the room. He looked terribly pale, and both his legs were suspended by a set of cables that kept them inches off the bed.

"Hi . . . How are you feeling?"

Jake stared at her hungrily. "Better than I was a moment ago," he groused. Shah looked positively frightened. He waved her into the room. "Come over. I want to know how *you're* doing." He almost said that she looked like hell, but it wasn't true. Shah looked beautiful in the clothes, the brown earth tones complementing her dusky skin, her black hair and her lovely golden eyes.

Shyly Shah handed him the flowers. "Here, these are for you." And then she laughed a little, nervously, as the small bouquet was swallowed up in his large hands. Hands that had touched her, made her body sing and her heart take flight. Swallowing, Shah choked out, "I guess you need a vase. I'll go get one from the nurses' desk, and—"

"Don't go."

She halted, a few feet from the door. It was agony to be with Jake, to be around him. Taking a ragged breath, Shah turned back.

"I can ring for a nurse to come in." Jake examined the flowers and smiled. "That was thoughtful of you, but then again, I'm finding out you're that way with everyone. It's a nice trait, Shah. Take off your coat and stay a while."

Like a robot, Shah took off her coat and hung it over the chair beside Jake's bed. The room was large and comfortable, painted pale blue rather than a cold hospital white. Outside the window, the trees were coated with a light dusting of snow—the first of the season, she'd heard from the bellman in the hotel lobby who'd called a cab for her.

Jake watched Shah in silence. He laid the pretty bouquet of yellow mums and purple asters on the tray by the bed and pushed them aside. She was so nervous, clasping and unclasping her hands, wringing them unconsciously. The darting look in her eyes told him she felt like a trapped animal. He patted the side of the bed.

"Come over here and sit down," he coaxed. "We need to talk."

The words sent a cold, splintering sensation through Shah. Trying to steel herself against what Jake might say, she turned and moved to the side of his bed. Sitting gingerly on the edge, she saw that his eyes were dark with pain and, although he'd recently shaved, his cheeks were gaunt, testament to his recent operation and past week of physical stress. Shah picked up a corner of the blue bedspread and played with it, still unable to meet his searching eyes.

"How do you feel?" she asked, casting frantically about for some safe topic of conversation.

"Lousy. But what really hurts is my heart, Shah."

Her head snapped up, her eyes widening. The blue spread fell from between her fingers. "What?"

Jake longed to reach out and caress her suddenly rosy cheek. "I said," he told her quietly, "my heart hurts."

"But...your legs were cut up by the boar..."

Patience, Jake cautioned himself. "My heart's taking a worse beating, if you want to know the truth." He looked deeply into Shah's golden eyes and tried to gauge the depth of her inability to believe that someone could love her. Jake knew in his heart that Shah had heard him say those words to her in Manaus. He'd spent all morning replaying the sequence of events, feeling his way through it.

When Jake reached over and claimed her hand, Shah swallowed convulsively. "I don't understand," she whispered.

"I know. At least I think I know." Jake's heart started a slow, almost painful pounding. "Tell me something. Did your father ever say he loved you?"

Startled by the question, Shah laughed a little. "Him? No. His way of showing his love was taking off his belt to punish me, and telling me it was going to hurt him worse than it was going to hurt me." She gave a bitter laugh. "I never understood that one."

Jake scowled heavily. "What about Robert? Did he say he loved you?"

"Yes."

"But you knew six months later that he really didn't."

"I guess I wanted to believe he loved me, Jake. I guess the truth is, he said it to get me into bed. When I realized that, I felt betrayed. He lied to me. He used the word *love* to lure me into his arms. I never forgave him for that." Shah compressed her lips. "That lie made me realize how little men value the word."

Jake held on to his very real anger at the callousness of the men in Shah's life. "I thought so."

She tilted her head. "Jake, what's going on? You're going somewhere with this conversation, I can tell."

He lifted her hand to his mouth and kissed it. Instantly he saw the golden fire flare in her eyes. Jake took hope, and plunged forward with his plan. "In Manaus, when I was just coming awake after you kissed me, I whispered something to you, Shah." He looked up and captured her startled gaze. "What did I say to you?"

The silence deepened, and Shah sat transfixed. A part of her, a large part, wanted to run. Just as she had run from Robert, and, earlier, from her father. She watched as Jake took her hand and gently stroked it with his fingers. The tingling sensation went all the way up her arm, and she pulled in a strangled breath.

"What did you hear me say to you?" he repeated quietly.

Licking her lips, Shah whispered, "I—I'm not sure, Jake. I thought I was making it up."

"You didn't make it up."

Oh, what if she'd heard it wrong? What if her heart and her foggy brain had made up what she wanted to hear, and it wasn't what Jake had said at all? She was going to appear to be a bigger fool in Jake's eyes if she mouthed those words. Bowing her head, Shah closed her eyes and whispered, "I think you said you loved me...."

Tipping her chin up so that she was forced to meet his patient gaze, Jake said, "That's right, I did." He watched surprise flare in her eyes. Why surprise?

"I didn't want to believe you said it, I guess."

"Why?"

Shah gave an embarrassed shrug, unable to hold his burning, intense gaze. "I was so tired. You have to understand, Jake, I'd gone without sleep for almost three days. When I kissed you, it was wonderful. When you woke up, I was so happy. I didn't see how someone like you could love someone like me. So I thought I'd made it up in my groggy head . . ." Her voice trailed off.

Jake whispered her name and framed her face. "I love you, Shah Sungilo," he said, his voice cracking with emotion. "I love you with my heart and all of my soul." He caressed her cheek. "This time, you know your mind didn't make it up. This time, you can't deny it."

With a little cry, Shah pressed her hand against her lips. Jake's mouth curved into a tender smile, and she could only stare at him in the silence.

"All your life," Jake began heavily, "men have abused you in one form or another, sweetheart. I couldn't, for the life of me, understand why you didn't respond when I said I loved you. This morning—" Jake shook his head and gazed around the room "—I lay here a long time trying to figure out why you hadn't heard me. And then I realized, you had, but you've been so hurt so many times by men who were incapable of loving that you didn't believe your ears. Am I right?"

Ashamed of herself, Shah hung her head. "Yes . . ."

With a sigh, Jake captured her clasped hands in his. "Only time can prove to you that I love you, Shah. Not because I want you beside me in bed. I want that, too, but sex is only a small part of what love is all about. You need to know that I love you for you, not for what you can give me, or what I can take from you.'' He saw tears forming in her eyes.

"I have a plan I want to share with you. The doc told me I'll need two months to recuperate. I want to go home, Shah. Home to the Cascade Mountains of Oregon. And I want you there, with me.'' He watched her face closely. "In a way, we both need to heal from a lot of wounds we've accumulated in the last decade. I need to come to terms with the loss of my family—and you need to realize that you can trust me,'' he added with a small, hopeful smile. "I can't undo what your father and Robert did to you, Shah, but I can show you a whole new world, a place where love is shared. Let me give you that chance to heal.''

Shah sat for a long time, assimilating Jake's words and, more important, the feelings behind his words. Her heart burst with such joy at the knowledge that she hadn't made up Jake's whispered words that she could barely think, much less talk. "I guess,'' she joked nervously, "I'm more Indian than I ever realized. I can't get out how I feel about this, Jake. We don't talk much, you know. We let our actions speak for us instead.''

"Your walk is your talk. Fair enough,'' Jake told her. "Let me prove that my walk is my talk, too.'' And it would be. "Then you'll come home with me? To Oregon?'' he asked again.

She gave a him a small smile. "If I didn't, who would take care of you? You're strung up like a Christmas goose ready to be baked in an oven, Jake Randolph.''

He laughed. Every movement hurt his legs, but Jake didn't care. His laughter boomed and rolled around the room. Shah was going to come home with him! He loved her more than she could possibly know. He smiled up at Shah. Her face no longer seemed as haunted as before. There was happiness there, along with uncertainty. "I'm not going to be a very good patient," he warned her. "I hate being bed-bound."

"I think I can deal with your grouchiness," she told him seriously. The joy written on Jake's face simply amazed Shah. He was like a little boy who had gotten the most wonderful gift in the world. She didn't feel like a prize, though. In fact, she didn't know what he saw in her. "I'm not used to living with someone," she warned him.

"We'll take it a day at a time."

Shah hung her head as she felt her way through a myriad of emotions. "It's such a chance. I don't know if I'm capable of that kind of risk."

Patiently Jake said, "You risk your life all the time in the name of worthy causes. Don't you think *you're* a worthy cause?"

His insight into her wounded heart astonished her. Weighing his words, his observation, for several long, silent moments, she whispered, "I think I am worthy."

"So do I."

Rallying beneath his beaming smile, Shah felt as if the sunshine were coming out in her life for the first time. "Okay," she said with a shy laugh. She looked forward to Oregon, to seeing Jake's home there. And yet Shah couldn't help wondering if she was being trapped in a new and different way. Only time would tell.

"I still will work on rain-forest issues, Jake."

"Fine," he agreed. "Maybe I can do something to help you. You never know. I'll need something to keep me occupied while I'm mending. I have a fax, a computer, a modem and several phone lines for business purposes. You can use them all you want."

Shah was pleased and surprised by Jake's enthusiasm, and by the sincerity burning in his eyes. "Well," she stumbled, "I'd planned on working with the Sierra Club on this issue, getting petitions signed and learning to lobby Congress, once I came back to America."

"I was a little worried you might be bored out in Oregon, but I can see you'll be busy."

Shah was unable to stop staring at Jake's mobile mouth, which was wreathed in a contented smile. She longed to kiss him, to share the joy bubbling up through her. But to be fair to Jake, to be fair to herself, she couldn't succumb to the heated kisses that had kindled that unknown but welcome fire in her body. Robert had trapped her that way, and she had to prove to herself that Jake wasn't like that. Her paranoid head warned her that he knew she loved his touch, hungered for it and wanted more. Her heart, that soft voice that acted on feelings alone, told her that she loved Jake with a fierceness she'd never felt before, and that because it was such a new and overwhelming experience it was scaring her, making her overly cautious.

She trusted Jake to keep his word, and she understood that he wouldn't trap her. Reading between the lines of his offer, Shah realized that if she wanted him it was she who would have to take the initiative. For the first time in her life, she held power, her true power, in her own hands. It was a giddy, euphoric feeling to know that Jake wouldn't stalk her, manipulate her with words or touches to get her to do what he wanted. No, he'd respect her, give her the time she needed to be sure, first about herself, then about him.

"You'll be going from one extreme to another," Jake said, humbled, as Shah slid her hand into his. There was such intimacy between them, strong and good, that it left him shaken in the wake of it. "From the tropics of Brazil to the snow and winter of the Cascades."

With a little smile, Shah said, "My life's always been one of extremes. I'll adjust."

Jake wondered if Shah realized that such flexibility wasn't something a whole lot of people possessed. It was one of the reasons she'd survived thus far, and he applauded her ability to bend, not break, when new situations presented themselves to her. "I'm going to call the Butterfields, who take care of the house for me, and tell them we're coming home." He squeezed Shah's slender hand, and an ache seized him. The need to love her, to introduce her to the realm of true love, was eating away at him. Jake knew he had to control his physical hunger for Shah, or he'd scare her away. "It's December first. You realize we're going to spend Christmas together?"

There was a wistful tone to his voice. Shah met his boyish smile. "Can we have a Christmas tree?"

"Just take a walk out into the front yard and take your pick," he chuckled. "That cedar A-frame of mine is stuck deep in the heart of big-tree country. We're surrounded by Douglas firs for as far as the eye can see."

"It sounds wonderful," Shah whispered, a little dazed by the sudden and unexpected turn of events. "Like a winter wonderland, a fairy tale..."

"You're my dream come true," Jake said, his throat tightening. "You're coming home with me. I never thought, I never imagined, that any woman would ever share that house with me.''

Shah understood Jake's emotionally charged statement. He'd lost his family, he'd lost everything he'd ever loved. How many times had he come off a mission to be alone in that cedar A-frame? How many? Her heart bled for Jake, for the terrible loneliness he'd endured. As she sat there, Shah began to realize that they were very much alike in some ways. That small revelation tore down another barrier of Shah's fear, and she looked forward to going home with him with a new eagerness.

''If I have to spend one more day in this bed, I'm going to turn into a bear,'' Jake grumbled unhappily.

Shah grinned as she brought Jake his breakfast tray. ''You've been home exactly two weeks, and I think you've already turned into a grumpy old bear, Jake Randolph.'' It was seven in the morning, sunlight barely showing on the horizon outside the window of the small first-floor bedroom where Jake stayed. He'd just awakened; his covers were in twisted heaps, and both his bandaged legs were exposed. Shah tried to keep from looking at his powerful, darkly haired chest. Jake had informed her once they got home that normally he didn't wear anything to bed, but in deference to her he'd wear pajama bottoms only. Shah had tucked her smile away and tried to be serious about it.

Placing the tray on the bedstand, Shah patiently smoothed the covers across his legs and tucked them around his waist. Jake was already sitting up, several goose-down pillows providing backing for him against the cedar headboard. Some of the grumpiness had left Jake's sleepy features when she'd entered his room.

"I'm going crazy," he muttered, taking the pink linen napkin Shah offered and spreading it across his naked torso.

"The doctor said fourteen days in bed, Jake. You've only got one more to go." She placed the tray on his lap. She found such joy in small things like making Jake's breakfast. Actually, Shah thought, laughing to herself, it wasn't that small: he ate enough for three people.

"This is a nice touch," he murmured. In a little white vase, Shah had placed a sprig of holly with red berries. "What did you do? Get up early and tramp outside in the snow to find them?"

"Yes. I had a lovely walk in the snow this morning. It was beautiful, Jake. The stars are so close at this altitude, so shiny and bright." She gazed out the window. The sky had been clear early this morning, but it had clouded over in the past hour, and now snowflakes twirled thickly through the gray morning sky.

"Wish I could've joined you," Jake said.

Shah smiled understandingly and sat carefully on the edge of the bed, facing Jake. She usually took her breakfast with him in his room. It was something she looked forward to, because Jake had insisted she take the lovely master bedroom up on the second floor. Shah felt cut off, being a story away from Jake when she went to bed at night. It was lonely in that big queen-size bed, with its massive cedar posts. All the furniture in the place, Shah had discovered, had been made by Jake. After the death of his family, he'd used the building of his home as therapy.

"One more day," she repeated patiently.

Jake dug hungrily into the stack of pancakes Shah had fixed for him. She'd put red raspberry syrup nearby, plus a small basket of well-fried bacon. "You're one hell of a cook, you know that?" He glanced up at her as he began eating the light, fluffy pancakes. "You get all this talent from your mother?"

"I guess. Actually, it was my grandma. Because my mother is a medicine woman, she's often traveling to people's homes, so my grandmother taught me how to cook and keep house."

"Your grandma still around?" Jake thought how beautiful Shah looked. She wore a bright red cable-knit sweater, and her long black hair was flowing around her. Her light tan slacks were loose, but still reminded him of her long thoroughbred's legs. She also wore a pair of lightweight hiking boots, a necessity for winter in the Cascades.

"Yes, and I hope you get to meet my whole family someday soon. Gram is ninety-four, but you wouldn't know it. She's sharp and spry." Shah surprised herself. Now, where had the invitation to meet her family come from? Glancing over at Jake, whose forkful of pancake had halted midway to his mouth, she realized her mouth was getting ahead of her brain—something that happened too frequently when she was around Jake.

"You mean that?" He saw a high flush come to her cheeks.

"Well . . . sure . . ."

With a smile, Jake popped the pancakes into his mouth, savoring them. Shah had put some piñon nuts in them; it was a trick that made even the most ordinary of pancakes taste great. "You're hesitating," he said with a grin, baiting her.

Clasping and unclasping her hands, Shah studied them intently. "Foot-and-mouth disease," she muttered.

"Oh, then you didn't mean the invitation?" Jake's grin widened. He hadn't teased Shah very often in the past two weeks, because coming here had been such an adjustment for her. Still, things were settling into a comfortable routine, and he saw her relaxing more and more every day. This morning he wanted to test Shah's security about being here with him.

"Sure I did!" she protested. "It's just that sometimes my heart gets ahead of my brain, and—"

"I thought you said Native Americans always speak from the heart, not the head."

Befuddled, and aware that Jake was teasing her, Shah managed a short laugh. "They do. I mean, they should. I mean, they don't always, but that's what my mother taught me. We're right-brained, and that side of the brain has no voice, like the left brain does. Did you know the left brain contains the nerves that lead to our voice? The right brain has no voice—at least not a loud one. Mother always said that our heart is this side of the brain's voice." Shah smiled fondly, recalling that particular conversation with her mother.

"No, I didn't know that. Sounds interesting," Jake murmured, impressed. He quickly finished off the pancakes and held out a strip of bacon to Shah. She took it and thanked him. The pleasure of sharing the morning meal with her was something Jake always looked forward to eagerly. But, then, he savored each and every moment with her. "So, if Native Americans are right-brained and heart-centered, what does that make white men?" he baited.

"Left-brained and vocal," Shah said with a wry grin. After finishing off the strip of bacon, she wiped her fingers on the pink linen napkin draped across Jake's torso. "Except for you."

"What am I?"

"I feel like you're a nice balance between the two," she answered seriously. Shah saw the dancing light in Jake's gray eyes. "Somewhere along the line, you disconnected from the general male stereotype and embraced your heart and feelings."

Jake handed her the tray with his thanks and watched as Shah stood up. She had such gazellelike grace that he never tired of simply watching her move. "That happened when my family was killed," he told her quietly. "Bess had been working on me for a long time, though, to get me unstuck from the male mode."

Shah stood near the dresser where she'd placed the tray. "I thought so," she said softly, not wishing to open up that wound. Lately Jake had talked more often about his family, and she could see that those conversations, though painful, were healing him before her very eyes.

"Do me a favor?" Jake pointed toward the upper level of the house.

"Sure." Shah saw his face grow pensive. What was he up to now?

"Go to the large cedar dresser opposite the bed. In the fourth drawer is a huge photo album. Bring it to me? There are some things I want to show you, share with you."

Suddenly shaky, Shah nodded and left. As she climbed the stairs that led to the huge master bedroom up in the loft, her heart started a slow pounding. As she gently opened the drawer and took out the leather photo album, she realized that this was about Jake's family. Her mouth dry, she descended the stairs, the album pressed protectively to her chest.

Jake's face mirrored vulnerability as she handed him the album. Her heart wouldn't stop its rapid beating as she sat on the edge of the bed next to him. He hesitantly touched the album, which was now resting in his lap.

"I've been wanting to share this with you for a long time," he rasped. "It's the family photo album." Running his fingers along the well-worn leather cover, Jake managed a sad smile. "It was Bess's idea—our beginning, middle and ending, she said."

Gently Shah reached over and placed her hand on top of his. Jake's voice trembled with emotion. She understood, and she hoped her look conveyed that as he risked a glance up at her before he opened the album.

Clearing his throat, Jake managed a weak smile. "I just never thought there would be an end," he said as he opened the album. "Bess was a lot more realistic about life than I was. Or maybe I ought to say that I was so in love with her that life's realities never really hit me until she was gone."

Words were impossible for Shah. All she could do was wrap her arm around Jake as he sat there with the album in his lap. Feelings were vibrating around them, and she understood as never before the depth of the love Jake had had for his family, for his wife. As he gestured to the first page of the album, Shah devoted her full attention, her heart, to what Jake was sharing with her.

"I never showed this album to anyone after they died. I couldn't look at these photos, our marriage, or the baby pictures of our kids." Tears blurred Jake's eyes, but he went on. It was so important that Shah understand his past. "Here's Bess and me on our wedding day."

"She was very beautiful," Shah said. The woman was petite, with light brown hair. Her white wedding dress emphasized the joy radiating from her oval face. Jake looked so very young, proud and tall in his dark blue Marine Corps dress uniform. "You both look so happy."

Jake smiled fondly. "We were. Young, idealistic, and carrying the hope of a happy future." Oddly, the tears left his eyes and a new kind of calm filled him as he went on to the next page of the album. "Katie was our first-born. She weighed ten pounds at birth. Look at the head of hair on that kid."

The baby in the picture had dark hair, just like Jake. Shah smiled gently, because the photo had been taken with Jake at Bess's bedside, the baby cradled lovingly between them. "The three of you look very happy."

"Bess probably looks more relieved than anything," Jake commented dryly, meeting and holding Shah's warmth-filled gaze. "She swore up and down she'd never have another baby because the labor had been so long with Katie." He laughed appreciatively, feeling another weighted cloak dissolve from around his shoulders. "Of course, then Mandy came along, two years later."

"And did she weigh in like a ten-pound sack of pota- toes?" Shah asked, smiling and feeling Jake's joy. It was as if showing her the album and talking about his family were healing him before her eyes. Grateful for whatever was happening, Shah felt the tension in the room dis- solving. In its place came an incredible sense of subdued joy that they could share this album filled with happi- ness.

With a chuckle, Jake nodded and turned another page. "Mandy weighed in at exactly ten pounds. Bess blamed me for that, and I gladly took the blame. Look at her.

Katie had my dark hair, and Mandy had Bess's lighter hair. The kid was a beauty.''

And she was, Shah thought. Mandy had her mother's delicate features, but her eyes were Jake's in shape and color. Relaxing, her hand unconsciously moving up and down Jake's back, she listened as he shared his family years with her. On the last page, he became choked up.

"There's Katie in her pink tutu. She was crazy about becoming a ballerina. At ten years old, she was the star of her class." Gently he touched the picture of his smiling daughter. "This was taken by Bess just before the recital that Katie starred in."

"Were you able to see her recital?" Shah asked. She saw Jake's mouth compress into a thin line and knew the answer. Sliding her hand across his shoulder, she allowed him to lean upon her.

Jake felt Shah's hand move on his shoulder. He reached over and embraced her, the tears in his eyes going away as he held her, the pain from the past seeming to disappear beneath her healing touch and the love she held for him. In the moments that followed, poignant and bittersweet, Jake realized that sharing the album, his life and his family with Shah was a catharsis for him. It was as if he had finally been able to place the wonderful memories and feelings into a chamber of his heart to be held there forever. That was the past.

Somehow, he realized, meeting Shah and falling in love with her had helped bring his past full circle, to completion. As he drew her more deeply into his arms and felt her sigh and rest her head against his shoulder, Jake felt a new flow of feelings through him. The past, his past, had finally been healed. Now he was genuinely able to step forward and dare to dream of a future with her.

"Thanks," he told her gruffly, kissing first her cheek and then her brow, "for sharing this with me."

Easing out of his embrace, Shah fought back tears. With a soft, unsure smile, she whispered, "I wouldn't have it any other way, Jake."

"They're in my heart," he told her quietly. "Forever. But I'm at peace with myself now, thanks to you, to us."

Touched to the point of being unable to speak, Shah could only nod and grip his strong, scarred hand. She didn't want to break the beauty, the healing, of this moment, but there were chores that had to be attended to. "Peace is another word for healing, Jake. In our own ways, we're still healing from our pasts, but at least we know it's possible to do that." Then, sliding off the bed, she said, "I've got to get your legs taken care of."

Shah bent down, opened a drawer in the lovely cedar dresser that Jake had made and drew out clean dressings. The bandages on his healing legs had to be changed daily.

Jake brightened as Shah leaned down after he'd removed the covers from his legs. "Hey, how about I try a walk outside? I'm only a day away from when the doc said I could start moving around in earnest." Jake gestured toward the window. "I like cold weather. I like the snow." Every day he'd been puttering around the house, extending his time out of bed and exercising his newly healed muscles. Shah would catch him standing forlornly at a window, looking out with a wistful expression on his face. Jake really was an outdoor person, and her heart bled for him, because she knew how hard it must be for him to remain house-bound.

"You like anywhere but this bed," Shah reminded him as she expertly cut away the old dressings and put them aside.

"I warned you—I'm not one to be tied down. Especially when I'm sick."

She smiled absently and looked at the many curved pink scars on his leg. All the wounds had healed nicely, but she regretted the hundreds of stitches required to patch Jake back together again. The scars would be many, and most would never go away. Gently she ran her hand down the expanse of his calf.

"How do they feel today?"

Jake tried to smile. Every time Shah touched him like that, he wanted to groan with pleasure. Did she realize how healing her touch was? How lovely her slender hand was as it caressed his ugly, scarred flesh? "Great," he muttered, praying that he could control himself. The bulk of the covers would hide his reaction to Shah's touch, but Jake lived in fear that one day, she would discover what her light caress did to him. Thus far, he'd been able to keep his hands off Shah. Every day she touched him a little more, and that told him that his decision had been right—for both of them. Every day Shah's confidence in herself, as a woman, as a human being who could show her feelings without threat, was increasing. To Jake, it was like watching her blossom before his very eyes.

"I want to put that calendula oil on them before I bandage them back up," she told him.

"Go ahead." He pointed to his leg. "The scars are a lot less noticeable since you've been putting that marigold juice on them."

With a smile, Shah brought the bottle of calendula, an essence of marigold, over from the dresser. "I'm glad I

called my mother and she sent this to us right away,"
Shah said. She poured the glycerine that contained the
brownish-colored liquid into the palms of her hands.
Leaning down, she gently bathed Jake's leg with it.
"Mother said it always took away scars if used early
enough after an operation," she murmured. "And she
was right."

"Your mother puts regular doctors to shame," Jake
told her. Jake lay there in abject pleasure. Just being
touched by Shah sent wave after wave of longing through
him. All too soon she had replaced the dressings and was
retrieving a pair of jeans and a dark green polo shirt from
his closet for him.

"What's on your agenda today?" Jake wanted to
know as he eased his feet to the golden-reddish cedar
floor.

"I'm expecting a call from the Brazilian embassy today. They've got the video of Hernandez using chain
saws." Shah frowned and laid the clothes next to Jake.
Although his legs were outwardly almost completely
healed, he was still weak. Each afternoon she worked
with him on several exercises designed to strengthen his
legs. "They're supposed to let me know if they'll send the
police to arrest him. I just hope they'll prosecute."

Jake saw the frown on her face deepen. "They will,"
he assured her confidently. When she gave him a distrustful look, he grinned. "How about we go find a
Christmas tree after you get that call? To celebrate your
victory?"

"Jake, you're not supposed to be going outside yet!
The doctors are afraid you'll slip on some ice and tear
those newly healed muscles."

"Now, Shah . . ."

She watched Jake slowly get to his feet. His routine was to shave, dress, and then move into the den to watch television, which he hated doing for any length of time. Then he would read books to stay mentally engaged in something. At other times he'd play secretary on one of her projects, folding letters and licking envelopes and placing stamps on them. Her heart went out to Jake; he just wasn't the sedentary type. He groused because she split wood every morning for the huge earth stove that sat in the living room. He complained when she swept off the red-brick steps that led to the garage and the fieldstone sidewalk that led to the snow-covered dirt road. He groused a lot, but Shah knew it was because he considered those responsibilities his, not hers.

"Just one more day," she pleaded.

He glanced at her as he moved slowly around the bed. "We'll see," he said, and then smiled at her. "Did I tell you how pretty you look in red?"

She grinned. "Matches my temper, don't you think?"

"What a smart mouth you have, Ms. Travers."

Rallying beneath his teasing, Shah said, "I'll see you later. I'll be working in your office if you need me."

Jake stood at the floor-to-ceiling windows in the living room. The snow had stopped falling, the sky was a light shade of gray, and the evergreens were swathed in their white winter raiment. It was almost noon, and he was bored out of his skull. There was only so much television a man could watch, only so many magazines, newspapers and books he could read, before he got restless. Very restless.

He crossed his arms, well aware of what lay beneath his keen restlessness. He wondered when Shah would gather enough courage to lean over and kiss him again. How many times had he seen the desire in her lovely, shadowed eyes? The hesitation, the fear, the longing? His own body fairly boiled for her, and it was all he could do to force his mind onto anything other than making long, slow, delicious love with Shah. But it had to be on her terms, Jake reminded himself savagely—her time and her decision. Intuitively he knew that once he got her in his arms, in his bed, she would never leave again. It was just that first time, overcoming her fear from the past, that was the sticking point. Jake had lost count of how many times he'd cursed her father and her ex-husband.

He was feeling strong again. Strong and powerful and incredibly vital. Jake turned, a plan in mind, a slight smile working its way across his mouth. The Brazilian embassy had just called to inform Shah that Hernandez was under arrest, and that he would indeed go to trial. That meant they would be going back down to Brazil as witnesses, but not until at least three months from now. Shah had put down the phone, thrown her arms around Jake and laughed in triumph. He'd hugged her long and hard, and both of them had been a little breathless after he released her. Yes, the time was ripening.

Jake hummed softly, feeling lighter with each step he took. If only Shah would go along with his plan, he felt it might be the turning point in their relationship.

Chapter Thirteen

Shah had just entered Jake's office, euphoric over the fact that Hernandez was being indicted by the Brazilian government. She hummed softly as she drew a file from the file cabinet. The phone rang.

"Hello?"

"Shah? This is your father."

Her heart plummeted. Automatically her hand tightened around the phone. "What do you want?" she asked, standing stiffly. She'd been unprepared for the anger she'd heard in his voice.

"Want? You know what I want! How could you do this to me, Shah? You took those damned pictures of Hernandez cutting trees down with chain saws! How could you?"

Anger sizzled through Shah, and she sat down, her free hand clenched into a fist. "How could I? How dare you!

You didn't want me down there in Brazil because the stock you bought is all tied up with Hernandez and several other landowners. And don't deny it. I have proof that you bought heavily into the Brazilian rain forest timber trade.''

"This is going to cost me millions! You don't care, do you, Shah? You're just like your damned mother—bull-headed, single-sighted, and you absolutely refuse to see anyone else's point of view.''

Her heart throbbed at the base of her throat, and when she spoke again her voice wobbled. "You've lied to me, you've tried over the last year to have me kidnapped out of Brazil. Why couldn't you have told me the truth in the first place?''

"Would it have done any good?''

"No, but at least there would be honesty between us. That's a start.''

"There is no start, Shah. I can't believe you would be this disloyal to me.''

Shah nearly choked. Every muscle in her body was tense with fury. "Disloyal? What about your disloyalty to Mother Earth?''

"Stop talking that drivel—''

"No!'' Shah said tightly. "Father, you hate women of any kind. You don't respect Mother Earth. You can't even respect my mother, much less me.''

"Cut it out, Shah. I called to ask you to remove your charges against Hernandez. My company can't afford to lose the millions we've invested in timber in Brazil.''

"I'll *never* do that.''

"Shah, you can't do this to me.''

Tears marred Shah's vision, and she released a harsh bark of laughter. "Do what? Allow you to continue to rape our mother? Allow you to help alter the quality of our air? Of life itself? I will never lift those charges against Hernandez. Not for you, not for anyone." Shah was breathing erratically, and she was trying to stop the quaver in her voice, but she couldn't.

"If you love me, you'll drop those charges."

Shah sat back and shut her eyes tightly. Gulping back a scream of pure frustration at his unfair tactics, she was silent for a good minute before she could control her voice and her feelings. "Love?" she whispered. "You don't know the meaning of love, Father. You never did. You never loved my mother, or me. You never respected us as human beings. I won't allow you to use love as an excuse for forsaking everything I live for and believe in, just to please you."

"You're just as fanatical as your mother!" Travers snarled. "Fine! I'll fight you in court on this, Shah. I'll use every penny I have to defend Hernandez and the other landowners in Brazil. This is war. You're not my daughter. You never have been."

The words cut deeply into Shah's heart. She had known that one day this would happen. The hurt seared through her, and for long moments she grappled with the truth of the situation: Some men were incapable of being fathers, much less decent, kind ones, such as Jake had been. "You do what you have to do," she said. "You might be my biological father, but you've never been a real one to me. I'll see you in court—on the opposite side, as usual."

Shah dropped the receiver back into the cradle and sat for a long time, allowing the grief, rage and hurt to flow through her. Hanging her head, she realized that Jake had given her the strength to stand up to her father. He was the polar opposite of Ken Travers in every way possible. She was so glad Jake had shown her that album, shown her that parents could really love and respect their children.

With a ragged sigh, Shah stood up on shaky knees. She locked them, her hand resting on the desk, until she got the strength to move. She wanted to find Jake and share the conversation with him.

Jake sat in the overstuffed chair, the magazine he'd been reading lying idle in his lap as he listened to Shah recounting the upsetting phone call from her father. She sat on the stool where his feet rested, almost doubled over, her elbows planted on her thighs, her chin resting on top of her clasped hands. When she'd finished, the silence ebbed and flowed around them. Such sadness and abandonment were clearly etched on her features that Jake ached for her.

Reaching forward, he gently eased her hands apart and held them in his own. Her golden eyes were marred by darkness, and he felt her grief and injury. "You did the right thing, Shah." Jake shook his head and gave her a gentle smile. "Sometimes life tests you on what you really believe in, and you've got to make choices. Hard choices. You made the right decisions for the right reasons. Your father was the one who was dishonest with you. Not vice versa."

Sniffing, Shah nodded. "It hurt so much when he said that if I really loved him I would withdraw the charges."

"I know.... Listen, when someone like him is stuck in such a dysfunctional state, everything he sees is interpreted with the same emotional skewing," Jake explained quietly. "Travers never knew what love was,

Shah. The man can't love himself, and therefore he's incapable of knowing how to love others, even you.''

The hurt in her heart mushroomed with Jake's calm words. "It's the alcoholism, Jake. That's the root of it."

"No, that's a symptom," he said. "I'll bet if you went into your father's past, the way he was raised, he was probably beaten the same way he beat you and your mother. Inside, the man's a cowering animal, hurt and frightened."

"Well, so am I, but I try not to take it out on others," Shah murmured.

"The difference is that you want to get well, Shah, and your father doesn't. And until he does, he's going to continue to play these kinds of games with you. He's using the word *love* when it's not really love at all, just a manipulation of you." He smiled a little and gripped her hands more firmly. "You didn't fall for his game, and I'm proud of you."

Shah held Jake's warm gray gaze, feeling his care wash across her raw feelings. "There's no easy end to this. No easy answers. My father sees me as this horrible villain ruining his life, his business."

"Maybe," Jake said, "someday, he'll realize he's got a disease that's poisoning not only himself and how he sees the world through those eyes, but his relationship with his daughter, his ex-wife, and probably everyone around him. Until he does, Shah, you'll remain the villain in his life. He won't win this court fight, even though he'll try. After he loses, he'll probably hate you until the next problem in the guise of a person comes along, and then he'll train his diseased focus on that poor target."

"And then he won't hate me as much," she muttered, seeing his faultless logic.

Pulling her forward, Jake guided Shah onto his lap. She came without fighting and he was grateful. As she settled in his lap, her arm went around his shoulders and she pressed her brow against his hair. He held her in an embrace meant to give her protection and love.

"It's so hard to know that he hates me. That he sees me as a bad person."

Jake patted her gently. "I know, honey, I know. But you have to listen to me, to your mother and your grandmother about how good a person you are. Try not to listen to your detractors—that will only tear you down, and if you buy into it heavily enough, it will end up destroying you." He closed his eyes, absorbing the vulnerability Shah was sharing with him. "You stick to the high road on these things, Shah. You didn't set out to deliberately or knowingly hurt your father. You happen to have a different reality about how to live your life, and that's allowed. You didn't try to manipulate him the way he did you. You stuck to your guns, your beliefs, and walked your talk."

She smiled a little and hugged Jake. "Sometimes I think you are part Native American. You seem to understand me so well."

He sighed and closed his eyes, content as never before. "That's because I love you, strengths and weaknesses combined. No one's perfect, Shah. And you can't march to someone else's idea of how you should live your life." Opening his eyes again, he said, "Come and help me find the right Christmas tree?" Shah lifted her head from where it was resting against him, her eyes widening at his request.

Jake held up his hand to stop the protest he knew was coming. "I know—I'm not supposed to start walking outdoors until tomorrow. But one day isn't going to kill me, Shah.''

She laughed. ''You're such a bad boy when you want to be. You know I can't stop you.''

Jake wove invisible designs on her hip and thigh with his light touch. ''I more or less had you contributing to helping me go outdoors.'' He sighed and looked around the large, airy room. ''The place looks naked without a tree in the living room,'' he complained. ''Christmas is always something special. I miss not having the tree decorated. Usually, the tree was set up around the first of December.''

''You,'' Shah said accusingly, ''could get a rock to walk if you wanted to, Randolph.''

''It's not a rock I want at my side. It's you.''

The instant Shah met and held his warm gray gaze, she felt a ribbon of heat flow through her. The last of the hurt over her father's phone call had evaporated. How could she say no to Jake? Did he realize how much sway he had over her? Placing both arms around his shoulders and giving him a quick hug, she muttered, ''Oh, all right, Jake. You just keep chipping away at me until I break down and say yes!''

''I believe,'' he said, with a rather pleased expression on his face, ''it's called nagging.''

The snow was fresh, fine and powdery, and it was knee-deep in places as they walked in search of just the right tree. Shah remained close to Jake's left arm—just in case he should slip and start to fall. But she kept her worry to herself, because he was such a little boy about getting to go out in the cold, crisp winter air. Jake wore a brightly colored Pendleton wool jacket, a red knit cap thrown carelessly over his head, and a pair of warm gloves. His cheeks were ruddy from the temperature, which hovered in the high twenties. Each time he exhaled, a mist formed around his mouth and nose.

"Jake," Shah pleaded, "we're almost a quarter of a mile from the house. You shouldn't overextend yourself this first time. Dr. Adams is going to throw a shoe when he hears what you've done!"

Jake halted and turned. Shah wore her red nylon jacket with a dark green knit cap and gloves. Her black hair flowed around her shoulders like an ebony cape, in stark contrast to the jacket. She wiped her nose with a tissue and stuffed it back into her pocket. Without thinking, because he was overjoyed to be outdoors again, he caressed her flushed cheek.

"Maybe you're right," he murmured. Then he gave her a happy grin. "Which one do you think will make a good Christmas tree?" He swung his arm outward to encompass the thick stand of evergreens that surrounded them.

The worry Shah felt evaporated beneath Jake's touch. She ached to lean up and kiss his smiling mouth. Never had she seen Jake so happy, so vital, as now. The past two weeks had been a sort of living hell for Shah. She so desperately wanted to kiss Jake, to walk into his arms and discover the love he'd promised her. But she was afraid. Too afraid.

"How about that one?" She pointed to a seven-foot blue spruce.

Jake sized it up, his ax in his left hand. "Looks pretty good to me."

Shah moved over to the tree and gently touched its snow-covered needles. "Now, don't laugh at me, Jake, but if you really want this tree, we have to ask it permission to give its life for us." When she saw his brows lift, she added breathlessly as she stroked the evergreen's limb, "We believe everything has a spirit, Jake. And we never take without asking permission first. If the tree says no, we have to find another one. All right?"

He tramped over to where she stood. There was such anxiety in her eyes that he wanted to reassure her that he wouldn't laugh at her explanation. Leaning down, he kissed the tip of her cold nose. "I like the way Native Americans see the world. Yeah, go ahead. Ask it."

Her nose tingled from his brief kiss, breaking loose a portion of Shah's fear. She moved the few inches that separated them and threw her arms around his broad shoulders. Pressing herself against him, her face nestled against his shoulder, she whispered, "I knew you'd understand. Thank you..." She moved away quickly, before his arms could wrap around her. Though embarrassed by her boldness, Shah was struck by the sudden hunger and need she saw in Jake's narrowed gray eyes. It made her go weak with longing, and she struggled to stop herself from moving back into his arms.

Jake anchored himself. He ordered himself not to move a muscle after Shah's surprising embrace. It had happened so fast that it had caught him off guard. And then he smiled to himself, joyous over Shah's thawing toward him. Maybe it was the pristine air and the scent of the forest that encompassed him, but he was sure something special was happening. Sunlight broke through the low gray clouds, sending blinding, brilliant shafts across the mountain where they stood.

Shah closed her eyes and tried to concentrate, her hands gently touching the tree. For her, everything was alive, and everything had a voice. Maybe not one like a human being's, but a voice, a feeling, nevertheless. Shaken by her unexpected spontaneity with Jake, she tried to concentrate on mentally sending a message to the tree asking if it would give its life to them. Her heart was pounding, but gradually it slowed as she formed the explanation and the question for the tree.

Jake stood silent, watching as Shah closed her eyes, her hands reverently cupping one of the branches of the blue spruce. There was something natural and touching about Shah's belief system and her practice of it. How many spiders had she found and carried out to the garage? She wouldn't throw them out in the snow for fear of killing them. One didn't kill one's relatives. Moved, Jake wondered if Shah knew just how special she was. Probably not, but he longed to be the one to show her, to tell her.

"It's okay," she whispered after several minutes, opening her eyes. She dug into a small bag she always carried in her pocket. "This is tobacco. We always give a gift to the tree, no matter what its answer is." Shah liberally sprinkled the tobacco across the tree. With a smile, she tucked the leather pouch back into her pocket. "Ready?"

With a nod, Jake came forward. He approved of the respect Shah held for all living things. The gifting of tobacco was an added thoughtfulness. With quick, sure strokes, Jake cut the tree down. In minutes they'd shaken the limbs free of the snow. Taking the spruce by the trunk, they walked side by side down the long, gentle slope back toward the house.

Halfway down the slope, Shah slipped. With a little cry, she threw out her arms. She'd hit a patch of ice hidden beneath the snow. Jake reached over to try to catch one of her flailing arms. Instead, he slipped on the same patch of ice. Snow flew upward in an explosion as Shah landed unceremoniously on her back. The tree slid on by them. Jake landed on top of Shah.

She gasped as he fell on her. He rolled onto his side to keep his massive weight from striking her fully. Reaching out, he made a grab for her as she continued her slide down the hill. They ended up several yards down the slope, tangled in each other's arms and legs, covered with snow.

"Jake! Are you all right?" Shah had a horror of him tearing those just-healed muscles. She lay beneath him, excruciatingly aware of him as a man, his weight not alarming, but sending heated, urgent signals throughout her.

He grinned carelessly, enjoying the intimacy the accident had created. "I'm okay. In fact, I couldn't feel more right," he gasped, mist forming as he breathed. "And you? Are you okay?" Shah was in his arms, her body pressed against his. She'd lost her cap in the fall, and her eyes widened beautifully as he reached over with his gloved hand and slowly began to remove snow from her hair near her temple.

"I—I'm fine," she whispered breathlessly, hotly aware of his powerful body covering hers, his arms pinning her against him. Shah's heart was pounding like a wild bird's, and as she looked up and drowned in Jake's hungry gaze, she felt the last of her fear disappear. His smiling mouth intrigued her, drew her, and without hesitation she leaned upward. The smile on his mouth changed, and she felt his arms tauten, drawing her even more tightly to him. Her lips parted, and she leaned upward, closing her eyes.

The world focused for Jake as he covered her lips with his. He tasted the coolness of the air on her soft, opening mouth, tasted the evergreen and a sweetness that was only Shah. Their ragged breath met and mingled as he deepened his exploration of her ripe, willing mouth. Heat twisted and knotted deep within his body, and Jake groaned as Shah's arms slid shyly around his neck, drawing him down against her. The snow cradled them gently, the cold air in direct opposition to the heat he felt welling within him and Shah. Tipping her head back a little more, Jake unconsciously allowed his hand to move across her jacket, to caress the curve of her breast, and he felt her tremble. It wasn't out of fear, but out of a fiery longing that was consuming her.

Jake tore his mouth from hers, his eyes narrowed upon her dazed features. He saw the undeniable desire in Shah's half-closed eyes, saw the glistening softness of her parted lips asking him to kiss her again. Pain throbbed through him, the pain of wanting her more than life itself. With a shaking hand, he caressed her fiery red cheek.

"Let's go home and finish this," he murmured in a rough tone.

With a nod, Shah reached out, her gloved hand briefly resting against his cheek. "Oh, Jake, I love you so much.... I was so scared to say it...."

Those words echoed through him, the sweetest music he'd ever heard. He gave a little laugh of relief, rested his brow against her hair. "I know you do, and I know how scared you've been."

She clung to him. "I've been so blind. So stupid."

Jake kissed her with all the tenderness he possessed, and afterward he whispered against her lips, "Blind, maybe, but never stupid, Shah. We had to have the time to build our trust of each other.''

Closing her eyes, her body like a vibrant, burning flame in a way she had never experienced, Shah whispered, ''Love me when we get home, Jake? I know I'm not very good but—''

''Hush,'' he murmured against her lips, silencing her self-doubts as he captured her full mouth against his. Whatever Shah thought she lacked, Jake was going to try to show her she was wrong, today, this hour. Reluctantly he eased his mouth from her wet lips. ''Come on,'' he coaxed, helping her sit up and brushing snow off her jacket, ''let's go home. Together.''

The tree was placed in the garage, and Shah held Jake's hand as he led her in the back door of the house. Her heart was pounding so hard that she thought she might be experiencing a cardiac arrest. Jake's smile, bestowed upon her as he allowed her to walk ahead of him, soothed her frantic anxiety. On the porch, they shed their outer gear and hung their coats on large brass hooks. Their boots were left there, too, and they padded in their stocking feet through the warm, fragrant kitchen.

''Sweetheart?'' Jake pulled her to a halt at the entrance to the cathedral-ceilinged living room. He settled his hands on her shoulders. ''This is your call all the way. Understand?'' His voice was low, off-key. He wasn't trying to hide his feelings from her. The need to love Shah was nearly overwhelming, but his concern for her welfare tempered his needs.

She gazed up into his strong, harsh features. ''No. . . everything is right about this, Jake,'' she whispered, ''I'm ready. . . . I want this. I want you.''

With a nod, he murmured, "Let's go upstairs."

Shah had already conceded that Jake's bedroom was the loveliest she'd ever seen in her life. Jake had made the stained-glass panes that graced the floor-to-ceiling windows. Broken sunlight shafted through them, lending a softened kaleidoscope of color to the large, open room. The gold-and-red cedar floor glowed as the sunlight slid across its polished surface, creating more warmth. Perhaps most touching to Shah was the dark green knitted afghan that served as a spread across the cedar bed. Jake had told her that his mother, who had died many years ago, had knitted it for him just before her unexpected death, and that he could never part with it, or the memory of her.

Sitting down on the edge of the bed, Shah ran her fingers across the worn expanse of the afghan. Jake knelt beside her and peeled one sock, then the other, off her feet.

"You have such pretty feet," Jake said quietly, and he ran his hands across them. "Strong, yet dainty." He lifted his head and smiled up at her. "Like you."

She framed Jake's face between her hands. "You find beauty in everything," she murmured, her thumbs caressing his cool cheeks. Drowning in his lambent gray eyes, Shah felt his hands slide up her arms and around her shoulders. In one smooth movement, he brought them both across the bed. She lay in his arms, looking up at him, her hand pressed to his chest, the soft polo shirt transferring delightful warmth to her palm.

Threading the thick strands of her hair through his fingers, Jake leaned over, caressing her lips. "Everything about you is beautiful," he murmured, moving his tongue to first one corner and then the other of her softly smiling mouth, teasing her, tempting her to respond. He felt her slight intake of breath, felt her fingers curl against his chest, and saw her eyes become a deeper gold. "Taste me if you want," he invited hoarsely. "Touch me like you want, Shah. Explore me. I'm yours...."

Dazed by the molten fire his mouth wreaked upon her lips, Shah drew him down until her lips met and fused with his. The instant they met and molded to each other, Shah relaxed bonelessly into Jake's arms. His body pressed against hers, urgent and hungry. Her breathing growing ragged, she felt his hand trail down her neck, eliciting tiny tingles, then turn hot and burning as it skimmed the crescent shape of her breast. A little gasp escaped her, kissed away by Jake as he continued to allow his fingers to linger, to caress her until she felt mindless with explosive needs she could no longer control.

Her hand moved of its own accord, and Shah longed to feel him, to tangle her fingertips in the dark, curling hair that covered his broad, massive chest. Sliding her hand beneath the green polo shirt, she felt Jake tense. He groaned as she boldly slid her hand across the flat, hard skin of his belly. Her fingertips slid upward to caress and outline his magnificent chest. The shudder that racked his body incited her, and Shah helped him tug off the shirt.

"You're just as beautiful," she whispered raggedly, her fingers buried in the fine, dark hair of his chest. She could feel the thundering beating of his heart, too, and his urgency spread through her.

Jake smiled a very male smile as he eased her back onto the bed. "I like your boldness, your courage," he told her thickly as he began to remove her red sweater. The moment his rough hand slid beneath the sweater, moving against her rib cage, he saw Shah's eyes grow drowsy with desire. His smile deepened as he nudged the sweater over her head and her black hair spilled around her like an ebony waterfall. To his surprise and delight, Shah wore no bra, just a white silk teddy. The thin fabric outlined her nipples and made her look even more desirable.

A sigh shuddered through Shah as Jake bent his head, his moist mouth capturing the peak of one nipple through the silken material. A little cry of pleasure tore from her, and she arched upward into his arms. The jagged heat, like powerful bolts of lightning striking down through her, made her weak, and she tipped back her head, surrendering to his caresses, to his loving. She forgot everything, wildly aware of the ache building in her lower body, the hunger stalking her. All she could do was frantically open and close her fingers against Jake's taut shoulders.

Winter sunlight burst through the stained-glass windows, the colors ripening and darkening across them. Shah felt the warmth of the sunlight, tasted the power of Jake's mouth upon her own, and felt his hand moving downward, releasing her jeans and nudging them away from her waist. Lost in the heat, the color, the amazing fragrance, she utterly surrendered herself to him. All she could do was react, incapable of thinking coherently enough to try to please him as he was pleasing her.

"That's it," Jake said, his voice an unsteady rasp, as the last of their clothing was swept off the bed. "Just enjoy it, Shah. Let me love you this time." Humbled as never before in his life, he felt her arch into his arms. Her little moans each time he caressed her drove him into a frenzy. She was like a highly sensitive instrument. Somewhere in his barely functioning mind, Jake had to remind himself that Shah had probably never experienced the enjoyment a woman could experience if the man took the time to bring her to that pinnacle of pleasure. Savoring her moans and responses, Jake absorbed the beauty of her half-closed eyes, the parted lips that were silently begging him to continue his intimate exploration.

As Jake's hand trailed down across her rounded belly, easing her thighs apart, Shah felt her world crack and splinter into a shower of rainbow colors. Each caress, each tender movement, made her cry out, wanting more of him. Frantic, she gripped Jake's shoulders, begging him for something she couldn't have defined. Speech was impossible; all she could do was move, press herself to his hard length and plead with her eyes. His smile was tender and knowing as he moved above her. Jake framed her face between his large hands, slowly allowing her to adjust to his greater weight.

Driven beyond her own barriers of fear, Shah arched upward, wanting, needing, Jake. The instant he met and filled her, she closed her eyes. The feeling was shattering, transforming and consuming. With each rocking movement of his hips, he moved deeper and deeper, until Shah truly understood the power of a man for the first time. But this was more than just physical sensation. As Jake slid his hand beneath her hip, angling her upward to meet his thrusts, pleasure burned and consumed Shah. Her head thrown back, a gasp drove through her. Her hands gripped him, and a cry, sweet and low, escaped from her lips.

Jake prolonged the pleasure for Shah, watching her face glow, the sudden flush covering her cheeks as her hands tensed against him. When he felt her begin to relax, only then did Jake release the hold he'd placed upon himself. Plunging deeply inside her, sweeping her uncompromisingly into his arms, he buried his face in her strong, soft hair and released his life within her loving, giving body.

Moments spun and glimmered together like rainbow beads of dew caught in the spiral circle of a spiderweb for Shah. She lay breathing raggedly, pinned by Jake's weight, his arms holding her tightly against him, his breath punctuating against her face and neck. Weak. She was as weak as a newborn kitten! Wave after wave of incredible pleasure sang through her newly awakened body. She felt Jake's mouth press against her damp temple, and she unconsciously inhaled his male scent, glorying in his tenderness in the aftermath. The beauty of their being one brought tears to her eyes that slipped out from beneath her dark lashes. Jake kissed each of them away.

Spinning in his embrace like sunlight captured by a cloud, Shah didn't want to open her eyes—she simply wanted to feel, and then feel some more. Jake's weight was like a heavy blanket across her. The thudding of his heart raced in time against hers. The power of him still filled her, reminding her that this was what true harmony was all about. Slowly she lifted her lashes. Jake's eyes were nearly colorless as he tenderly surveyed her, but his pupils were huge and black. His hair was damp, clinging to his brow, and her mouth stretched into a tender smile as she reached up and smoothed those damp strands away with her fingertips.

"I never knew," she whispered brokenly. "I never knew...." She slid her hands upward to touch and outline Jake's harsh-featured face. She watched his eyes narrow, and she felt his smile long before it appeared on his strong mouth.

"I didn't, either," Jake admitted, his voice rough. "Not like this. Not ever like this." He captured her full, sweet mouth against his in a long, cherishing kiss that brought a sound of pleasure from Shah. Her moan was like a song to him. Even as they lay there, still coupled, Jake felt himself growing strong within her once again. He eased his mouth from hers, drowning in the sunlight of her eyes. "I want you to be the mother of my children." He touched her hair, smoothing it away from her face. "I want to fill you, Shah, with myself, with my love. I want our love to grow in you."

The idea of having his children shimmered through her like a rainbow after a violent storm. Her eyes widened with surprise, and then grew lustrous with pleasure as she felt Jake move his hips. A soft smile touched her mouth as she slipped her arms around his shoulders.

"Yes..." she murmured. "Yes..."

Night had fallen long ago, and the firelight in the stone fireplace was dancing out across the large living room. Jake was in his blue terry-cloth robe, barefoot, and Shah stood in her pink chenille robe next to him. The Christmas tree standing in the middle of the huge room was now fully decorated, the lights bright and colorful.

Jake slipped his arm around Shah's waist, drinking in her shadowy beauty. The firelight graced her smooth features, emphasizing the clean lines of her face. It was a face softened by love, he realized humbly, the love she held for him alone. As he led her over to the large sheepskin rug that lay before the fireplace, Jake brought a bottle of white wine with him.

Just the idea, the hope, that Shah was pregnant with his child filled Jake with such euphoria and humility that he felt on the verge of tears. Loving Shah was like holding sunlight in his hands. Whatever fears she'd had, she'd relinquished earlier, in the heat of their loving. As she sat down next to him on the sheepskin, the firelight reflecting across them, Jake understood the courage she had shown.

He filled two crystal glasses with wine and handed one to Shah. Barely touching the rim of her glass with his own, he said, "To our love, and to the courage it took you to love me in return."

The words, like a warming blanket, enveloped Shah. She smiled up into Jake's shadowed features, feeling herself respond to the burning look of desire in his eyes. Holding her glass against his, she whispered, "And to the man who gave me the courage to love..." Taking a sip of the wine, she put it aside and touched Jake's cheek, now in dire need of a shave. The darkness of the stubble only made him look more dangerous, more alluring, to her.

"What if I am pregnant, Jake? We didn't take any precautions."

He shrugged and set the wine aside, drawing Shah into his arms. She came willingly and languished within his embrace, her head resting against his shoulder as they watched the fire dance before them. "Wouldn't bother me." He tipped his head so that he could see her expression, which was thoughtful, and perhaps a bit worried. "Would it you?"

She smiled tentatively. "No..."

"Then what has you worried?"

"I— Nothing, really. It's just all so soon, so new..."

Jake held her for a long time. "You're right," he admitted. "We love each other. We have the time now."

Turning in his arms, Shah faced him, his eyes dark with disappointment. "We do, but I don't feel you believe that."

He caught her hand and pressed a kiss to it. "I don't understand what you're saying."

Tears touched her eyes. "Jake, you had your family torn unexpectedly from you. I feel that now that you love me you're afraid something terrible will take me from you, too." Smiling gently, she caressed his cheek. "I won't disappear on you, but you've experienced otherwise. You love children. And you were born to be a family man. It's written all over you."

Jake squeezed his eyes shut and hung his head, Shah's hand warm against his face. She was right on all counts. At the time, he hadn't thought of protection for Shah. Unconsciously he'd made the decision for both of them, and that hadn't been right. Raising his lashes, he stared into her wide, compassionate eyes. "You're right, sweetheart. We do have the time. I'm sorry."

"Never be sorry," Shah begged him. "I guess I'm just now understanding how very deeply you love me, Jake. You knew from the moment you met me. But I had to let you grow on me, because I was leery of you as a man." She leaned over and pressed a kiss to the grim cast of his mouth. "We'll grow together, Jake. A day at a time."

He nodded and ran his hand down the textured surface of her robed arm. "What if you are pregnant?"

"Then," Shah whispered, placing her arms around his neck and forcing him to look up at her as she knelt between his thighs, "you and I will be parents sooner rather than later." The joy she saw in his eyes made her heart break. Smoothing his hair, she added, "Did you know twins run on my mother's side of the family?" Grinning suddenly, Shah gave him a little shake. "Serve you right, Jake Randolph, if I do have twins! Instant family!"

With a rumbling laugh, Jake caught Shah in his arms and laid her gently on the rug. Her laughter was breathless, and undying love for him burned in her dancing eyes and in the sweet curve of her mouth. "Marry me, Shah."

The sincerity, the pleading, in his gaze tore whatever hesitancy she had left within her completely away. The word whispered from her lips, low and trembling. "Yes..." She threw her arms around him and hugged him with all her womanly strength. He buried his head beside her, nuzzling into the silk of her ebony hair.

As Shah lay in Jake's arms, the firelight flickering over them, she had never felt more happy. Her heart was open, receiving, and Jake was responsible for it, for freeing her from the prison of her past. Shah realized that not every day would mean forward progress, because wounds took a long time to heal properly. As she lay there, feeling his heart's steady beating against hers and his powerful arms snugly around her, Shah felt a contentment she had never before known.

"I love you," she said, kissing him with all the tenderness she held within her. As she eased away from his mouth, Shah met and held his warm gray gaze. "Forever..."

*   *   *   *   *

by Lindsay McKenna

Morgan Trayhern has returned and he's set up a company full of best pals in adventure. Three men who've been to hell and back are about to fight the toughest battle of all...love!

You loved Wolf Harding in HEART OF THE WOLF (SE #817) and Sean Killian in THE ROGUE (SE #824). Don't miss Jake Randolph in COMMANDO (SE #830), the final story in this exciting trilogy, available in August.

These are men you'll love and stories you'll treasure...only from Silhouette Special Edition!

Take 4 bestselling love stories FREE

Plus get a FREE surprise gift!

Special Limited-time Offer

Mail to Silhouette Reader Service™

P.O. Box 609
Fort Erie, Ontario
L2A 5X3

YES! Please send me 4 free Silhouette Special Edition® novels and my free surprise gift. Then send me 6 brand-new novels every month, which I will receive months before they appear in bookstores. Bill me at the low price of $2.96 each plus 25¢ delivery and GST*. That's the complete price and— compared to the cover prices of $3.50 each—quite a bargain! I understand that accepting the books and gift places me under no obligation ever to buy any books. I can always return a shipment and cancel at any time. Even if I never buy another book from Silhouette, the 4 free books and the surprise gift are mine to keep forever.

335 BPA AJJ2

Name	(PLEASE PRINT)	
Address	Apt. No.	
City	Province	Postal Code

Silhouette®

SPECIAL EDITION®

WILD RIVER TRILOGY

by Laurie Paige

Come meet the wild McPherson men and see how these three sexy bachelors are tamed!

In HOME FOR A WILD HEART (SE #828) you got to know Kerrigan McPherson. Now meet the rest of the family:

A PLACE FOR EAGLES, September 1993—
Keegan McPherson gets the surprise of his life.

THE WAY OF A MAN, November 1993—
Paul McPherson finally meets his match.

Don't miss any of these exciting titles—only for our readers and only from Silhouette Special Edition!

Silhouette Books has done it again!

Opening night in October has never been as exciting! Come watch as the curtain rises and romance flourishes when the stars of tomorrow make their debuts today!

Revel in Jodi O'Donnell's STILL SWEET ON HIM—
Silhouette Romance #969
...as Callie Farrell's renovation of the family homestead leads her straight into the arms of teenage crush Drew Barnett!

Tingle with Carol Devine's BEAUTY AND THE BEASTMASTER—
Silhouette Desire #816
...as legal eagle Amanda Tarkington is carried off by wrestler Bram Masterson!

Thrill to Elyn Day's A BED OF ROSES—
Silhouette Special Edition #846
...as Dana Whitaker's body and soul are healed by sexy physical therapist Michael Gordon!

Believe when Kylie Brant's McLAIN'S LAW —
Silhouette Intimate Moments #528
...takes you into detective Connor McLain's life as he falls for psychic—and suspect—Michele Easton!

Catch the classics of tomorrow—*premiering* today—
only from V. *Silhouette*

**Relive the romance...
Harlequin and Silhouette
are proud to present**

by Request

A program of collections of three complete novels by the most
requested authors with the most requested themes. Be sure to
look for one volume each month with three complete novels by
top name authors.

In June: **NINE MONTHS** Penny Jordan
Stella Cameron
Janice Kaiser

**Three women pregnant and alone. But a lot can
happen in nine months!**

In July: **DADDY'S
HOME** Kristin James
Naomi Horton
Mary Lynn Baxter

**Daddy's Home... and his presence is long
overdue!**

In August: **FORGOTTEN
PAST** Barbara Kaye
Pamela Browning
Nancy Martin

**Do you dare to create a future if you've forgotten
the past?**

Available at your favorite retail outlet.

HARLEQUIN®   Silhouette

REQ-G

MEN MADE IN AMERICA

Fifty red-blooded, white-hot, true-blue hunks from every
State in the Union!

Beginning in May, look for MEN MADE IN AMERICA!
Written by some of our most popular authors, these
stories feature fifty of the strongest, sexiest men, each
from a different state in the union!

Two titles available every other month at your favorite
retail outlet.

In September, look for:

DECEPTIONS by Annette Broadrick (California)
STORMWALKER by Dallas Schulze (Colorado)

In November, look for:

STRAIGHT FROM THE HEART by Barbara Delinsky
(Connecticut)
AUTHOR'S CHOICE by Elizabeth August (Delaware)

You won't be able to resist MEN MADE IN AMERICA!